WILD ONES

Alexander Reed

TREATY OAK PUBLISHERS

ALSO BY ALEXANDER REED

Burning Son

As reviewed on Amazon:

"*Burning Son* has wonderfully developed characters and enough twists in the plot to to keep you guessing, I found it so engrossing that I could not put it down and finished it in a day and a half. I could see West Texas, the life of the ranch hands, the sunrise… I just hope there is a sequel as I did not want the story to end."

"Always loved Texas stories, and now I'm in love with cowboys, too. Everything came alive in this book: the fascinating characters, the setting, the raw emotions. Some of the writing is absolutely lyrical, while the drama of the conflict between the two brothers kept me up late reading another chapter, and another… "

PUBLISHER'S NOTE

This is a work of fiction. None of the characters, business establishments, or events are based on actual people, either living and dead, and their lives or circumstances. All material is a product of the author's imagination. Any resemblance to actual people, businesses, events, or places is merely a coincidence and purely unintentional.

Cover design by Will Bakke

Printed and published in the United States of America

TREATY OAK PUBLISHERS

ISBN-13: 978-1-943658-26-8

ISBN-10: 1-943658-26-9

Avaliable on Amazon

ACKNOWLEDGEMENTS

Thanks to

My parents for all their endless support and encouragement.

Cynthia Stone at TREATY OAK PUBLISHERS for her help and guidance.

Jesus, for the rescue.

Jannis Hegenwald and Jenni Rose for showing swagger in the title photo.

Will Bakke for his design work on the cover.

All the musicians who provided the soundtrack to which I wrote.

And, as always, Mr. Daniels, my writing buddy.

WILD ONES

Part 1

THOSE DAMN WILD ONES

CHAPTER 1

A bump in the road shook the van, jarring her awake. The sun forced her to squint as she brushed dark locks behind her ear. Of the other seven passengers, five were asleep while the other two engaged in conversation. But this did not surprise her; she rarely saw Dr. Bernice and Dr. Patrick sleep.

Up front in the captain's seats sat the two security personnel assigned to their team by the World Health Organization. The driver kept his eyes on the horizon while the other examined the big gun strapped to his chest, his face set in a permanent grimace and veins bulging off his neck.

She looked out the window. As a girl watching *Prince of Egypt* or *Aladdin*, she had seen the Middle East portrayed as an ocean of sand: golden currents turning in the wind. But not so. Most of the Afghanistan she saw was mountain and rock. This was not her first time around mountain and rock, but the ones in Colorado seemed more welcoming, while these appeared older, more foreboding, and harsh. She watched as the van passed a village and witnessed a small shepherd boy leading his goats.

A knot twisted in her stomach. She was not scared, just nervous. The majority of the villagers she met in the country were wonderful people. Though she often donned a hijab, village girls loved to touch her hair and she felt a connection to the other women with whom she shared tentative smiles and soft laughter. But she realized many dangerous men waited out there as well, hidden in mountains and hidden in crowds. She witnessed the atrocities these men were capable of inflicting, even on their own countrymen and women.

Her stomach eased when the village disappeared from view. Wanting to make sure her next article was ready to be emailed and published, she pulled her laptop from her backpack. As she retrieved the computer, she studied the case engraved with the insignia "BU" for her alma mater: Baylor University. Now, the sorority parties and fun days in the quad were distant and unrecognizable.

She considered the suburban house in which she would be baking cookies right now had she not followed her journalism major away from a MRS degree and toward her job as a correspondent for *Horizon World Magazine*. She was never against the MRS degree if it came from him, but he had never offered. She always knew it was not something he was capable of giving anyway. And while he conquered mountains and stood unflinchingly against the wind, their moment seemed to pass.

As she pulled the computer cover away, she once again found and read the note her mother had stuck inside the computer the day she said goodbye to her parents in Houston.

Brynn,

We love you so much and will pray for you every day. You're such a wonderful woman and we couldn't be prouder! (But the second you want to come home, we'll buy you a ticket from anywhere in the world).

XOXO,
Mom & Dad

Brynn had received that note five years ago, on the day she moved from Texas to New York. After years of copy editing and begging, she became a correspondent. And following a particularly good article that drew the chief editor's attention, he had assigned her to the international team.

So here Brynn was, covering the World Health Organization team as it made its way through war-torn Afghanistan, sticking to areas declared "safe" by coalition forces. She often considered the eleventh day of September and the sophomore biology class interrupted by the fallen Twin Towers.

Brynn opened the computer and reviewed her work.

"What's that article about, Miss Greene?"

The sound of a voice was a welcome relief from the droning of the van. She looked up. Dr. Bernice and Dr. Patrick grinned at her.

"About the brilliant medical care of Dr. Bernice and Dr. Patrick, of course! Two of the W.H.O.'s finest." She smiled.

The two men laughed.

Dr. Bernice's smile glowed bright and white, juxtaposed against his dark Morrocan skin. "I thought you were a journalist, not a novelist!" He chuckled more. "No one is going to believe that work of fiction!"

Brynn was relieved when they didn't inquire further. She didn't like her answer because she didn't have one. Everyone back in New York had so many opinions. So many people knew exactly what should be done in the Middle East and in Afghanistan. Countless hours passed in editorial meetings as everyone voiced their opinions. The problem seemed so small to all those philosophers back in America, mere products of groupthink.

Brynn never offered an opinion, instead always waiting and watching. Now that she was here, she observed how complicated the war and Middle East was. The diversity was expansive. The good, better than she had expected. The bad, worse than anyone had imagined.

Brynn knew exactly what she wanted to type but wasn't sure it was worth the fight. As she stared at the screen and mused, the machine went into sleep mode and she stared blankly for an hour.

The rustling of the sleeping body next to her woke Brynn from her trance. The passenger further stirred and sat upright.

Brynn rolled her eyes in anticipation.

"I had a dream I met a pretty girl," said the team's pharmacist, Weston,. "And here you are." He bounced his eyebrows at her as he sat up straighter. He swept his long brown hair back with both hands and put on his wayfarer sunglasses.

"Easy there, drugstore," she said. "The dry air is getting to you."

"It's not the dry air." He grinned. "It's those baby-blues."

"I think you'll have more success dreaming," she said.

"Dreaming. Awake. It's all you, Brynn." He winked.

"Weston, I'm just the flavor of the day, the only American girl you've seen in five months."

He gave a toothy smile. "And I have fate to thank for that!"

She thought him a skirt-chaser. Still, she secretly welcomed the cheesy banter and his shameless advances. Days without showers and weeks without makeup often made her feel far less than the belle of the ball.

"I'm a realist, Brynn. Time is on my side. And we've got miles and miles until this trip is over. I'll wear you down." He crossed his arms and leaned his head back on the seat. After his eyes were closed, he said, "We could be very comfortable in my mother's basement in New Jersey."

She laughed. "I don't think you could handle two women in your life."

"Fine," he said, keeping his eyes shut. "I'll make Mom move out."

Brynn shook her head and chuckled. Closing the lid of her laptop, she decided the article could wait until later. Instead she pulled out her iPod and let Ryan Adams sing to her as the country drifted by.

Hours later, the group was wide-awake. They sat in the van as the journey continued, and at Brynn's suggestion, each told of a story and lesson they learned as a child. She found activities like this translated cross-culturally more easily than games like truth or dare. Dr. Patrick was just in the middle of describing an incident with a horse in Dublin when Clint, one of the security personnel, interrupted.

"Okay, folks. We're approaching the base in five clicks. Ladies, go ahead and put your hijabs on and everyone get your paperwork and passports ready. The liaison should be there to meet us."

"Is this an American base?" Brynn said.

"No. Canadian-British forces."

"Holy Hell. I hope they have syrup!" Weston called out.

Clint stared at Weston. "Finished?"

Brynn laughed as Weston whispered, "Looks like I'm not teacher's pet anymore."

When the van rounded another pile of rocks, the landscape gave way to wide-open land. Approaching the base, Brynn could tell it was not as large as many of the bases they'd been to, perhaps only a mile long.

The driver flicked on the dome light, allowing those outside the vehicle to see its passengers. As they neared the main gate,

Brynn noticed the red and white maple leaf flying proudly alongside the Union Jack.

Troops shuffled near the entrance. Brynn knew the men were trained not to fire, but it was still uncomfortable having all those guns pointed at her.

A man stepped out from the guard shack. Standing in the middle of the road, he held up his hand and signaled the van to stop. The brakes squealed as the vehicle halted. The man approached the driver's window.

"If it isn't the World Health Organization," the man said in a playful British accent from behind his gray and black mustache. "Captain Beckett. Welcome to Forward Base Snowfall."

"Thanks for having us, Captain Beckett." Clint said. "You should have gotten our itinerary and roster from Paris."

"Oh, we did." Captain Beckett nodded. "But be a good sport there and turn off the dome light. Taliban snipers have taken to shooting at valuable-looking aid workers." He shook his head and grinned. "It's like they're trying to kill us or something."

Brynn caught the famous dry British humor.

The dome light clicked off.

"There's a good chap." He walked around and opened the passenger door to the rear of the van. He read the occupants' names from a paper in front of him, shining his flashlight on their faces as they replied.

"…Brynn Greene?"

"Here, sir."

He looked up from his photo of her, shining his light on her face. After reviewing everyone in the van, Captain Beckett gave the signal and the gate was raised. The van pulled inside.

Sympathy for the troops welled up inside Brynn. This base was far less elaborate than the many others she had seen with all the conveniences of the West. Plywood paneling loosely lashed together comprised many structures. An old basketball goal stood in solitude with its chain netting barely clung to the rim. The officer charged with the W.H.O. group's care led them to the mess hall, more a tent from which food was served, and outdoor tables.

Brynn looked down at her tray while haunting memories of elementary school cafeteria cuisine flooded her thoughts. But she never wanted to seem ungrateful in front of soldiers who gave so much. Though always one of mild appetite, she tried to clean her plate out of respect.

Thoughts of scorpions and bugs greeted her as she entered the tent designated to her and the other female member of the group, Liz. The sleeping cot hovered a foot from the ground. Plugging her computer into the tent's outlet, she spattered off a few pages of text for her editor back in New York. She looked up

"Liz. On the way in, did you see anywhere that looked liked they had a satellite uplink?"

Liz lowered her copy of *East of Eden* and looked at Brynn over the brim of her glasses. "If I had to guess, I'd say it was over to the north side of where we ate dinner."

"Thanks." Brynn left the tent and stepped out into the arid night. A cold breeze drifted down from the mountains. She responded by zipping up her fleece. The night sky was high and dark over her head as a few stars established themselves. A sharp blade of smoldering orange cut across the horizon, as the sun bid farewell to the Afghan countryside, the last sliver of day.

Finding the communications center was not hard. Passing soldiers fell over themselves just to give her directions. Eventually, seven of them led her to the place she wanted to go.

The communications center hummed with computers,

radios, and telephones. Bulbs burned brightly, illuminating the plywood walls and canvas ceiling. She passed a bank of troops sitting at phones.

"All right, Mum, one more month and I'll see you," one of them said into the receiver.

Brynn ascertained the officer in charge and batted her eyes a few times. The military had no obligation to allow her to send her story, so she relied on her smile to ensure the article would make it to the other side of the world.

The message indicator popped up on her screen verifying a successful submission and she thanked the staff.

"Our pleasure, miss." The Lieutenant nodded towards a folding table on the far side of the room. "You're welcome to the cookies Private Shanklin's mother sent him."

"Thank you so much!" Eager to be agreeable, she made her way across the room. The table was away from the computer bank, cradling a sole tin of cookies and a coffee machine that Brynn thought might be her same age. The spread sat against a draped canvas wall. She approached.

"…it doesn't seem like such a good idea that your people should head that way." The voice came from the other side of the wall.

Brynn froze.

"The Taliban has a strong presence in Shindand and I'm not sure you should be traveling in those mountains."

"But we've been cleared to travel." Brynn recognized this voice as Dr. Patrick. "Has that changed?"

"Technically, no," said the other voice, a Brit. "But patrols in the region have taken fire more often than I'd be comfortable with for you to travel there."

"But Colonel, there are children in those villages who need

our help," Dr. Patrick said.

"The Taliban won't care why you're there."

"Bullets can only do so much. Eventually the healing has to begin. We all knew this was not going to be a vacation."

"Doctor, that's easy to say now. It won't be so easy when a tribesman has a scimitar on your neck."

There was a moment of silence. Brynn could feel the uncomfortable air of the situation wafting through the canvas. She searched the tent to make her eavesdropping went unnoticed.

"We're a little more than Boy scouts." Brynn knew the voice to be Clint's.

"...so are they," said the Brit.

"But we're on a humanitarian mission. We're non-combatants." Dr. Patrick's tone turned insistent.

"I told you: they do not care."

"Well, as I said, Commander, we did not join the W.H.O. because we thought it'd be safe."

"If you're mind's made up, then I can't stop you. Statistically, it's more likely than not you'll arrive safely. The likelihood of an incident is low. I just want you to be aware of the facts."

"Then you've done your job, sir." Dr. Patrick said.

"Well, that settles it."

Brynn heard the men shuffling.

"In that case, would you care to join me for a night cap?"

As they seemed to disperse, Brynn scurried away, clutching her computer close to her chest. During her walk back to her tent, the base seemed more desolate. She knew she'd encounter risks in Afghanistan but this felt more real as she replayed the conversation in her head. Since leaving the United States, she missed the veil of protection.

The cot creaked beneath her as she lay back. Liz breathed

deeply by her, lost in sleep. But sleep never found Brynn. She stared at the ceiling of the tent, haunted by the words she had overheard.

Hours later, Brynn stirred from her thoughts only when a loud diesel engine rolled by outside their tent. The morning surprised her as sunlight crept back into their tent.

Liz turned over on her cot and passed her hand over her face, rubbing her eyes. "I can't wait to be back in Tel Aviv. I'm going to sleep for three days and gain ten pounds on room service." She sat up. "Then hate myself afterwards."

Brynn laughed. "Remember how great pedicures are?"

"I'd just be happy with a hot shower." Liz chuckled. "Well, I'm sure Dr. Patrick wants to get going early."

As Brynn and Liz rolled up their sleeping bags, they shook the unexplainable and unavoidable dust into the air. Then they carried their duffels to breakfast.

Her companions ate a military breakfast. But she was nervous and could not join in, even to show her appreciation.

Too soon, the W.H.O. van pulled away from the base. Brynn felt exposed. She turned in her seat to watch the safe haven as long as she could, until it was out of sight.

Clouds overhead blocked the sun. The sparsely colored landscape appeared even more monochromatic. Miles didn't pass fast enough for Brynn.

"How long until we reach the village?" Liz said from where she sat, three bench rows ahead of Brynn.

"Just go ahead and get settled. We'll be lucky to make it in under eight hours," Clint said from the front. His gaze swiveled back and forth in a disciplined fashion.

A moan rose from the group.

To try and keep morale high and to distract herself, Brynn

called to her fellow passenger. "Dr. Bernice, what's the biggest holiday in Morocco?"

"Eid al-Adha."

"What do you and your family do on that holiday?"

As she calculated, Dr. Bernice went into a long explanation of the holiday. The van seemed entertained and the story helped the time pass.

Hours and miles intertwined and blended. Conversation came and went. The bumps in the road created a rhythmic swaying of the vehicle's passengers. In unison they leaned to and fro as if choreographed.

Somewhere in the monotony, Brynn looked out from the vehicle and smiled. A crystal mountain stream cascaded off a nearby cliff. As it fell over earth, splashes of water jumped through the air. The light of the now brilliant sun overhead refracted in those droplets and illuminated them in gold, like sparks flying.

Brynn found it beautiful.

"Kind of majestic," Weston said from his seat next to her. "Isn't it?"

"Yeah, it's a lovely waterfall."

"I was talking about you," Weston purred.

Brynn smirked at his desperation and gave him the most exaggerated eye roll she could muster.

"No worries. Refuse me now." He shifted in his seat. "But our kids are going to laugh about—"

CRUNCH! Glass failed and shattered. In disbelief, Brynn watched half of Weston's head disappear. His body slumped and folded sideways. He was there a moment ago. And then he was gone. She tried to scream but became too distracted as the inside of the vehicle erupted into chaos.

"CONTACT!" Clint yelled from the front.

The air filled with screeching bullets, the high-whistle emanating as they pattered and penetrated the steel of the vehicle. Light poured through the peppered holes. Another screaming bullet tore the side of Liz's neck. Blood sprayed everywhere and coated the interior, painting the seats scarlet. Liz grabbed the wound.

Brynn couldn't breathe. *What's happening?*

"GO! GO! GO!" Clint yelled.

The engine revved as the hulking vehicle charged forward. Lead tore apart the windows. Brynn's eyes watered.

Horrifically close, a cloud of dirt jumped towards the sky as a loud concussion hit the van. Brynn felt the front of the vehicle collapse into a crater. Her ears rang. The moments were deafening.

"SHIT!" Clint yelled. The passengers in the van were either riddled with bullets or climbing over each other to get to the floor. Clint and the other security contractor kicked their doors open, used them as shields, and shot back at unknown assailants.

Liz shook violently. Brynn found enough focus to grab her scarf and compress Liz's wound. She watched the life drain from her friend.

All she could do was try and force her fingers to hold the scarf in place. She wept and whimpered. "LIZ! HOLD ON!"

"Brynn… I can't… I can't…"

"LIZ!"

Dr. Bernice forced the passenger doors open and jumped out into the light. So many bullets hit him that his arm detached and fell away.

Brynn laid her body on top of Liz, as though she could save her. The horrors around her tried to steal her soul.

"BRYNN!" Dr. Patrick yelled in the distance.

She tried to look around but the air was filled with too much smoke, dust, and blood.

Another concussion hit the vehicle as a second grenade exploded. She jerked sideways. The driver's body flipped through the air next to the van like he was performing acrobatics. His scream left no questions.

"DAMMIT!" Clint yelled. He clicked something on his gun. Then he turned, sent out a hail of bullets, and ran up the hill towards the attackers. He made it six feet before he fell, never to get up again.

"Oh God, please" Brynn whispered.

At that moment, the bullets stopped as though her prayer was answered. But the silence that followed was louder than the chaos before.

Brynn forced her eyes open. She realized Liz was no longer struggling. "Liz?" She reached for the woman. "Liz?"

No response.

Outside the vehicle, someone yelled in Farsi. Brynn whipped her head in every direction, looking out the windows.

With guns raised and slow, steady steps, warriors drifted down the embankments. The heavily armed guerilla fighters hid their faces with brightly colored shemaghs. They seemed everywhere, like vultures descending on a carcass, draped in a mess of robes and camouflage fatigues.

"Oh no," Brynn said. The gravity of the situation rested on her. Terror seized her soul. She would have vomited if she had not been too afraid to move.

The men barked orders to each other. They came closer and closer before two entered through the passenger door. They yelled fierce words at Brynn.

She winced and stuck her quivering hands into the air. She knew her death was close. They were so, so angry.

One of the two men swung his gun and jumped towards one of the bodies at the front of the vehicle, screaming Farsi.

"Doctor! Doctor! I am Doctor!"

The intruder reached down, seized Dr. Patrick, and jerked him from where he was between the seats. He cowered as he was pulled up. The other man shook his gun at Brynn and screamed incoherently.

"Nurse! Nurse!" she pleaded. "I am nurse!"

The anger in his eyes turned to inquisition, as his brow softened. He lowered his gun and gestured for her to follow him out of the vehicle, waving his hand sharply. For the moment, he didn't kill her.

As she emerged from the van into the sun, arms raised. She did not think she'd ever see the sky again. Someone behind her threw her to the hard ground. She cowered in the desert dust, sickened at her own powerlessness.

It seemed as if twenty men stood around the two of them, pointing their weapons and arguing about what to do with the infidel. A few men gritted their teeth, while others yelled at each other in Farsi.

Tremors took Brynn as she shivered on bent knees, huddled next to Dr. Patrick. It was all she knew to do. Her teeth chattered. Nausea attacked her insides. Snot and tears ran down her face.

"It's going to be all right, my dear," Dr. Patrick whispered, as he put his arm around her.

His words were not reassuring. She felt so vulnerable, exposed in front of all these hateful men. Death was terrifying, but not as terrifying as what they might do to her if they kept her alive.

But she had no time to think. Someone put a hood over her head and gave her a fierce knock across her temple. Then there was nothing but sand and darkness.

CHAPTER 2

I t hurt, but it was the right kind of hurt. Connor West rounded the last corner and looked at his destination, 200 yards away. It seemed far and hard, just as he preferred.

"I like my odds," he said to himself as he beheld the task. His muscles burned. The 80-lb dumbbells he held in either hand fought to be dropped. Some would consider it insane to carry that amount of weight for a mile, but insane was what he wanted. His body needed to deal with the insane, so he would train for it.

The sun high overhead beat down on Connor, taunting him. It teased him, telling him he would never make it. But the sun and the distance didn't know Connor. The sun did not realize it would only light his way. And the distance did not know it would only tempt him.

With swift and steady steps, he gained ground, hauling the weight every last inch. It hurt, and that only pushed him harder. He ground his teeth and growled. He'd be damned if he would give up.

He looked over at his companion. "Let's go, Remo."

Remo nodded and they continued forward. All it took was one step after the other. The hurting grew, but overcoming the hurt grew closer as well. Their feet kicked up dust.

Years and years before, Connor's middle-school coach use to

tell him and his teammates to unleash the lion they had inside, to let it all out. It did not take Connor long to realize he didn't have a lion inside, but a squall, a hurricane. And moments like this made him feel it welling up inside.

They closed the distance and crossed the line. But Connor didn't drop the weight. He tricked his body and made it carry the weight 20 yards farther. And when there, he calmly and in control set them down. His limbs wanted to collapse in relief, but he wouldn't let them.

"Ooooh, hell yeah!" Remo said. "Hurts so, so good."

Connor looked over his at his friend. Remo reached for the ground, stretching out his body. The man's blonde hair and beard were matted to his face with sweat.

The two bumped fists in satisfaction. The fierce heat pulled sweat from Connor's body following the lines of his scars and muscles, before dripping off into oblivion. Perspiration glistened on his fingers, over the numbers tattooed on his pinky, ring, and middle finger, "2-0-7," an unending reminder of his greatest accomplishment: BUDS Class #207. His other hand bore "E-K-I-A." And on his shoulder, the Eagle and Trident perched proudly.

Connor gazed across the vast Afghan base. He squinted at the endless rows of trucks and tanks, hangers and tents, helicopters and jets. Concrete went on as far as the eye could see, giving a foundation to this war machine metropolis. Hundreds of diesel and generator engines hummed on the fringes of his world.

War scared most. Yet, he had never felt more at peace. After years of restlessness, it was so sweet to have an outlet. He loved walking in satisfaction.

A cheer drew Connor's attention and he searched his surroundings. Nearby, across the dust and stone, a group of soldiers played football in an empty field, blanketed in scorched grass. The players had only a pigskin, no pads. The entire group wore the regulation military shorts.

The players began methodically heading for a touchdown at the far end. The line of scrimmage assembled fifty or so yards from where Connor and Remo cooled off.

The team Connor stood behind had the ball and were about to call "hike."

"They don't know what's coming." Remo said, reading Connor's mind and grinning.

Connor shook his head. "Probably not."

His depleted body trembled with fatigue. All he wanted to do was collapse and chug water. To sit down would be such comforting relief.

And that was why he must push on. Countless times before, and he knew countless times to come, he would need his body to produce more than it should. So today, he would force it to as he always did. He pushed the pain away.

From the back of his mind, his father's voice recited the words he told Connor as a child. "Son, you don't have to be the fastest or the strongest. You just have to keep going when all others have stopped."

Turning towards the football field, Connor demanded his limbs obey. The center lineman snapped the ball and the soldier playing quarterback faded towards the rear. Then the troop let it fly.

Connor was already tearing across the barren field, cranking his body in perfect form to maximize speed. Without time to breath, he instead focused on winning. He determined his body would listen to him, or else. The misery was exhilarating. He slipped through the line of scrimmage like a deer hopping over a fence.

Thirty yards ahead of him, the receiver and the cornerback watched the ball linger in the air as they raced towards the end zone. But Connor let loose, pouring out his swiftness. Then, as they leapt for the ball, so did he. The two other players were taller, but he used his strength to find height. And when the three of them came back to earth, Connor's triumphant hands clutched the ball.

Connor held his prize.

"What the *hell* are you doing?" one of the players harassed him.

"Thanks." Connor flicked him the ball. "That was fun."

The other two looked him over, their faces twisting on the cusp of anger. But whatever hostility they held drifted away with the hot desert wind. Connor jogged off, nearly euphoric at the pain he overcame.

Heading across the pavement, Connor spotted his next stop. Clean lines and neat construction comprised the base, confined to its regulation parameters. But one area stood out as chaotic and in disarray. The shell of a rusted-out bus barricaded one side while a long hanger incorporated the other.

Thirty-two men gathered. Their wild appearance contrasted with the strict structure, cleanly shaven faces and trimmed haircuts of military life. A few men stood barefoot, in polo shirts and athletic shorts. Some were shirtless in bathing suits. Others wore hula shirts and grass skirts. One inexplicably had a tuxedo from the 1970s. Some of these men stood by a barbecue pit that surged with smoke while others lounged around an outdoor TV smoking cigars, watching others play video games. Many sat in worn out couches and chairs that had been destroyed by the desert weather. Others perched at picnics tables running oil over weapons.

Connor laughed as some of them gathered with a skateboard, a rope, and a dirt bike. He approached a group of his teammates lounging under makeshift sunshades.

"Lt. Junior Class, Connor West!" a voice called from a nearby couch. "Felt like some football?"

Bear, named for his impossibly hairy body, balanced a Coors Light on the arm of the couch. "They looked flustered. Should have told them you're a legendary running back."

"Just tell them that I'm never out of the fight." Connor said as Bear tossed him a Coors.

Connor turned and fist pounded Lt. Ryan, who had the body of a rugby player and jollyness of Santa Clause.

"Holy hell, Connor! You just gave me a hard on!" Petty Officer Darby called from his recliner and slapped his knee hard.

"Aw, your husband is going to get jealous!" Connor smirked as he popped the can open.

"Nah, Connor, that ain't his husband." Lt. Ryan said. "That's his wife."

Darby nodded with a pensive look. "Understandable. She's not an attractive woman."

The whole group laughed loud without apology.

Connor glanced around, quietly grateful to be surrounded by so many others who shared his drive and love of the misery. Half a world away and in a war zone, he never felt more at home.

"Grab some shade, Connor," his teammate, Mike, said. "Congressman daddy won't be happy if we let you burn in the sun."

"Actually, as of midnight Tuesday, it's *Senator* daddy," Connor said to the group as they ooohed and ahhed.

"Are y'all kidding?" Remo said. "His dad loves this stuff. Connor and I were in the same BUDS class together. I met his parents a few times. Good people." He nodded at Connor. "I saw his dad interviewed on some MSNBC show and someone asked, 'Congressman West, would you sign your son up to fight in Afghanistan?' And without missing a beat, Connor's dad is like, 'No. My son went on his own. SEAL Team 3. And his mother and I are proud of him every day.'"

The group laughed. "Preach!"

"Your dad got elected to the Senate?" Mike said.

"Yeah. Texas decided they liked him."

"Damn, West. Didn't know I was in the presence of royalty," Petty Officer Dodge said. "What'd they do? Fast track you through training?"

"More or less. I spent most of BUDS playing *Call of Duty* in the Admiral's office, sucking down his scotch, and sleeping with his wife."

The group laughed.

"It sucks though. Only had a 42-inch screen. What am I, homeless?"

"Don't listen to him," Remo said. "During training the masterchief called him out and begged Connor to try and hit him."

"Did you?" Bison said.

Connor nodded.

"And what happened?"

"He beat the shit out of me." Connor smirked. "Any chance to fight, right?"

"Preach it, reverend!"

Connor knew that this group understood his reasoning more than anyone else on earth. "All right, you sack of dicks, keep circle-jerking, I'm going to shower." Connor turned away and flicked his empty beer can at them.

"It's all right if you think of me in the shower," Mike said.

"I wouldn't cheat on your mom like that." Connor said.

The group cracked up in laughter as he walked away. Entering the shower facility, Connor found warm water. Most of the troops showered on shift change so he caught a break. But he cranked the water cold. He worried if he gave in to one creature comfort it would spiral him into desiring things that made him weak.

He heard his dad's voice. "It's only the cold, son. Just ignore it."

Stepping out of the shower, he surveyed himself in the mirror. The dark untamed hair and beard from months without shaving, coupled with sun-worn skin and countless scars made Connor fear that his outside finally mirrored the savage within. It was good to be himself.

He threw on athletic shorts and an old Henley before retuning to the rest of his team outside.

"Hey, Bison. Grab me a burger." He called to his teammate working the grill.

His friend wiped his hand off on his Ohio State University apron. "Cheese?"

"Duh."

He sat down on one of the broken couches and turned to his teammates, Baker and Dodge, who played darts.

"I got winner," Connor said.

"So you'll be playing me," Dodge said.

"Dodge. You can't handle darts *or* women." Baker said as he threw.

"What are you talking about? Ladies love them some Dodge."

"Tell that to Sarah," Baker said as the group laughed.

Easing back into the couch, Connor put on his sunglasses and helped himself to one of the cigars in the humidor. After a burger and another beer, he sat up when a humvee screeched to a halt by the group.

Rue Roberts, their Commanding Officer, stuck his head out the window. "Hey, girl scouts. Bourbon Street, ten minutes."

"Awww, Commander, I'm just starting to get a base layer," Bison said.

"You'll still be an ugly son-of-a-bitch. Ten!" He slapped the side of the vehicle twice and the humvee sped off.

"Well, boys." Bungee turned off the grill and put away his spatula. "Let's go to work."

"I was bored anyways," Remo said.

Nine minutes later, the SEAL Team sat in the rusty hanger that served as their command center. They spread out on the beanbags and janky armchairs they'd spent months acquiring.

"Gentlemen," Commander Roberts began, while the briefing screen displayed an image of Afghanistan, then zoomed in on the Tatsu mountains.

"This is my favorite movie!" Bison called out.

"It gets better," Commander Roberts said.

The screen changed to an image of a white van on some lost Afghan road, all shot to hell.

"Three days ago, at approximately seventeen hundred hours, a World Health Organization aid mission was ambushed ten miles south of the village of Shinnt. The roster we received from the W.H.O. has ten names on it."

A series of pictures sequenced showing numerous dead bodies. Most faces barely distinguishable due to mutilation.

"Our friends, the Army Rangers who found the vehicle,

counted eight bodies. All passengers were identified except two: Dr. Augustine Patrick of Dublin, Ireland."

The screen showed an I.D. photo of a man with red hair and beard, who might as well have been standing by a pot of gold at the end of a rainbow.

"And a news correspondent, along to document the trip, from New York, a… Miss Brynn Greene."

The screen displayed the picture of a beautiful and happy young woman, with dark hair and eyes an epic shade of blue.

Connor froze. The pencil in his hand snapped. Fate punched him in the gut and he was sure the ground shook. His entire body tightened and heart raced. But he caught himself. It was very important he not give anything away or he would be taken off the mission. If the intelligence guys had not figured it out already, they probably wouldn't.

Connor knew those eyes and that smile, because they were with him every day of his life. The person on the screen was the one he cared for most in the world. And now he must go and get her.

"Sorry, boss." He had to be sure. "What was her name again?"

"Booooo!" some of the crowd scolded amid guffaws.

"Sorry, guys, sorry," Connor said as if he agreed with their jesting. An empty soda can hit him. Every one was supposed to understand details the first time.

"Yeah, come on, Connor!" Bison jeered. "Be a SEAL, dammit!"

"My bad, won't happen again." Connor bowed, mimicking a penitent hermit.

"Uhhh, *Brynn Greene,*" Commander Roberts said again. He cast a comical look on Connor as though he truly were incompetent.

Connor eased back. He had verified it was Brynn, and he mentally forced himself to appear calm, although his grip tightened on the arm of his chair.

What the hell was Brynn doing here? Had he really not checked on her in that long?

"C.I.A. intelligence in the region says Taliban members were seen entering a compound south of Jarbar two nights ago. It has not been confirmed it's our missing doctor and reporter, but we're rolling anyways. Besides," Commander Rogers turned and nodded towards Remo. "You look bored."

Remo was stuffing his lip with a fat dip but nodded.

"Satellite imaging puts twelve hajis on ground. Best guess is they think we don't know they're there. And abra kadabra, the structure is a former school built by a Russian firm so our friends in Langley sent us blueprints. Aerial insertion two miles east, drop down the ridge. Blackhawks at twenty-mile standby with gunship air support. Bison, Gibbs, Charlie, Remo, Bungee, West, Mike, Denver, Tarda go in, grease the hajis, rescue the girl and the doc. The rest of you ready to support."

He looked around at them. "Build it out. Learn the packets. Wheels up in twelve hours. Get to it."

The screen turned off. Some SEALs grabbed the briefing packets and began reading. Others took the blueprints and started arranging the movable temporary walls they had piled up in the hanger to make a rough copy of the compound.

Connor helped with the construction, forcing conversation so as not to appear compromised. Next, he took one of the briefing packets and read through the 57-page document. Shortly thereafter, he had memorized what he needed to know. Under the hostage information, the packet only listed Brynn's residence as New York. And for some other reason, it didn't list her educational background. She worked for *Horizon World Magazine* as an international correspondent.

Where else had she been?

Commander Rogers put Connor in charge of the insertion team. After two hours of practice, the team had the infiltration down to instinct. They moved as one, continued whole, a form of liquid steel with a common purpose. Connor's mind kept going back to Brynn, but he pushed those thoughts away. For her sake, he needed to focus.

When practice finished and the men were required to rest before take off, Connor slipped away to the bunkroom he shared with Remo. Their plywood quarters featured a pair of twin beds and a desk between, much like the tree house version of a dorm room. The fluorescent light overhead had not worked in several months, so they relied on lamps. Connor's Texas flag hung on the wall over his bed, paired with the Tennessee flag Remo had nailed over his. Remo littered his walls with pictures of home and family. Connor had not taken the time.

When he was certain he wouldn't be disturbed, Connor sat on the edge of his bed and pulled his trunk out. After lifting the lid, he examined the contents. He sifted through items: a few pictures of family his mom had sent, an old map of Texas, his music and his books, including the latest he had read, *The Reckless Outlaw, Will Kelly.*

A moleskin lay buried at the bottom, coated in dust. Connor opened the cover as the scent of stale paper reached out. He read the words she wrote to him: "I hope you find what you're looking for."

He pulled a photograph from its pages. The image drew him in and Connor remembered.

A college kid, who looked a lot like Connor, sat leaning against the statue of Judge Baylor at the university named for him. Brynn perched on the kid's back with her arms around his neck. It didn't matter if Connor smiled, Brynn smiled enough for the both of them. He remembered taking the photo, plagued by the energy and uneasiness inside him at odds with the girl's gentle touch.

Connor recalled the day he was to show up for the corporate job his dad arranged, but instead ran off and enlisted. The moment he did his first pushup in basic, he was finally free. He never felt the need to explain it; no one would understand him anyway. But Brynn was different. He owed her more. He couldn't exist alongside her, because he needed the misery too much. Still, of all the people on earth, she was the only one he hoped could understand. Brynn was more and better than them all. Before the teams, she was his only friend.

And now she was here. And they would dare hurt her. The storm inside him rumbled.

HOURS LATER, THE C-130 plane passed through dark skies over an unsuspecting earth. The planet had no idea that soon the steel beast would open its belly and spill havoc upon the land. No one could guess the killing force cradled within, a group of very professional and deadly heroes.

Connor sat in the red interior lighting, tightening his assault gloves. He made sure his Sig Sauer was snug on his leg and checked his modified M4. For a brief moment, Brynn's face appeared in front of him and his anger grew as he considered what might be happening to her. But he must control himself.

Every step of his role must be carried out with precision, so he focused.

"Two minutes!" the jump engineer yelled from the back of the plane, holding up his index and middle finger.

In unison the smiles and conversation faded as the warriors stood, each rechecking every strap and buckle. Remo scooped chewing tobacco from his lip and tossed it to the floor.

"Let's go to work." He winked and slapped Connor on the back.

The red interior light shut off as the back of the plane opened. A rush of wind filled the hull as outside came in. Dark sky went on forever. The empty void dared them. Then the indicator light turned green, and as one they charged forward.

With a leap, Connor fell into the grip of gravity. "I am death incarnate," he whispered. And he descended.

CHAPTER 3

I t was night. In slow steady rhythm, water dripped from the ceiling and collided with a puddle on the floor. Ripples danced across the surface. A thick and stale stench plagued every breath. The cement ground pushed back, causing pain while it rubbed against her bones. Nausea destroyed her from the inside.

And Brynn was cold. So cold, her fingers ached and were useless as they clutched the scarf she held while trying to channel her pain and neurosis into some tactile action. She quivered and shook. Terror, her constant companion, caused her to jump and whimper at every sound and every change. Because every sound and every change might be one of them coming.

Brynn hurt from the inside out. She did not count her time by days, but by atrocities. Being raped was the worst experience of Brynn's life. It happening twice was even worse. Two of those holding her captive had taken turns ravaging her. Since the moment they pulled her from the van, she was frequently beaten. But the times she was forced into submission, before they assaulted not only her body but also her soul, broke her. Violated did not begin to describe her emotions. She felt dirty, cheap, less than human. The powerless feeling swarming within her haunted her as they pushed her down and pinned her wrists to the floor.

Now, she did not know if she were alive or dead. But if alive, she wished she were dead. Brynn begged God to take her life. Surely, it would be more merciful.

She stared at a moldy piece of bread that rested alone in the middle of the floor. But she refused to eat it, considering perhaps they wanted her strength up so they could use her again. She would show them, by choosing instead to die. Maybe, just maybe, if they looked away long enough, she could race through the door and perish at the hand of the desert.

When she closed her eyes, she saw her parents. They watched old movies together in their living room. The lights were dimmed and the fire burned. A big, spacious couch cradled the pair while they sipped red wine and enjoyed each other's company. She sat near them. Shadows bounced against the cathedral ceilings.

Yet she knew it to be a fiction, regardless of how she wished it to be true. By now her family would have received word she was missing. Certainly the military found the crippled van and reported it. Ironically, she was probably the headline of her own network's newspaper.

Drifting in and out of consciousness, she often hoped to wake and find her dreams were her reality. They failed her time and time again.

A rat slunk across the floor on the far side of her room. It sat up on its haunches and seemed to study her. How odd to be pitied by a rat. The creature scurried away.

On the wall hung an old chalkboard. Brynn guessed this place use to be a school or something of the like. Try as she might, it was hard for her to imagine happy children sitting there learning subtraction.

Among all the evil surrounding her, the element that

shattered Brynn the most was the eyes of her captors. Flashes of their disdain, contempt, and anger burned. As she considered them, Brynn wasn't sure the hope, happiness, and kindness she saw in other Afghans' eyes could compete with the hate. The Taliban and her world would never find reconciliation.

The only guard in the classroom sat in a chair with his feet propped up on a rickety table at the far end near the exit. He crossed his legs next to an oil lamp that cast shadows across the barren room. His folded arms hung still as he slept.

An arid breeze blew through the glassless window. Each time it did, a subtle layer of dust lifted. And when the breeze blew harder, the guard stirred slightly.

Brynn watched him closely. She wanted him to sleep, to leave her alone. He was not one of the ones to violate her, but who knew what kind of villainy he was capable of?

When he did not wake, her nausea subsided, just a little. It roared back a moment later when the patter of boots on the concrete outside let her know someone approached. Every muscle in her tensed up.

Moments later, another Taliban fighter entered the room. He wore ratty fatigues and a shamarg around his head, a worn-looking machine gun slung over his shoulder in a haphazard fashion. He glanced Brynn's way. He was one of the two who changed her forever.

Her heart shuddered. And while she feared him more than anything on earth, she also hated him to the same degree.

He took the cigarette out of his mouth and said something to the guard at the table. When the other guard did not respond, he leaned over his companion and slapped the sleeping insurgent hard across the back of the head. The guard sprung awake, losing his balance in the chair. He fell to the floor and paused on all fours like a lost infant. He looked every direction and straightened himself up. The other guard yelled at him in Farsi.

The man got to his feet and gathered himself. He shuffled towards the door.

No. Don't leave me alone with him.

But the disheveled man could not hear her thoughts and slipped through the entrance, leaving only her and the monster.

He had his back to her, appearing in no hurry. He let his cigarette fall to the floor. Then he turned and looked at Brynn. Enjoyment and playfulness covered his face, as though to taunt her. Grinning, he exposed his yellowed teeth. He said something rhythmic and licked his lip, taking one step closer, and then another. Each footfall thundered in Brynn's ears as he drew near. She knew this time would end her. This was it.

Her hands shook and teeth chattered. She wished she had enough strength to run, but brokenness overwhelmed her. All she could do was cry.

He took the gun off his shoulder and set it to the side. Then he unbuttoned and removed his heavy coat, dropping it to the ground.

Brynn's vision narrowed. All she could see was the man and the night around them. He was larger than life.

The man pulled at his belt and loosened it. He said nothing now, just looked at her in hate. His belt came off. Then his fingers reached for his pant's button.

"Save me," she whispered to the darkness. *If only it would.*

The insurgent raised his eyebrow, hesitating. Tilting his head, he studied Brynn. Three seconds later he unbuttoned his pants and edged forward to descend upon her.

Brynn wished for insanity that she might escape this

moment. Death would have suited her as well.

He reached towards her.

"Please," she begged the night.

There was nothing to be heard but her own beating heart. She tensed. He was *so* close.

But then the night reached out, taking hold of him and wrapping two unstoppable arms around his neck. The hatred in the villain's face fled before the fear replaced it, his face twisting in terror. His eyes bulged. He grabbed at the arms that constricted around his throat, but to no avail. They were too swift, too confident, and too surgical. The insurgent was helpless and powerless. Then the night's arms jerked in a sudden, contorted way. And with a sickening pop, her rapist's neck bent sideways.

As the body fell away, Brynn saw what saved her. She looked up at the giant, not in stature, but in the energy and capability that radiated off the figure, a slayer of monsters. It had taken the thing she feared most and extinguished it without effort. The figure was a menace, a killing machine. Weapons and technology clung to every inch of it. And as her eyes adjusted, she discerned two others behind it, searching the area with guns raised to their shoulders.

Then, from on high, it came down to her level, kneeling close. The thing leaned forward and whispered in her ear, "Don't tell them you know me."

It leaned back and reached up its hand, taking a hold of its mask and pulling it away. The thing had a face, and she *knew* it; the eyes gave him away. They were the same green eyes that made her dreams, both waking and sleeping. They were ones that owned her years before and followed her ever since, beautifully fierce.

So many questions, but she remained silent as he instructed, too weak to inquire.

"Miss, are you Brynn Greene?" he said in a loud voice that filled the room.

"Yes," she whispered.

"Miss, what does your father do?"

She found it a weird question. He already knew. Her father was a… a… She struggled a moment before she could answer. Her dad's occupation seemed distant and to elude her.

"He's a doctor."

The warrior nodded. He touched a mic on his neck. "This is 6. Confirmed. Swan recovered. Repeat, swan recovered. Moving out."

He turned to her. "Miss Greene, my name is Lt. West. We are here to take you home." He reached into his vest and withdrew a plastic rod. "Miss Greene, this is adrenaline. I have to give it to you to help you move. It will hurt."

Connor's quick and steady hand shoved the needle into her leg. Yet before the pain settled over her, life resurged within. She jolted up in the whirlwind of awareness. Connor cradled her neck and body. Her heart beat strong in her chest. The dim fringe of her surroundings suddenly came into focus.

"Miss Greene, do you think you can stand?"

She looked up at Connor and nodded. He clasped her arm and waist, lifting her from the ground. Her body still ached, but it felt distant, almost weightless.

"This way." Connor led her across the room. One of the soldiers put an old laptop from the table in a bag and the other dragged the dead body through the door behind her and Connor.

She followed Connor's lead. They emerged from the room and into the hall. A collapsed roof allowed the bright moon to pour in. She was careful not to trip on rubble.

A clear sheen and wetness glimmered on the wall. The irregular tint splashed across the surface and down onto the floor where it pooled, as though someone had flung fresh paint everywhere. Brynn realized it was blood, evidence of a massacre. Down the hall, she saw another one of unstoppable soldiers dragging the body of the insurgent who had fallen asleep while guarding her. They traveled the length of the hall and rounded a corner toward an open door.

As Connor escorted her through the exit, the cold, cleansing night air wrapped itself around the strands of her hair and touched her neck. She breathed deep, baptized in what she dared to believe was relief.

Lunar rays exposed a row of terrorist corpses that lay side-by-side, face up and bloody. One by one, a team member made his way down the line and, with a flash of his camera, took pictures of their faces. A German shepherd pulled at a leash, leading another soldier around the building. Before, the structure seemed like a guarded fortress, now it appeared broken and pathetic.

Brynn looked around in disbelief. This was the worst place she had ever been and this group of men had cast it to ruin in minutes.

So, this is what Connor does, she thought. She peered up at him, but he did not return her gaze.

"Wrap it up! Helos inbound!" he called on his mic.

The pair stood near three captured insurgents. They sat with their hands zip-tied behind their backs, slumped over in defeat. One SEAL stood as sentinel over them, ever watchful.

The insurgent nearest turned his face just enough. He was the other one who assaulted her.

Brynn quivered as a whimper escaped her. She clung tight to Connor as flashes of her torture plagued and tormented her. *Look at that monster, just sitting there, trying to hide. It was me you did this to!*

Anger crept into her veins. She knew she'd never sleep again while he lived. He had to pay. He shouldn't exist in the world and she would end it.

The Americans had laid their enemies' weapons in a pile near Brynn and Connor. She pulled away from Connor ever so slightly. He was still engaged with the operation. Slowly, she knelt and wrapped her hand around a pistol. The metal felt cold and dull. She remembered just enough of what her father taught her. Standing, she raised it towards her devil. He had to pay. She could erase him forever. It would only take one bullet.

But try as she might, she couldn't seem to keep her hand still. The gun shook.

"Brynn?" Connor whispered over her shoulder, speaking with more familiarity. "What are you doing?"

"He made me dirty, Connor," she said. "He made me so dirty."

"He did?" Connor said darkly.

She knew he understood. "He doesn't deserve to live." She pleaded.

Connor slipped his arm around her and ran his hand from her elbow to her wrist. She didn't struggle. "Trust me," he said as he gently took the gun away. "You don't want to live with that."

He drew Brynn closer into his chest. She surrendered.

"Charlie," he called.

The SEAL next to the prisoners looked up. Connor gestured with his head and the SEAL stepped away.

Connor pulled a gun from the holster on his leg. This gun

had a silencer. Connor raised the weapon towards the insurgent and pulled Brynn closer. "Don't look."

She closed her eyes and buried her face in his vest.

A light pop was followed by a heavy thud. She knew the beast who would occupy her nightmares was dead.

"Charlie, looks like there's one E.K.I.A. we forgot to photograph. Take him over to the line up."

"Roger." The SEAL cut the body's bonds with his knife and dragged it away.

The ground trembled. The sound of turbines grew deafening as two helicopters appeared over the ridge. The windstorm they created blew a blizzard of sand. They slowed and hovered overhead before lowering to the ground.

"Mount up!" Connor called across his mic. He and Brynn hunched over as they approached the near helicopter. A massive door on the side slid open and a crewman reached out and offered his hand. She took it, but clung with the other to Connor. She refused to let go of him. Connor followered her and took a seat next to her.

"Miss!" A crewman yelled over the sound of the helicopter, holding up a blanket. Brynn leaned forward while he wrapped it around her shoulders. In seconds, other SEALs took seats around them while the rest headed to the second helicopter.

The pilot looked back with a thumbs-up. Connor responded with the same gesture and in moments the vehicle lifted from the ground.

Reality shifted for Brynn. The men sat in the helicopter, appearing ever so relaxed, and conversed like it was any given day at the office. She wondered how they could all look so business-as-usual. Why weren't they as overwhelmed as she was? One of them even yawned. But she gave up.

And as the aircraft droned on, she leaned against Connor, smothering herself in his shoulder. She closed her eyes and took steady breaths, inhaling his aroma of canvas, metal, and gun oil. Resting against his powerful arm, she dared to feel safe. Her racing heart slowed and her limbs hung heavy. When she stared out the helicopter window, moonlit mountaintops drifted by. She grew numb to the sound of the roaring engines.

The vehicle slowed. Rows and rows of lights cut through the night as though a city rose from the desert. It expanded and went on forever. The helicopter descended through the air and touched the ground. The engines eased while the men filtered out of the choppers.

Brynn stepped onto the tarmac. A group of individuals stood waiting, dressed in long white lab coats. A female soldier with a red cross on her arm pushed a wheelchair toward her.

"Miss Greene. I'm Lt. Daley. Please come with me," she called over the sound of the slowing helicopter. "We need to make sure you're all right!"

Brynn looked at Connor. *Why is this woman trying to pull me away from him?* Connor never acknowledged Brynn. He tried to step away once, but she clung to him. When he paused, she slowly loosened her hands.

So Brynn sat down in the wheelchair while the staff bombarded her with questions, but she could not listen. She watched as Connor joined the rest of the SEALs. One of them from the other helicopter carried the motionless body of Dr. Patrick and laid it on a gurney, as though the hefty doctor were no more than a pillow.

Now in the bright light of the base, Brynn could see her rescuers better. They carried themselves so rigid, so final. Their strides reminded her of victorious cowboys walking away from a gunfight, a pack of modern day gladiators. And then they left together, vanishing into the darkness and night from whence they came.

The next few hours became a whirlwind of fluorescent lights, examinations, and shots. Brynn tried to focus as they asked her what hurt and where. They offered her food, but she did not feel like eating. At times, uniformed individuals, not part of the medical staff, would approach and ask questions about her time in captivity. They wanted to know if any other insurgents had come and gone or if she understood any of their dialogue.

Eventually she was alone with a female doctor. From the moment they landed, Brynn was scared of this encounter and the questions that would inevitably arise.

"Miss Greene, did they ever sexually assault you?" The mechanical manner in which she spoke seemed impossible. Brynn didn't want to talk about it, not with this stranger, not with the person who had run through a list of questions from a book. Because this question would never be enough.

Brynn wanted to be asked if a piece of her was murdered. She wanted to tell the world her dead attackers got off easy, as she was the one condemned to walk the earth in punishment. She wanted to speak of her silent pleadings, her pulled hair, and her slapped face. No one asked about the moment she felt abandoned by God. Or when she wanted to know where He was on the night it was cold and gray but all she could see was the back of her eyelids as she tried to escape the horror. She wanted to know how to live feeling dirty from the inside out.

But not here, not among these strangers, however good their intent. The soldiers rescued her body while her soul lay casualty in some forsaken corner of the world.

"No. No, I was not."

The doctor checked a box on her form. "Okay. Did you ever—"

"I'm sorry," Brynn said. "I'm extremely tired. Could we continue this tomorrow? I'd like to go to sleep now."

The physician exhaled. "Well, yes. Of course." She turned her head. "Private Winters, please escort Miss Greene to her bunk."

An individual, smaller than Brynn, who looked like he had no need of a razor, stepped up in an oversized uniform. "This way, ma'am."

Brynn nodded to the physician and followed Private Winters across the tile floor and beneath the harsh lights. The beeps of medical devices and dividing curtains accompanied the pair, until they passed through the doors.

She followed him into an SUV. They drove a mile to a different part of the base. Then Private Winters led her to a recently erected structure, not painted so its plywood construction showed clearly.

A few other civilians sat outside in chairs, cleaning electronics and video equipment. They did not look towards her.

Private Winters shoved a door open and flicked a light switch. The room was tiny, with a single bunk built into a wall, and a lone light bulb cast a tired glow. The assembled shelves waited bare. A pitcher of water and plastic cup sat on the table. On one end of the bed lay a folded blanket, and on the other, a pillow with no case.

"Sorry it isn't much. But we've notified your family and you're scheduled to fly out of here tomorrow at 10:00 a.m. If you need anything, just talk to some of the M.P.s stationed over there."

"Thank you."

Private Winters closed the door behind him.

Brynn stood in her room, too tired to get in bed and too overwhelmed to care. The light bulb caught her gaze and entranced her, as visions of her last three days plagued her.

A knock came from the door.

"Yes?" Brynn arrived back to the present.

The door opened and Connor stepped in from the night.

Her heart drew back. In the years since they last saw each other, she had forgotten what it was like to be in his presence. *How could a single man fill the space like that?* The room bent away from him, strained by the energy that surrounded him. She saw it first when they were kids. No one else ever seemed completely at ease around him, as if he were an animal choosing to be docile, to perhaps change at any moment.

"Why didn't you tell them we grew up together?" Brynn said. Starting mid-conversation felt odd after being apart for so many years.

"Because if they were aware we know each other, they never would have let me come." His voice was calm and raspy. He had discarded his fight gear, wearing a black fleece and the Hoyt ball cap he'd owned since they were fifteen.

She looked across his familiar face, weathered by the sun. In their separation, he'd found a new scar for his chin and one for outside his right eye. The green in his irises burned with all the ferocity, fearlessness, and immortality she once blanketed herself in.

She never questioned that Connor had both great and terrible things inside him. And discovering the instrument of destruction he'd become, Brynn guessed he'd done both.

But to her, right now they weren't a war machine and international news journalist. All Brynn wanted was to be the girl who followed him around hopelessly from the day she met him, and him to just be the wild one that owned her dreams.

Emotion fought through and she lost control. But she didn't care. They sat down on her bunk as she soaked his shirt with tears. When he put his arms around her, Brynn went limp.

She knew she might look silly to him, so shattered and so crushed. He didn't understand fear or defeat, and he had never faced a thing in his life and seen it as insurmountable. He never would. He had dragon skin, on loan from Siegfried. But she didn't need him to understand. All she wanted in this moment was for him to let her cry. So she cried.

CHAPTER 4

"Death is my craft, and destruction is my wake," Connor whispered to himself, squeezing the trigger of his modified M4. The insurgent in his sights fell back as a high-velocity round smashed his face. Then Connor found another Taliban fighter and let the lead fly. Chips of brick and mortar tore off the wall next to him as enemy fire peppered its surface. One flying shard cut his ear lobe, but he chose to ignore it and never broke his firing rhythm. Another insurgent fell.

The team fired from the remains of a blown-out building in a small town of the Kunar Province. In the distance, concussion from artillery fire split the air, filling the town with the sounds of Armageddon. The blasts were deafening. Fire danced in the streets.

Taliban fighters had Connor's team pinned down from two rooftops across the street. A bothersome individual sprayed bullets from a mounted .30 caliber machine gun in the back of a pickup. Wave after wave of bullets berated the frogmen.

"THAT SHIT STAIN IN THE TRUCK IS REALLY PISSING ME OFF!" Bison yelled over the madness.

Connor nodded.

Bison counted off with his fingers. On the count of three and in a second's time, the pair popped out from behind their wall, aimed, and fired, then immediately ducked behind the wall. The machine gun fire stopped as the body slumped forward.

"I LOVE OUR JOB!" Bison yelled.

"I KNOW!" Connor shot twice and turned his head. "I can't believe we get paid!"

Firing at the rooftop across the street, Connor emptied a clip and switched mags. The gunfight was too intense to keep counting, but he guessed he was up to eleven kills for the day, doing his job as hunter.

"Call all those marine cobras and tell them where we are. Tell them we need those houses to be parking lots!" Lt. Ryan yelled from Connor's left, behind a column. Fabric tore across his pant leg as a bullet grazed his right thigh, drawing a thin, scarlet line.

Mike looked up from a radio, giving a thumbs-up and indicated the fighter helicopters had received the message. "INBOUND! MARK IT!"

Connor popped a smoke grenade and heaved it onto the roof across the street. A second later, the yellow indicator drifted into the air, marking the insurgents. Connor gunned down two men who tried to pick it up and remove it. After he fired the next bullet, one man exploded. Knowing his bullets were not capable of such feats, he realized the helos arrived. Connor looked up at the great machines hovering above the violence, like angels of death waiting for their turn. The pilots opened fired and swept the rooftops clean before sending a blizzard of rockets to tear apart the concrete.

A great burst of dust seeped from the demolished buildings and blanketed the SEALs in a shroud of darkness. Soon, wind carried it away. In the aftermath, a pile of rubble was all that remained. Connor trained his weapon down the narrow street, daring someone to stick his head out.

"I'm bored." Remo said as he spit tobacco juice on the ground.

"Let's move," Lt. Ryan said.

They worked north, half on one side of the street and half on the other. Connor focused straight ahead, which for the moment was his only job in the world. He didn't have to worry about the rooftops, as they were his teammates' job. Nor did he have to be concerned about their rear, that was someone else's job. His team could handle it. He needed only to look forward.

Despite the storm of explosions on the other side of town, the block they walked was quiet. The patter of their boots provided the only soundtrack of their movement.

A door to the street flew open as an insurgent with an AK-47 rushed into the alley. Before he could raise his gun, three of Connor's teammates shot him in unison. Connor stepped over the body as they proceeded forward.

Connor saw the next insurgent standing in a window at the same time as the insurgent fired his RPG. He didn't have to time to dive for cover. The explosive force sent Connor through the air, head over heels. A flash of white light stole his clarity, and in an instant all he saw was her blue eyes. He slammed hard into the ground, ears ringing and his team's voices muffled.

"CONNOR!" Bison reached down and grabbed Connor's vest to drag him out of the middle of the street. The air sang with gunfire as other insurgents arrived.

"Connor! Can you hear me? Connor!"

In his haze, Connor forgot where he was. Everything hurt terribly and his arm was numb.

Get up. Get up, you pussy. Just stand, it's not that hard. They didn't count on someone as strong as you.

Connor rolled over and pushed himself off the ground. He shoved the pain far and away, for now was not the time to deal with it. Now was the time to make war.

"Are you still in the fight?" Bison called from where he crouched below a pile of rubble.

"I *am* the fight!" Connor spun around the corner and let bullets fly. "And I like my odds!" Every shot was surgical, intentional. *Why does she plague my mind?*

After the group of insurgents was eliminated, the team moved past the bodies they just dropped. They turned left at the cross street to realize that the battle had demolished the buildings in their path. The SEALs came to a dead end, mountains of wreckage surrounding them. They crouched and covered different directions.

"We're going through that building." Lt. Ryan pointed towards a dark doorway in the building ahead of them, which seemed to be the only way through.

The street before the door turned right, around a corner.

A touch on his shoulder let Connor know to proceed. He rose and moved forward, spinning wide around the turn's corner to cover right, leveling his gun.

Instincts fired. PERSON... HOSTILE?... No. Connor identified the little Afghan boy who startled him as a non-threat. The boy appeared as surprised to see the SEALs as they were to see him.

With a terrified look on his face, the boy put his body between Connor and the goat he led. He looked up at Connor, the killing machine, with big, brown Arab eyes.

"This sucks," Mike said. "Leave the kid alone here to try and survive a warzone. And even if he does make it, he'll just grow up to try and kill us later. Classic Monday!"

As his team moved passed, Connor kept his eye on the child. He reached into his vest, removed a protein bar, and tossed it to the boy. "Here, kid. If we end up friends, I want you to eat. If we end up enemies, I want you strong."

Then Connor followed the others into the building. Blinking, he waited for his eyes to adjust from the bright sun to the dark interior. The musty stench of mildew stunk the air.

The team stopped communicating and moved through as a silent killing unit, sweeping rooms as they went. The rush of not knowing what was around the next corner, death or victory, caused Connor's heart to race.

They traveled down a long corridor. Various doorways opened off the left side. On the right side was a straight wall. Every twenty feet the wall was glass, floor to ceiling, but dirty and impossible to see through. On the other side of the wall ran a street.

The team moved methodically, hoping to find a way out in the direction they wanted to go. Rusty old desks and chairs lay askew across the floors. Papers, once white, now yellow with age, littered the rooms.

Connor, along with his companions, turned on the laser sights attached to their weapons. The beams swept and painted the interior. Every corner, closet, and cabinet became a potential hiding spot for a haji.

Turning into a small room, a closet door splintered as someone fired a shotgun through it. The spread hit Connor in the chest. His vest stopped the lead but the force hit him like a wrecking ball and launched him off his feet like a rag doll. Despite flying backward through the glass wall, he fired mid-air at his attacker, killing him.

The glass shattered. In an instant, Connor was awash in

sunlight and slammed hard into the street outside. After impact, he looked around, assessing his new surrounding.

Forty yards away, a group of militants had gathered in the street. Their eyes opened wide and they raised their guns.

All Connor could do was use momentum and roll through an open door on the far side of the street. Collapsing backwards through the door, he jerked his legs inside as bullets ricocheted at his feet.

The firefight tore the street apart. Connor looked around his refuge room, assessed it was empty, stood, and fired down the street.

"We're playing my favorite game," he grunted through clenched teeth.

After relentless fire, no insurgents remained alive. Back with the team, Connor and the team moved up the street. His shoulder felt sore so he looked down to see himself bleeding. One of the twelve gauge pellets that missed his vest had pierced his arm.

He savored the hurt. It was such a rush, a high, to overcome it. His enemy would need bigger bullets.

They neared a three-story building, tall for this town. They needed the high ground to verify their location. As they wove their way towards the structure, gunfire and a thumping sound came from the top. Connor guessed insurgents must be shooting bullets and mortar rounds at the Marines on the far side of the town.

The team filtered into the lower floors like poison into veins. The resistance was minimal. Minutes later, Connor stood before the door that led onto the roof. He and Mike forced the door open and handled the group of insurgents shooting in the opposite direction.

Connor and Mike decorated the remaining insurgents on the roof with bullet holes. Half the team was on the roof while the others guarded the lower floors and their way out. The remains of the town's square smoldered in front of the building.

Lt. Ryan pulled out his satellite screen. Connor peered over the edge at fires that blazed a half-mile away. Smoke lifted from the streets. The Marines were doing their thing. Down to his left, a mother ran holding hands with children on either side.

"All right." Lt. Ryan looked up from his screen. "It's that one, the pinkish one. That's where he's at." He pointed forward.

"This guy better provide the intel he promised and make the trip worth it," Bison said.

"The Brass want him. We're here to get him," Lt. Ryan said. "Plus, at least you're not shoveling shit in Louisiana. Move out!"

After leaving a grenade behind to destroy the mortar weapon, they descended the stairs and the team rolled out across the old square. Rubble crumbled under their feet. On the far side, they reached another street and traveled north. Two hundred yards more and they came to cross streets. Before rounding the corner, they knelt and covered different directions while Lt. Ryan waved Dodge forward.

"Trident in position," Lt. Ryan called over the radio to command.

"Stand by," Commander Roberts voice crackled back.

They waited, allowing the robot drones to do their work from the skies above. Effects from the nearby battle rattled the town.

Pictures the drones took finally registered on Lt. Ryan's screen. Thermal images of their target building informed them of the layout and its habitants.

"Shit," Lt. Ryan said. "Six hostiles. Should be four."

Connor peered through the shattered window. A narrow walkway separated their building from the target building, while both structures were two stories.

As he studied it, another artillery shell landed in the neighborhood. Its energy shook the building, raining dust down on them as foundations trembled.

"Well," Lt. Ryan said. "Looks like we're gonna have to cowboy this one."

They took ten minutes and devised a plan. Connor and Dodge found a ladder among the wreckage and carried it to the roof. With quiet, controlled movements they laid it across the narrow alley so it connected to the roof of the pinkish building.

When Lt. Ryan signaled them, they crept across. The ladder creaked and bowed beneath Connor. He kept one eye on the door and the other on the alley below. At the last rung, he put his boot against the roof. After a bit of testing, it seemed like it could hold his weight.

With Dodge coming next, Connor approached the door to the lower level and slipped his inspection mirror under the door to make sure the coast was clear. Then he gently pulled on the door and cracked it open. He clicked his mic three times to let the team know he and Dodge were inside. Connor drank in the excitement.

They waited. A crash came from the first floor and gunfire unleashed. Connor and Dodge slipped down the stairs, coming in behind men who were in a firefight with the other SEALs. The pair allotted one bullet each and dispatched them.

"Clear!" Lt. Ryan said after the enemy was neutralized.

The team moved through the house. Connor posted against the window, checking for insurgents drawn by the gunfire.

At one point, the building may have been very well

maintained, but war had not been kind to it. Empty jars and spent cans of food littered the floor. A dim light came through thick curtains. Huge vacant spots remained where kitchen appliances once operated.

Connor surveyed the unusual collection of porcelain dolls sitting on a shelf, as well as masked trinkets. They reminded Connor of an art project Brynn once did in high school. *No, stop! This is not the time to be thinking about her. You gave her up years ago.*

"He should be under there." Lt. Ryan pointed to the kitchen table at which sat three bullet-ridden Taliban corpses. Connor seized one of the bodies and hulled it to a corner. Remo and Bison moved the table away. All that was left was a tattered, dust covered Persian rug.

Lt. Ryan pulled the carpet away. Beneath it, the rusted metallic trap door seemed out of place. The SEALs in the room stepped back and raised their guns.

"Omar Al Chalabi!" Lt. Ryan called toward the trap door. "Omar Al Chalabi! This is the United States Navy! Come out!"

A few moments passed without a sound.

"Maybe he left."

A loud snap resonated and the door lifted open.

"Keep your hands raised!"

Two small, olive-colored hands crept over the edge, followed by arms and a head. The moment the man cleared the trapdoor, two SEALs swept in and made sure no one else was down the hole while another patted him down.

Connor checked Omar Al Chalabi over, deciding he resembled the Arab version of a sleazy car salesman. Though extractions were rare, he enjoyed it more when they rescued people who looked like they didn't cheat at cards. Connor did not care for him and sure as hell didn't trust him.

"Omar Al Chalabi?" Lt. Ryan stepped forward.

"Yes." Al Chalabi answered in perfect English.

"Put your thumb here." Lt. Ryan held out a small electronic device and directed Al Chalabi in scanning his fingerprint.

Lt. Ryan read the machine. "It's him." He reached for his radio. "Nest, this is Trident, Santa Clause recovered. Repeat, Santa Claus recovered."

"Roger that. Move forward to extraction," said the radio.

"Copy." Lt. Ryan turned to the men. "Move out. Mike, Minetti, stick on him like glue."

Connor locked eyes with Omar Al Chalabi. To Connor, Al Chalabi didn't look as relieved as he should. A certain calculating air lingered.

Again, they took to the streets. Minetti and Mike dragged Omar along. As they neared the edge of town, the buildings were spread farther and farther apart. The Marines' battle grew distant. The team wove systematically between the ruins, hoping to go unseen.

Their route sloped upward at the edge of town as the settlement approached the mountains. The team weaved through the rusted shells of cars toward the rise. Dodge took his place at the front and up the ridge.

Connor felt exposed out in the open and the daylight didn't help.

Dodge peaked over the ridge before throwing up his hand. Connor tucked down and monitored their rear, his kneepad crunching against the stone.

"Thirty Hajis between us and the L-Z," Dodge said through the mic. "They aren't supposed to be there. Why didn't a drone pick them up?"

Lt. Ryan pulled out his radio and grinned. "Time to bring in Dad." He worked the mechanism. "Skyhammer, this is Trident. Do you copy?"

"Skyhammer here, we copy."

"Detachment of hostiles between us and the L-Z. Send in the thunder. Coordinates 33°97'96", 61°31'46"."

"Roger that, Trident. Let's see if we can't clear the road for you. Inbound, three minutes."

Connor hated waiting. Instinct told him to keep moving forward, never stay still, always take the ground. But he knew now was the time not to change position.

Three minutes later, the sky roared with the approach of dawning destruction.

"Skyhammer on site. Ready to drop the thunder, Trident," the voice came over the radio.

"Roger. Drop the thunder, Skyhammer," Lt. Ryan said into his radio. Then he turned to the team. "Dad's here."

Dodge pulled out a cigar and lit up. Nodding to Al Chalabi, he winked. "Watch this."

Connor looked up into the sky. The herculean aircraft rumbled overhead in its wide rotary pattern. Then came the unmistakable sound of the C-130 gunship dropping lead on the target, as lightning rained. The ground shook.

Connor wondered if ancient warriors had ever guessed how easy killing would become one day.

The team climbed the ridge and watched the destruction from 500 yards out, standing shoulder to shoulder. The huge aircraft dusted the desert with fire, reaping a tidal wave of sand. When the firing stopped and the cloud settled, nothing remained but twisted metal and a memory of where the enemy once walked.

"You are clear to proceed, Trident. Skyhammer out."

"Much obliged, Skyhammer," Lt. Ryan said. "Hear that command? Ready for evac."

"Roger that, Trident. Osprey inbound."

Connor's team trotted down the road as the V-22 Osprey troop transport floated in and waited for them, pelting them with gusts of wind. His boots hit the ramp and then settled into his seat.

"Well, that was a *fun* one," Remo said before loading his lip with dip.

"Yeah. Who would've ever thought a dumb shit redneck would make such a great SEAL?" Connor grinned.

"Back at you, silver spoon, prep school bitch."

They laughed and bumped fists.

The aircraft lifted them away from the chaos and swept them across the landscape. An hour later they landed at base. Connor walked away, momentarily satisfied. His itch was scratched. But he wondered why he couldn't shake Brynn as he normally could.

Later that night, after he and his team watched *Old School* together and smoked cigars they had bartered for, Connor returned to his bunkroom and sat down at his computer. He pulled out the photo of Brynn and him and ran his fingers across her face.

Half a decade before, when he disappeared, it made sense. He had spent his lifetime pulled in two directions. One was towards her, and the fantastic mystery it was to know her and hear her thoughts. To walk, uninterested in the rest of the world, but fascinated by her. She was layers and layers, endless roads to explore.

The other was his irrepressible need to struggle and overcome, to have his back against the wall while facing gods and titans. He needed to fight. And more than that, to fight chaos or create it. Stillness unsettled him. The steady patterns of the conventional were torturous to him. To explain it was impossible, so he never tried. But Brynn seemed to understand.

Too many times, these two directions had been at odds. He would have been blind not to see what Brynn endured.

Unsure which direction would win, the outcome had not mattered. Instinct took Connor to the military. Long ago he realized he couldn't have both.

But that was years ago. He'd grown and changed, as had she. He'd found a path. His issue was handled. It no longer controlled him; he controlled it. Seeing her six months ago unlocked and returned something. Her essence lingered with him since she cried on his shoulder. Perhaps he could have it all. And she was his favorite person on earth.

After all, there was nothing he couldn't do.

In fourteen months at war, Connor had sent home only one message. It was six months ago: an anonymous letter that read, "While in captivity, your daughter was sexually assaulted. Make her participate in counseling."

He opened his email and wrote his second message in all that time. "I'm coming home on leave." He pressed send.

CHAPTER 5

Brynn tapped her fingers on the steering wheel. Reaching for the radio, she searched the stations for nothing in particular before giving up and turning it off.

As she fidgeted, the car felt stuffy, so she unrolled the window. She forced herself to sit back and take a deep breath. Then she flipped down the vanity mirror in the car, checking her makeup. Pausing, she questioned the shade of her lipstick, bolder than she normally wore. Was it the message she wanted to send?

She wasn't sure what message she wanted to send, but whatever it was, this particular shade wasn't right. She pulled a napkin from her purse and dulled the intensity. Besides her makeup, she also examined her hair, thinking she looked like she tried too hard. So she let it fall and pulled it into a ponytail.

Brynn regretted arriving so early. Maybe it was nervousness that caused her timing. Or maybe it wasn't nervousness, but anxiety or excitement. Perhaps it was just curiosity.

The anxiety, nerves, and excitement began the moment she had received a call from Senator West asking her to pick up Connor at the base. *Why wouldn't he do it? Or ask one of his aides to?* Plus, the Senator acted as though she knew Connor was coming in on leave. *What does all this mean?*

A soldier carrying a box of tools, the same one who had

walked by twice before, passed her parking spot on the tarmac. She really had arrived too early.

A glance at her watch told her it was 6 p.m., the time the plane was due to land. Minutes crept by. With the windows down, she felt like part of the evening. It was calm and quiet. The air was cool enough to be comfortable.

She sighed. "What am I doing here?"

Despite recent events, she needed to be on guard for her heart's sake. Looking down a familiar road, she refused to let her life become unfurled just because of a visit. Brynn thought it was good to stay cautious, even feeling a little proud of herself. Yet, she couldn't help but generate a little excitement about the unknown, possibilities that were unlikely but possible nonetheless. In the end, she just felt overwhelmed.

A dark shadow approached from the burnt orange clouds patrolling the horizon. Brynn knew it was *him*, she could just tell. It descended like a ghost. Eerily she could see it drift yet hear no sound until it was close enough for the engines to roar. A puff of smoke dissipated from the tires as the plane's landing gear hit the ground. The hulking aircraft traveled every inch of the runway before stopping and swinging around. Like a monstrous bull strolling through a meadow, it taxied over until it reached her end of the tarmac. As it settled, the engines slowed and eased. The great beast sat at a standstill.

Anxiety gripped her chest. The keys grazed her hand while they dangled in the ignition. It would be so easy to drive off. But she shook her head and rolled her eyes, then pushed her door open and climbed out onto the pavement. After she shut her door, she leaned against the side of her car, arms crossed as she waited on the black top. A tender breeze lifted hair off her neck. She forced herself to stand still and look calm while she watched through her sunglasses.

The cargo ramp on the plane creaked open inch by inch. Crews of men approached with forklifts and clipboards. Yet before they climbed the ramp, a lone figure descended. From a distance, his boot falls seemed heavy.

He walked across the tarmac like a giant. All the world spun toward him and yet spiraled away. She wasn't sure if the ground or her heart was shaking. Flashes of him walking off the field towards her after high football games dashed across her mind. Images of him leaving his latest frat house brawl soon followed. She couldn't believe she'd soon hear his voice.

Behind him, the setting sun highlighted his silhouette. A duffle bag swung high over his left shoulder. From his broad shoulders, his V-frame torso narrowed to his waist. His strides were calm and confident, as though he'd make the world match his pace. Some might call him a hero, but Brynn knew he was something else; something more *and* less. Though she couldn't hear it, she was certain the concrete broke beneath him. And as her knees grew weak when the spell of his presence fell upon her, she forgot all the carefully thought-out words she had planned to say.

At last he stood before her, casting his easy smile at her, grinning behind his aviators. He was every bit a neighborhood hunk, yet dark and dangerous. The shaggy hair and barbaric beard he had in Afghanistan were now replaced by his bare steely jaw and trim haircut.

So, there in the middle of some forgotten army base, the reckless boy and the girl who chased him stood before each other.

He set down his duffle. "Hey there, bright eyes."

She melted. "Hi, Connor."

The man pulled her in close. She felt so delicate and narrow in his embrace.

"Thanks for picking me up." He kissed her head above her ear, in a fashion that could be romantic or just friendly.

"Yeah, no… no problem." She wanted to say more but felt herself studying him, watching his every move and gesture, mesmerized.

Connor opened the back door and heaved his duffle inside like it weighed nothing. She reached for the driver's door handle.

"Whoa! What do you think you're doing?" He stretched out his hand toward her handle. "This *is* Texas after all. Guys open doors here."

She blushed as she slid in. "Thanks."

"Can't help it, Brynn. It's a rule, bigger than any of us." He smiled. Then he circled around to the passenger door and opened it.

"What's this?" He pointed to a small gym bag in the front seat, waiting to enter the car.

"I don't know. Your dad's aide sent me that for you after he called asking me to pick you up."

" Yeah, I don't know why he didn't make other arrangements instead of giving you this chore. Sorry he asked you to drive all the way out here." Connor pulled at the zipper of the bag. "Although it is good to see you." He gave her a playful look.

She was grateful for his sunglasses, worrying his eyes would cast her into dizziness.

Connor pulled open the bag, exposing a pair of well-worn Ariat boots and Wrangler jeans. "Nice call, Senator." He nodded. Without hesitation he dropped the fatigues from his waist and stood in his boxers before throwing on the denim and leather.

He slid into her passenger seat. "That feels better."

Brynn recognized the boots. He'd worn them for years and years, from high school through college. She considered all the concerts, bars, trouble, and adventures she and Connor had gone through with him in those boots.

"Ready?" he said.

"You look good, Connor." She wasn't as embarrassed as she thought she'd be to say such a thing.

"Think so?" He looked at her.

"Yes." She started the car and pulled away from their spot. Connor waved to the personnel at the gate as they exited the base and headed for the highway.

Every few minutes, Brynn looked at him, stealing glances at his profile.

"So, like, do you want to stop anywhere or need anything?" Brynn pulled the question from the flood of possible inquires pouring through her brain.

"We should head to my parent's house," Connor said.

"To your home?"

"Yeah, my parent's house." Connor said again, his T-shirt stretched to hold his bicep. "So, after we saw each other six months ago, I learned you've been living in New York. International reporter?"

"For a while." Brynn said, looking at him more than at the road. "I'm back here now. Things kind of changed after Afghanistan. Thank you, by the way."

Connor turned to her. "Sure. Just don't let it keep you down."

Is that it? Is that all we're going to say about what happened? Brynn hoped it'd be a much longer conversation, where she could talk about how much it meant to her and what it meant to him. Yet, Connor handled it in too succinct a fashion.

For twenty minutes, they drove. Connor spent much of their time commenting on all the new development in town. A few questions about what Brynn was doing these days. Yet Brynn was not getting what she wished for. For every word he uttered, Brynn had a thousand she wanted to say but didn't. And not just on the Afghanistan incident, but on the better part of a decade.

Connor looked out the window. "How, *how* many Starbucks does a town need—"

"Where did you go?" The question got away before Brynn could stop it. "*Like where?* I mean, six years! We were here, and then you were gone, in the blink of an eye and to the other side of the world." She hesitated. "You were going to take that job your dad had for you, move back to Houston. What happened?" She exhaled.

Connor lowered his eyebrows and tilted his head, then he looked forward. "You know, Brynn. It just didn't fit. It never did."

"But why there?"

"It fit."

Brynn fell silent, considering his words. Connor was so correct. Years before as she watched the lives of those around them, she witnessed a calming wave pass over when Connor disappeared. Things settled. There seemed to be less heartache around the neighborhood.

"Did you find what you needed?" she said.

"You better believe it."

How could that be all of it?

Brynn pulled her hand in from the open window. "Is it hard being over there?"

"In some ways, and it's easier in some. It's simpler. Being

that near to death puts things in perspective for a lot of men. 'Good bye' might really be just that. Things after walking by flag-draped caskets."

"It must be hard seeing that." Brynn said.

"It's just death. Everyone has to do it. At least they got to die heroes, fighting to the end, strong and free. Fifty more years makes no difference. Descendants always forget names, and gravestones become unreadable. You know?"

"What was it like, the first time you killed someone?" Her voice quivered as she realized the awkwardness of her question.

He sighed, as though contemplating what to tell her.

"Pretty easy. I grew up with my belief system and he grew up with his. We're both the 'good guys' from our own perspectives. Sure, I love America and he loves whatever back-ass tribe he's from. In a thousand years, neither will stand. We've been promised different paths to Heaven." He slowed. "But in the end, it's just him and me. We both volunteered for this game. And in the moment, it just comes down to who plays it better. Who's got better aim, who's stronger, who's faster. In the moment I don't have to be the best, just better; better than him, better than the guy coming behind him, and better than his son who will grow up to hate me someday." Connor fell silent.

His words felt so final and weighty, poetic and arrogant. What could she contribute?

She had more questions, but they grew fuzzy as she sat quietly content to be near him. The voice in her head sounded alarmingly like it did in high school. But she knew where her heart would go if she let it. She didn't know what to make of Connor's brief return. She promised herself to be strong.

As she drove, he gave her a brief overview of the years since he vanished, supplementing the stories Brynn once heard through gossip.

Before long, she pulled down the brick circle drive, of Connor's childhood home. Massive white columns held up the overhang of the roof, two stories and put one's mind to an antebellum south. Two all-black SUVs with dark windows were parked out front. A man in a suit stepped out of the front door.

"Looks like the goons are here." Connor opened his door and retrieved his duffle from the back. He walked in front of Brynn up the steps, his broad back swelling through his shirt.

"Lt. West, welcome home." The Secret Serviceman saluted Connor, which Connor returned.

"Is your boss here?" Connor said.

"Yes." The Secret Serviceman opened the door.

Connor waited for Brynn to enter first, then followed. A great round table sat in the two-story entryway, under a fantastic chandalier. The black-and-white patterned marble landing dropped away to a high-ceilinged living room. Florida windows reached up the walls. On the far side of the landing, halls extended to the right and left. A great, wide staircase wrapped up and around the living room.

A high-pitched yapping, accompanied by scrapes on wood floors, started slight and grew louder. Around the corner bounded a small white dog, stopping at Connor's feet. It continued to bark at him, not conceding ground.

"What the hell are you?" Connor's brow furrowed before he shoved the animal away with his foot. The barking stopped and it paced back and forth at the far side of the landing, staring at him.

"Connor!" Mrs. West came around the corner. Clearly once a beauty queen, she wore her age well. The petite woman approached her son with a big smile, holding her hands together and watching him. Her arms would start to lift, then dropped back to her sides, like she waited her turn in line.

Only after Connor opened for an embrace did she let herself give him a hug, exploding forward in a gush of emotion.

"Brynn!" Mrs. West turned to her after releasing Connor and hugged her as well. "It's been forever. I was glad to hear you moved back to Texas. And thank you so much for picking Connor up. I hope it didn't put you out too much."

"Oh, no, it's not a problem. It's nice to catch up." Brynn smiled, searching Mrs. West's face. She saw no pity or insecurity and guessed Mrs. West must not be aware of the details of her Afghanistan ordeal or the fact that Connor pulled her out. It must still be classified.

"Oh my Lord! All my kids back in my house!" she said, teary-eyed and holding her heart.

"Son?" An authoritative, clear, yet soothing voice filled the foyer.

Senator West entered, practically at a run despite his limp and cane. His salt-and-pepper hair was combed neatly back while his strong chin supported his wide, regal smile.

"Father." Connor stuck out his hand and looked up into his father's face.

Glowing, the Senator shook it heartily. "My Navy SEAL son! Took you long enough to visit."

Connor shrugged. "There's always another mission."

"You keep turning down leave," Mrs. West said. "We were beginning to take it personally."

"Brynn!" The Senator turned to her and hugged her. "Thanks so much for picking up this hitchhiker for us."

"It was no trouble," she said.

He stepped back and looked at her in a very fatherly way.

"You've grown into such a lovely young woman!"

"Thank you." Gathered with the characters of her youth, Brynn felt like she was vacationing in her teens.

Some of the Senator's staff walked in, one of which was a short, doughy man named David Richards. Around Connor's age, he had joined the Senator's staff years before. David always struck Brynn as earnest and passionate about his boss.

"Hello, Connor." David peered at Connor over thick-rimmed eyeglasses.

"Hello, Dave."

The two men could not be more opposite. Connor was carved from battle stone, weathered by years of a fierce lifestyle. David was soft, yet trying to perform a job that required a bear for the sake of the Senator.

Brynn had watched more than one instance of David responding to Connor's lack of interest in the Senator's business, annoyed that a son with so much to offer gave none of his potential to his father.

"Brynn, won't you join us for dinner?" Mrs. West said.

She wanted to, if only for minutes longer to wait and linger on his words. Yet she could interpret nothing from Connor's reaction, hoping for a clue about how he felt.

"No, no. That's very kind, thank you. But I'll let y'all have some family time."

"Well, I hope we'll see you soon," Mrs. West said.

"You bet." Brynn turned, hoping to share words with Connor but the Senator had already swept him away.

As she climbed into her car, the vehicle felt empty and stretched thin. She was not satisfied with the encounter. So much of it felt familiar, yet there seemed a wall between Connor and her. Their conversation seemed too professional, too much distance between them.

Rounding the first corner, she didn't bother with the seat belt as the Greene family home appeared in view. A long, lush lawn pulled the eye toward the red brick structure. But the greenery didn't stop there, reaching up the house through decades of ivy growth. A huge, second-story window just over the front door allowed in the eastern sun.

On her way inside, she checked her flower garden, a hobby she began a month before to stay busy. Satisfied, she entered through the back door, one her family never locked. In the kitchen something smelled freshly baked. The tranquil and peaceful aura of her home wrapped itself around her.

"Hey, princess." Her father looked up at her from the overstuffed leather couch where he watched TV. He tilted his head sideways, regarding her with his kind eyes. "How are you doing?"

"Just fine, Dad."

He pushed away the throw pillows, exposing a spot for her to sit. She accepted his hug and leaned into his slender frame. "How was surgery?"

"It's too soon to tell, but I'd guess Mr. Neff is going to live a long and happy life." His legs didn't reach much farther than Brynn's on the footstool.

"Good." Brynn said, ready to drown herself in the meaningless drabble on the screen.

"Well, did you drop him off?" Brynn's mother entered the family room holding a box of decorations, pushing some of her feathered brown hair from her face. "Don't know why the Senator asked you to do that."

"I did."

"Did you make any plans with him?" Her eyebrows shot up

like a principle critiquing the behavior of a child. She pursed her lips.

"No, I did not." Brynn smiled patiently.

"*Good*. And if he's got any sense, he'll leave you alone."

"My darling wife that I love, oh so much," Brynn's father said gently to her mother, with a subtle chuckle. "She's an adult, has been for some time now. She can decide who she spends her time with."

"Yes, she can, Eric. But she shouldn't decide on him. Or don't you remember the 22 years she spent waiting on him to be someone reliable? All she ever did was run after him, hoping for him to grow up. How many times did she break her heart? Or what about the three years she spent crying for him after he disappeared? He was a wild one as a boy and only got worse." She looked at Brynn. "He doesn't deserve your tears and never did."

"He never promised me anything, Mom."

"No, he didn't. Not with words. But he should have told you that you were wasting your time."

"Kathleen, that was years ago," her father said.

"And she's in a good place right now, and I don't want Connor to ruin anything."

"He's not a villain, Mom."

"You sure?"

"Don't worry, mom. I'll be fine." Brynn smiled. "That was a long time ago."

"Good." Her mother carried the box into the dining room.

Brynn eased back into the couch.

"She just loves you a ton," her father said.

"I know."

"And she just might have a point." Her father turned the

mute off.

Lost in memories, Brynn couldn't focus on the television. She thought back on every dance Connor took her to, only to have him leave for a parking lot brawl. Or all the nights they made plans, just for him to disappear without telling her and wind up arrested. He was her first kiss and her first time. She even followed him to college, never admitting that's why she picked Baylor. People always asked her if he was her boyfriend. She never knew how to answer. But then he would smile at her or touch her or break into the stadium for her and she would forget the ways her situation lacked logic.

"Brynn?" her mother called from the other room. "Did you invite Chris to the Spring Gala at the country club?"

Chris? Brynn had forgotten about the guy she'd been seeing for a few weeks. "Yes. He's planning on coming."

"Good!"

"I know you're unsure about him," her dad said in a low voice. "But I'm happy you're over what happened in Afghanistan enough to try dating again." He kissed the top of her head.

HER NEXT TWO WEEKS were a balancing act. As she ran errands around her part of Houston, she kept an extra eye on the crowd, considering what to do if she saw Connor. Other times she'd check her phone, hearing phantom rings and expecting a missed call. Or she'd look out her window to perhaps see him standing in her front yard waiting, as he once did. But it never happened, although she did go on two dates with Chris.

Yet still, why was she asked to pick him up? What did it all mean?

In the end, she convinced herself it was better that Connor ignored her. It would make her resolution easier.

★ ★ ★

SHE BLINKED AND THE Spring Gala was upon her. The lights of the vanity in her bathroom glowed warm against the white tile. Pulling away the curling iron, her last dark lock of hair fell into place. The blue, knee-length dress made the color in her eyes pop.

She selected a coral shawl and wrapped it around her shoulders against the chill of the evening. Her heels tapped against the hardwood floor as she descended the stairs.

"Brynn, you're every bit an angel, epically beautiful," her dad said as she made her way towards the front door.

"Thanks, Dad." She smiled.

"And you, wife of mine." He turned as her mother entered. "I'm definitely going to need some alone time with you tonight." He bounced his eyebrows.

"Eric! Not in front of our daughter!"

"If I remember, a dress like yours is the reason she's here," he purred.

The women laughed. A ring from the doorbell interrupted their humor. Her father reached for the handle.

"Well, hello, Chris." Her father led him inside.

"Good evening, Dr. Greene." He shook his hand. "Mrs. Greene, this is for you." He held a small brown bag out. "It's organic coffee, from a company in Jamaica that provides college textbooks for its workers."

"Thank you, Chris!" Her mother peeked inside the bag.

"Brynn, you look nice." Chris said and smiled. His tall narrow frame felt imposing in their foyer. As he pulled her in for a hug against his seersucker suit, she was careful not to mess up his peach-colored bowtie.

"Thank you, so do you," she said, wondering why he had shaved his beard into a mustache.

After a short trip in her dad's car, they arrived at the country club. The edges and paths of the impressive building were lined in flowers. They seemed odd and playful against the black tuxedos of the attendees. The walkways and lights channeled party-goers towards the entrance.

The energy of the party met them outside and accompanied them into the ballroom. Voices buzzed in the air as hundreds of people mingled. A jazz band played on the far side of the floor. The three-story room felt slightly like a fantasy. Waiters carried elaborate trays of appetizers in every direction.

The faces summoned memories, a result of spending her whole life in this community. She and Chris strayed from her parents when many people from her past approached to talk. They wanted to know about her hostage ordeal and if she was happy to be back in Houston. She kept things very general, and despite her best efforts, couldn't help but look beyond their shoulders for the soldier.

CHAPTER 6

Connor closed the great oak door behind him and entered a house that resonated with voices.

"Of course," Connor muttered to himself. He walked down the cherrywood hallway and entered the kitchen, grateful the room was empty. His mother's dog glared at him from its bed but never let out a peep. Turning on the faucet, he filled his water bottle and drank it dry. City water still tasted odd to him. Sweat ran down his temple.

"Not pushing it too hard, I hope." His father walked in, his usual suit and tie traded for jeans and t-shirt.

"There's no such thing." Connor sipped the water. "Just like you taught me."

"Did I say that?" His dad smirked.

"Yeah, I'm pretty sure I was nine and I thought Marl Lake was too wide to swim across."

"And what happened?"

"I swam across it."

"What did you learn?"

"I learned I could swim across anything."

"Or at least a lake as wide as Marl Lake." His father waved his hand.

Connor turned away and took a swig of water. "For starters."

"What are you going to do today?"

"I don't know." Connor walked across the kitchen, stuck his head in the laundry room, and tossed some of his dirty clothes into the basket. After peeling his shirt off, he added that as well. He gave his head one last wipe with his towel before he returned to the kitchen.

His father's face twitched. "What's going on there?" He pointed towards Connor's torso.

"These?" Connor indicated the multitude of scars across his body.

"Yes."

"Oh, just memories." Connor picked his bag up from the floor.

"Any of that hurt?"

"It might have." Connor said. "But it's just pain. No reason to stop." Connor found these questions from his father odd.

"You know, it's okay to ease up sometimes."

"'If you just keep going, eventually you'll be the last one standing.'" Connor looked at him. "Your words."

His father nodded, his politician smile wavering a little. "I did say that, didn't I?" He looked down at his hand on the counter. "I said a lot of things."

"Is there a problem?"

"No. There's no problem..." Connor's dad tilted his head sideways. "It's just... You know, kid, I'm really proud of who you've become. I know I put a lot of ideas in your head as you grew up. I hope I wasn't just trying to turn you into the person I wished I could be."

He lifted his cane. "I just hated watching life from the sidelines, jealous of those who got to participate in ways I couldn't. The kind of life I'd have if it had legs..." He leaned his weight against the counter. "I guess I... just..."

His father shook his head, replacing his contemplative look with a smile. "Nevermind. Just your old dad babbling. Anyways, I've been meaning to ask you. The Spring Gala is tomorrow and I'd really appreciate it if you were there. Your mom would love it."

Connor grimaced.

"I know it's not how you want to spend a Saturday night and I could tell you it's for the campaign, but it's not. Mostly, I'm just a father who wants to show off his kid."

"I don't think—"

"Now, now. No need to answer right away. All I'm saying is it would be enjoyable. Plus, Brynn will probably be there."

"We'll see," Connor said.

"Just think about it."

Connor left his father in the kitchen and walked down the hall toward the back stairwell. He reflected on his father's cryptic words but deciphered nothing from them. Mostly he didn't care, writing the words off as nostalgia from a father. He spent more time thinking about Brynn.

He'd been home two weeks without seeing her. She was his favorite person in the world. Years before, he left, conceding he couldn't have her and manage this thing that ran free inside him. It wouldn't be fair to get her hopes up. Connor couldn't control his issue, so he gave her space.

The water in his shower steamed up the bathroom. He ran shampoo through his hair. Through talkers around town, he learned Brynn was dating someone. To know she must be recovering from her traumatic experience made Connor happy. And as long as the guy was worthy, she was taken care of. In fact, the gala was the perfect place to say goodbye.

He didn't sleep much that night. Not because of any

particular thoughts, but because he had not spent enough of the wealth of energy inside him.

★ ★ ★

THE NEXT EVENING, CONNOR drove his own vehicle behind his parent's guarded SUV, in case he wanted to leave early. He had not worn cufflinks in years.

Inside the ballroom at the country club, marble pillars reached stories up and supported the massive ceiling. The crowd hummed in conversation. Mounted lamps and chandeliers cast a soft glow. Waiters carried trays of hors d'oeuvres and weaved in and out among the guests. Familiar faces appeared in every direction, from his pediatrician to former childhood acquaintances. They looked soft to him. The expanse of the room could not have been more spacious, and yet Connor felt tight and cramped.

David steered the Senator towards a cluster of people. Connor, still hooked on his mother's arm, was dragged along, quite certain she clamped down just a little to inhibit his escape. He rolled his eyes.

"Senator West!" A man in an unconvincing toupee turned from the group and extended his hand. "Welcome!"

The group opened to absorb the Wests. Names were thrown around and hands were shaken. Connor did not consider it a valuable use of his time to remember them.

"Thank you for your service, son," a short man wearing cowboy hat said with a pleasant demeanor. "I appreciate what you do for our country."

Connor felt like saying it wasn't about the country or about service. It was about his team, the struggle, the odds, and winning. He wanted to tell the man he didn't have to thank Connor because it was the most fun and satisfying job on earth. Saving the country was just a by-product. But Connor only nodded.

"Oh, I can't imagine!" Another woman in a long velvet dress said to Connor's dad. "You must worry about him constantly. How can you stand it?"

Connor's dad lost his wooing glow and looked over at him, switching his cane from one hand to the other. "You know, I've never seen that boy not get back up. I guess I just believe he'll always keep getting back up."

The people nodded. But looking in their eyes, Connor could tell only one man really understood what the Senator meant.

"But anyways, Mrs. McGee, how's the fundraising going for the zoo?" the Senator asked.

Connor took advantage of the crowd's shift in attention to slip away, preferring to create some distance from the high volume of individuals approaching his father. The bar drew him in. He posted against the dark cedar wood counter.

Although tonight was simply to say goodbye to a person who deserved it, he couldn't shake the excitement to see Brynn.

"Bourbon, rocks," Connor said to the bartender. The man nodded and reached for a glass, scooping ice cubes into it.

"You still fast?" a familiar voice called from behind him.

Connor turned around.

"Sometimes." Connor stuck out his hand. "Coach Brandenburg, you still making men out of mice for Memorial football?"

"It gets harder every year." Connor's high school coach wore the same unkempt hair and mustache he did a decade and more before, though gray was defeating the brown.

Connor reached for the other man. "Sammy."

"Hey, Connor, good to see you."

"Well, damn. Who would've thought?" Coach Brandenburg shook his head. "My star quarterback and running back, years later and respectable?"

Connor looked his old quarterback over. He clearly traded hours in the weight room for family life.

"What are you doing these days?" Connor said.

"Typical Houston. Doing the oil and gas thing over at Shell," Sammy said, eyes glazed. "Are you home on leave?"

"Yeah."

It seemed odd, his old coach talking to Connor like a peer.

"I'll never forget having to grovel in front of the principle and athletic association so they wouldn't kick you off the football team, when…" he turned and laid a hand on Sammy. "Well, *you* remember this. In that game against Oakridge when that linebacker took a cheap shot on you."

"It still hurts," Sammy joked, stroking his lower back.

"I bet. I was yelling at the ref for the call, then I turn and see our boy Connor here booking it across the field after that linebacker." The coach laughed. "That big ol' boy never thought a running back would chop him down like that. Took half the team to pull you off of him."

"I still got suspended two games," Connor said.

"Some wanted you expelled or in jail. Lost their nerve after that old dad of yours threw some weight around and made some calls. Good thing, too. We needed you."

"But hey," Sammy said. "In your defense, that linebacker never touched me again for the rest of high school."

"Anything for Memorial," Connor said in a sarcastic tone.

"Amen." Sammy looked across the room. "Oh, there's Rebecca. Find me later and I'll introduce you to my wife." He walked off.

"All right, take care." Connor had no intention of meeting Sammy's wife.

"I better find my wife, too. But Connor, while you're home, if you need a place to hit weight, the high school gym is yours." Coach Brandenburg nodded.

"I'll let you know." Connor watched him walk away.

Connor receded farther down the bar. The claustrophobia in his chest made his lungs feel small. He didn't mind tight spaces, but he was annoyed to be surrounded by so much nonsense. All these people gathered around the room and chatted. Connor could guess their conversations. They probably spoke of decorating their homes or sports. They described their children, a topic only interesting to the parents of the children.

Many times as a youth, Connor often heard the crowd speak of what a shame it was that certain parts of town had become "rough" and how it was no longer a good idea to go there. But Connor never understood the fear. All one had to do was decide to be a victim or not.

His muscles tensed beneath his tuxedo for a second. The storm rumbled. Running wild sounded good and freeing. But he took a deep breath and the thunder subsided.

At the bar, he ordered another Buffalo Trace and avoided eye contact with everyone. He wondered what his team was doing back in the field, probably out hunting the enemy. As he drained the amber liquid, his trigger finger twitched.

But he was hunting, too. He needed to find Brynn, the real reason he came tonight. And as though the universe heard his thoughts, the tides of guests parted and a flash of blue cut through the dullness of the night.

Connor straightened up.

She came down the stairs. *She came down the stairs*. Every step a dance. Her beauty erupted from the forgettable backdrop like a wildflower bursting through concrete. *Oh, to touch her.* She was a ballet of fire and ice, queen of the evening, and there was no one on earth but her, descending like the stars were for her alone.

Just go do what you came here to do. But in the light of her presence, Connor was having a hard time remembering his intentions.

She reached the main floor and stopped, looking in the opposite direction of Connor. As he approached behind her, Connor could tell she watched the Senator greet people. Every step towards her invigorated him. He took a deep breath.

"He's always working," Connor said, suppressing his excitement for her to turn around.

She spun. Her dark locks and the hem of her dress lifting upward in unison. Connor smiled calmly as he drank in her blue eyes. He had seen such ugly things in his years at war, ugly things that required effort to overcome. Brynn seemed the exact opposite, as though seeing the worst of humanity allowed Connor to truly celebrate the best.

"Brynn, someone could gaze at you for a million years, and when they were through, never regret a day." He leaned in and kissed her cheek. "And then start over."

"That's quite a compliment," Brynn said.

"Just speaking truth."

"I didn't think you'd be here. It's not really your thing."

"You're right." Connor nodded towards his father. "The Senator needed a mascot." Connor moved a step closer, a point at which most others cowered before him. Brynn stood her ground.

"So, you've been here two weeks," Brynn said. "What have you been—"

"Brynn, there you are!" Some other person interrupted her and entered their circle. "Who's your friend?"

Connor sized him up. The seersucker suit among tuxedos came off as obnoxious and Connor felt disappointment in the man's shoes, which were more slipper than formalwear. He might have let it go if he thought the man couldn't afford to better dress himself. But the expensive outdoorsman watch and tailored cut of the suit made Connor suspicious this man knew exactly what he was doing. He guessed him at 6 foot 3, 185 pounds, and noticed he was right handed. His instinct filed away five ways to bring the man to his knees.

"I'm Connor." He offered his hand to the man while Brynn squirmed, her smile accented by a wince.

"Hi, Connor, I'm Chris." The annoying man accepted the handshake. "Brynn and I have been dating for a few weeks."

Connor tilted his head back. "Yes, I've heard. I've managed to catch up on some of the Memorial gossip." Despite his better judgment, Connor gave the man more opportunity to speak. "Where did you two meet?"

"Houston book fair," Chris said.

Connor sensed anxiety from Brynn.

"And what do you do for a living, Chris?"

Chris pulled his drink away from his lips. "Until recently I was a human rights attorney for International Rise. It's an organization dedicated to promoting peace worldwide by bridging communication gaps."

Connor didn't want to hear anymore. "Until *recently?*"

Chris smiled and nodded. "Well actually, a month ago I accepted a position on Congressman Ned Parish's staff primarily to focus on his new *Conflict Resolution* campaign. Sort of a response to the pro-war crowd."

"I don't know that anyone is pro-war. Perhaps they just recognize a sad inevitable necessity for war," Connor said, sneaking glances at Brynn. "But tell me about this *Conflict Resolution* campain."

"Glad you asked," Chris said.

"Now, Chris, I'm sure you get tired of work." Brynn grabbed his arm. "Let's just have fun tonight. No need to talk about all this."

"Peaceful resolution is always important." He turned back to Connor. "It's an initiative to raise awareness of the need to put greater efforts into talks with other nations. I mean, just think of the trillions spent worldwide on weapons and defense. What if all those resources could be put towards something more important, like education or development of the third world? Or think of the senseless deaths and atrocities committed by armies foreign and domestic? It can all stop if we just believe in each other. What if instead of buying guns we bought books? It's in human nature to live in peace."

"And all we need to do is *believe in each other*," Connor echoed.

"Exactly!" He tapped Connor's lapel with his index finger. "But I've been talking too much. Connor, what do you do?"

"I'm in the military." Connor hoped this would be enough. He wasn't interested in Chris' opinions on the details of his work and loathed the idea of a drawn-out conversation.

"Oh." Chris nudged Brynn. "Shooting is easier than thinking, isn't it?" He laughed and tapped on Connor's arm.

"I'm just kidding, friend."

Connor fought not to roll his eyes. *One of these guys.* Fine. Connor would play with this guy.

Brynn's face twisted.

"What branch of the military?"

"The Navy."

"And what do you do in the Navy?"

"Oh you know," Connor sighed and tilted his head. "Jump out of planes, mine harbors, kill terrorists."

The confident smile on Chris' face faded, as though he was surprised Connor never broke to say he was kidding. "They got a name for that?"

"I'm what they call a SEAL operative."

"*A Navy SEAL?*" Bewilderment charged Chris' face. "Well, then. That's quite a career." Chris nodded. "So you've killed men?"

"Hundreds." Connor said without batting an eye. "Don't worry. They all deserved it."

Connor could see the sentimentalities boiling up inside Chris.

"*Deserved it?* Why? Because they're evil, just because they were born with different beliefs than you?" Chris squared off.

"No." Connor smiled. "Because we both wanted to win. I just wanted it more."

"Well," Chris said in sarcastic tones. "I hope you find it rewarding."

"Not nearly as rewarding as listening to your opinion on what's best for a people and country across an ocean and two continents away. A people you couldn't possibly understand from the few minutes a day you listen to your favorite pundits, impressing themselves with the sound of their voices. This, all before you get online and social media the hell out of all your thoughts, which believe me, the rest of the world is so grateful to be exposed to."

Connor winked at him. "And you'll keep bantering about peace, disregarding the fact that you and they will always have different, irreconcilable beliefs and wants."

Brynn stepped forward. "Okay, you two—"

"You know, it's people like you who hold back the rest of society," Chris said, pointing his finger in Connor's face. "You're so used to one way of thinking, so accustomed to fighting, you can't imagine a world without it. Peace *scares* you. You hate the thought of being obsolete. That's why you can't stand it when we try to settle conflict with words and diplomacy! You think war is good because you're nothing but a savage!"

"Wrong. War is the very worst thing on earth. And it's *your* job to prevent it. That's why I need you to beg, plead, bribe, negotiate, apologize, and deal at all costs to keep us from it. But once you fail…" Connor sneered. "You turn around, close your eyes, and shut your ears. Because war is *my* job. And I'm here to wreck shop, wreak havoc, and lay waste. Because conflict will always be in the heart of man. So *you* keep believing in others. And *I'll* keep dealing with them."

Chris stood wide-eyed and overwhelmed.

"By the way, that's a nice ironic mustache you have," Connor said.

"Why is it ironic?"

"I need a refill. Perhaps I'll see you later." Connor turned and left them.

After finding stairs, he climbed to the second floor balcony that wrapped around the entire ballroom. It was quiet. Below, the crowd mingled and chatted in a blur.

Connor strode toward the empty end. The lights weren't bright there and he felt reprieve in the shadows. He leaned against a pillar and perched on the railing, sipping his whiskey. Gazing down on the crowd below, he'd rather watch the party than be a part of it, if he had to be either. Two hours ago, he thought he could take one night of this. But he was mistaken; this crowd sickened him

Connor wanted to leave and he wanted Brynn with him. She was an adventure and the only good thing about this place. She was more than all this.

Rose oil drifted through the air and the floor squeaked, a sound almost lost to the chorus of the party below.

"Taking a break?" Connor said, still watching the gathering below.

"I haven't experienced what you've experienced," Brynn said as she approached. "But after you've seen other things, *worse* things, this gala stuff seems kind of mundane, doesn't it?"

"Yeah, I… know what you mean." Connor turned to her. The warm light painted her skin in a soft glow. She might as well be an angel. "So, where'd you leave the professor?"

She laughed. "He's not really up to par, is he?" Brynn shared the railing. "It's part of the therapy. Trying to be trusting towards men again…" She swallowed. "By the way, my parents received some anonymous note after Afghanistan." She looked down at the crowd. "Thanks for that."

"I knew you'd overcome, even though you may not have wanted it at the time," Connor said.

"I needed it."

Connor, what are you doing? Don't take responsibility for her heart if you're just going to break it.

She sat there in silence for a few moments while Connor

made up his mind.

"This night's getting old," Brynn said.

"It was never young." Connor looked at her, lost in a great deal of affection. "Maybe we should leave."

She nodded at the large and expansive crowd. "We'd never get past them all without someone noticing."

Connor got a slight rush, as he always did before lighting fireworks. He stood, walked to the wall, and put his hand on the fire alarm. He paused and winked at her, then he slid the lever.

In an instant, the ceiling tore open as water fell from the sprinkler system. The droning siren echoed through the ballroom while the hordes below quickly shuffled and shifted in confusion like turning tides cowering beneath the downpour. As an amorphous blob, they moved towards the exits, calling out and screaming.

Connor moved to the top of the stairs. Turning back, he offered his hand to Brynn. He would take her with him.

Brynn's arctic storm blue eyes looked at his hand, then back at his face, seeming uncertain as she exhaled, "I don't know. I heard you were a wild one."

"You should try it sometime." He smiled.

CHAPTER 7

There he was, in a tailored black tuxedo that made him nothing short of royal. The formalwear merged perfectly with the battle scars on his temple and chin. His green eyes looked out above an easy smile. In the midst of chaos, he stood calm and sturdy as the world around him fell apart. The hand he offered looked so strong.

Don't do this, Brynn! You're past all this! This will only end in heartache!

Her fingers tingled. But another voice told her it was Connor, and a moment with him was worth it. The energy that drove him finally landed on her. He was about to give in to his recklessness and desired to take her with him. The prince wanted to lead her down the stairs. And perhaps it was time for her to live as though tomorrow didn't exist.

Her heart trembled and nerves quivered, yet she couldn't help but smile as she took his hand. His fingers closed around hers, and she felt part of something invincible.

She stepped out of her shoes and picked them up with her free hand. "Let's go."

Connor winked.

They rushed down the wide staircase taking the steps two at a time and hit the main floor, joining the mess.

"This way!" Connor said. They headed away from the crowd

that struggled to exit through the main doors. Emergency sprinklers cascaded water on them as Brynn's bare feet splashed through puddles on the soaked marble floors. She looked at the crowd. Her father was the only one facing their direction, standing alone in the chaos. He looked at her and sighed, then shrugged and nodded.

"Don't worry," she mouthed. Then she turned and focused on Connor, letting go of the rest of the world.

Connor guided her towards the glass doors leading to the veranda.

"Sir, the veranda is closed. Please use the front exits." An attendant said over the piercing alarm as he held up his hands.

"It's fine." Connor never looked at him as he shoved the doors open.

"Sir!" The steward seemed baffled.

Connor pulled her through, plunging Brynn into the crisp night air. The cool wind and cold stone of the veranda titillated her senses as the pair weaved between wicker furniture towards the edge of the patio. There the porch dropped away to the lawn three feet below.

Connor jumped down, let loose his bowtie, spun and raised his arms up to Brynn.

"I got you."

She fell into him. And as he set her down, she felt delicate.

Now the soft, velvet lawn caressed her toes. She took a deep breath. The night was theirs. She could run miles and miles with him and laughed shamelessly.

In the parking lot, they dodged between vehicles. Three rows in, Connor pulled keys from his pocket and came around the side of a large SUV before stopping at the car on the far side.

"You still have this?" Brynn asked, eying the car that Connor raced around in during high school and college: some sort of old tire-burner, adding to his legend of chrome American prince.

"You don't throw away a classic, Brynn." He opened the door for her.

She scrambled in, the smell of cracked leather seats and faint aroma of gasoline both familiar to her. Connor slid in the other side and turned the key. With an aggressive roar, the car came to life. And with a shove of the pedal, they drifted away from the country club, the crowd, and the rules.

Connor pulled onto the highway and let the rocket ship go. The breeze came through open windows as Brynn ran her hand along its current. The repetitive pattern of streets lights flashed by, creating the illusion of hyper-speed in the world beyond her seat. She drowned in the surreal feeling of dreams coming true and years disappearing in instants and miles. She was eighteen again and he, the undisputed object of her affection. He had finally come back to her, just as she once whispered to herself in quiet moments.

They talked as they once did, and soon she felt as though they'd never been apart. At times, during long moments of comfortable silence, she'd just watch him drive, the urban landscape dwindling.

White lines and hours passed. Her heavy eyelids closed as she negotiated with herself to sleep, but only if she could awake once more to this dream. A rich, peaceful rest cradled her.

✳ ✳ ✳

SHE WOKE ON A lonely desert highway and glanced at him. Connor was still in the driver's seat and that was good enough for her.

Brynn sat up. "Where are we going?" Her hand brushed the hair from her face.

"Just trying to get good and gone."

A road sign read "El Paso 107."

"Are you hungry?" Connor looked over at her. He'd been driving all night but appeared unphased.

"Actually, yes."

"I thought you might say that." Connor slowed the car. It shook on the gravel shoulder and stopped. "Follow me."

What adventure does he have for me now?

He retrieved a paper bag from the backseat and a tray with coffee cups.

"Wait, when did you—"

"Hey." He smiled. "Sometimes things just work out."

After exiting the car, she followed him up the embankment next to the highway, before navigating a small rocky outcrop. They found a spot on the desert rocks, a natural seat that nature surely had made for them and them alone. She nestled in next to him as he handed her a coffee and pastry.

He glanced at his watch. "Should be soon."

Brynn sat there in bliss while the dark, eastern horizon was cut from the night sky by a pinkish hue. They waited and after a while the pinkish hue deepened as it charged across the sky. Then the first glimmer of sun danced over the desert.

"It's beautiful," she said. "What's the sunrise like *over there?*"

"Like it is here. It happens. Doesn't matter what happened the night before. It always comes, without apology."

"Do you want it to apologize?"

"Not today." He kissed her forehead. "Are you cold?"

"No, I'm perfect. Let's just stay here awhile." Brynn wanted time to memorize the present moment, desiring to forever remember the day the rest of their lives began. She was right about Connor, just like she always told herself. She should never have doubted he would come back to her. And he had. He was done chasing those other things. Now, at last, it was her turn.

"Connor?"

"Yes?"

"Do you remember the day we met?"

"I do." He rubbed her back. "What do you remember?"

She thought a moment. "I remember our whole house was draped in pink, just like I wanted. My mom found a birthday cake with all the Disney princesses on it and a giant number eight. There were presents everywhere. Mom and Dad must have invited the whole neighborhood. I was so excited because I got to wear this frilly princess dress that was—"

"Light blue," Connor said. "I remember."

"And my parents kept telling me to be nice to this new kid who had just moved to the neighborhood. They told me his daddy worked with the president. You were so shy and didn't say a word when you came in with your parents. You just kept looking at me. I took you to see my presents and then outside to the bounce house and crafts station. You stayed completely silent."

She laughed. "I was probably talking enough for both of us. Then Trevis Bakke, my older cousin, stole the balloon animal the clown had made for me. I cried and cried. But then you got it back." She took his hand. "Didn't you hit him with a... what was it?"

"The putter from the mini golf game." Connor smirked. "But you got your balloon back."

"Yes!" She slowed. "Afterward, the adults made us all

apologize to each other over and over." She shifted in her seat. "Then you were gone and I couldn't find you. Your parents wanted to leave and I looked for you. You were down the hall by yourself. I told you your parents were leaving. And you handed me a flower and—"

"And I kissed you right there." Connor touched her cheek with the back of his hand.

"That was the first time a boy kissed me." Brynn laughed at herself for blushing.

"Cooties," Connor said. "Gross."

"I know, right! But when you left with your parents, I was afraid I'd never see you again. Then you were in school on Monday."

"Ms. LaMarca's class. You loaned me your favorite pencil." Connor shook his head. "If you're trying to get it back, I refuse."

Brynn laughed. "No, you can keep the pencil."

★ ★ ★

AN HOUR PAST SUNRISE, they resumed their journey. As they drove, she joyously requested any and every whimsical stop she desired. Roadside fruit stands, antique galleries, art shows. Each time she requested one, he'd just say, "Of course."

The friendship, the love was back. And with each pass of a hand and graze of skin, every instant of eye contact and smile, the heat between them blossomed. The air was electric and the feeling of being within reach of him became intoxicating. His gaze was on her constantly like a warm blanket. Being around him reminded her of how untouched she felt. She'd encountered others since he disappeared, but none of them touched her, *truly* touched her as he could.

That afternoon, they found a department store somewhere in New Mexico. Not wanting to wear black tie attire for their entire adventure, they bought clothes and supplies.

At the register, Brynn reached for her credit card.

Connor put his hand on hers. "They can track that." Pulling out a roll of cash, he paid their bill.

"West still?" Brynn said as they climbed back into the car.

"I thought we'd try north for a while." He nodded down the road. At a red light, Connor looked to the left and right. No cars were coming. He pulled through.

Night approached, and the sun they had watched rise early that morning began to set, coating far-off mesas in an inferno. Hours later, dim neon light crept through the drapes of their roadside motel, 300 miles beyond being lost in some forgotten nowhere. The glow exposed Connor and Brynn to one another, their floor-bound shadows becoming one.

With intrepid hands she pulled his shirt away. The two of them had not ventured here together since college and she beheld for the first time the damage his body sustained in the time that had passed, convinced it wasn't years that did this, but miles. The tattoos and countless scars weaved a tapestry that whispered to her tales of a warrior. They spoke of how he lived. She ran her fingers over them, making them more real, and traced ridges of the hero's muscles. What a human. He was steel.

Brushing her lips, he caressed her neck and seized her. Her knees quivered. Her lungs heaved in the ecstasy of the moment and her heart raced, every movement watched in slow motion. She was ready and yearning. Her dress fell away. She knew no shame before her lover. He was hers for all time.

Then he surprised her. And it meant so much. She felt him

suppress his ferocity and hold back the wild. Instead he came at her slow and gentle, making love instead of lust. She felt so savored, tasting his lips again and again. Lost in sheets, they made up for time apart. Then the dawn cradled them to sleep.

★ ★ ★

DAYS AND ADVENTURES LATER, the two sat on blankets placed over lush lawns under a clear blue sky while Brynn lived her dream. Families and friends scattered throughout the park. Like Brynn, they seemed to be enjoying the day. One particularly cute little girl gathered daisies.

"Isn't Denver wonderful?" a dreamy-eyed Brynn said.

"I'm certainly enjoying it right now." Connor ran his hand through her hair.

"What do you think you'll do when we get back to Houston? I mean after your enlistment ends."

"I don't know." Connor rolled onto his back and looked up at the sky.

"You could be a police officer or sheriff."

"I could. That seems like it would right in my wheelhouse, doesn't it?"

"It does. Or there's a million-and-a-half oil jobs. You might try that." Brynn touched his arm. "Although, I can't see you behind a desk."

"Can't you?" Connor said towards the sky.

"I have a feeling it wouldn't do." She rolled over and laid her head on his stomach, and in turn, also observed the sky. Two sparrows spiraled and folded over each other as they dashed across the blue.

"I've also heard of guys in your position starting private security companies. Or start training courses for security personnel. I'm sure they'd love to be taught by you."

"I've heard of that, too. It's a pretty typical path for ex-special ops guys."

Brynn pictured them, tucked into a bungalow in the Heights of Houston. Long walks down the gentrified streets followed by evenings on the porch.

Among uncertainties, the future was a scary thing to her. When he had disappeared, and it seemed as though he wouldn't be part of her story, she never felt excitement for the future. She felt adrift. But now that he had come back for her, and knowing he would be there, the future wasn't scary. Indeed, nothing seemed scary with him there. The world had opened anew, rampant with possibilities.

"Your mom will be so excited to have you back permanently. Your dad, too."

"Yeah, they don't enjoy the distance." Connor chuckled. "Your mom would hate me for moving back."

Brynn laughed. "She'll come around."

She listened to his heartbeat, the very heart that drove her amazing man. As more families strolled by, Brynn imagined the two of them hand in hand, walking across a playground, chasing children of their own. *What a wonderful headache our son will be!* She pictured a little boy with his father's eyes and spirit. She'd try to be stern, but in the end she knew she'd spend most of her time smiling and laughing. Connor could teach their boy to do all sorts of things.

As she envisioned their daughter, she suppressed a laugh at the thought of high school boys coming to their house to ask Connor if they could date his daughter. She knew none of them would dare keep her out past curfew. The future seemed so exciting.

"I'm hungry," he said as he rolled back towards her.

She raised her eyebrows. Connor never expressed personal needs or discomfort.

"Me, too. You know what sounds really good right now? Seafood."

"I don't know. Is it wrong to have seafood when we're not on the coast."

"What are you talking about?" Brynn laughed.

"It's like eating spaghetti in China."

"You have a point."

"Great, it's settled. Seattle it is!" Connor jumped to his feet. "Let's go."

Brynn chuckled and rose, grateful for the impulsiveness that had become the charm of their trip.

They drove north on I-25 until Wyoming, then took a left through the arid prairie comprising the southern part of the state. After Utah they headed diagonally northwest towards Seattle. Saturated hills, moist and green, were a welcome change. Cloudy mists formed in the valleys while the tallest peaks reached through to bright skies. Shivering from the cold, Brynn put on her fleece.

Nothing bothered her anymore. She was happy inside and out, every second of every day because Connor was always there.

On a back road between Oregon and Washington, Brynn turned the radio off as they lost signal of any worthwhile stations. She dreamed through simultaneous adventures. One being the actual journey she partook in with Connor. The other being her future hopes and dreams.

North of Seattle, on a lonely two-lane highway, they lost

themselves in enough green foliage to drown. The road lifted and fell with the mountainous terrain, until their path snaked its way around the curve of a hill.

Brynn gasped. The Pacific Ocean shimmered like part of a fairytale. The water lay ghostly still under a calm dawn. Wildflowers interwove among the slopes, as though God dared artists to try to capture such a thing. Out in the middle of the lost bay protruded a pier, reaching toward the heart of the sea.

The moment was perfect. Brynn decided now would be the instant in eternity when she told Connor she loved him. She knew it in her heart, always had, since the day she turned eight. But now that he was back, now that she dared to believe, she would voice it. And she didn't need courage because love always works out.

"Hey Connor, I want to tell you something. And I don't want to put pressure on you or anything, but—"

"Hold on a sec." Connor turned his gaze from the ocean to her, giving her a wide grin. "Have you ever been in the Pacific Ocean?"

Brynn thought about it. "Well, no actually. I've been to California a few times but I never managed."

Connor yanked the gearshift and the tires squealed. The car whipped down a narrow road that dropped to the beach. He stopped in front of the pier. Not a soul in sight. He jumped out of the car, opened her door, and reached for her.

Hand in hand, they ran down the long pier surrounded by an ocean on fire, ignited by the morning sun.

"Why don't we jump in here?" she said between breaths.

"Can't do that. We have to jump in at the end. That way, it counts."

They hurried to the end of the pier. Connor led her over

the railing. She stood with him on the ledge above the sea, wary of what mysteries it contained. The thought of depths and creatures unknown shook her from her bliss and set an uneasy feeling in her stomach.

"I don't know if I can do this, Connor." She looked into the waters. "It makes me nervous."

"What?" He turned and drew her to him, squaring off and grabbing her shoulders. "Of course you can." He looked at her, emitting layers and layers of care. "You're amazing. You can't help it. It bubbles up from inside you. Amazing flows from you. It radiates from you and brings amazing out from those around you. *Of course* you can do this."

His eyes seemed so sure, without an ounce of doubt. So she took his hand and faced the never-ending waters. And on three, they leapt and fell into the cold dark.

CHAPTER 8

She slept on his chest. Her warm breath caressed his skin and bewitched him. He slid the tips of his fingers down her bare back; her skin so soft, so perfect.

His world was one of rock, sand, cold, and hot. He warred with that world. But her world welcomed him.

As he studied his hand, it seemed so out of place. His scars, the "Invictus" tattoo on his forearm, and "E.K.I.A." letters across his knuckles, made his limb monstrous. Touching her was as though the condemned reached up from the filth to experience something angelic. Limp white sheets clung to her edges and curves. She smelled sweet, clean, and floral. Connor lay in bed and looked out the window. Of the miles they traveled and the motels they haunted, this one was his favorite. It was quiet and far away. The Cabinet Mountain Range rose high on the other side of the glass. Light blue paint inside the room bled into the sky outside. The dresser sat free of a television, a feature he didn't miss since he preferred a reprieve from the bombardment.

Brynn was his longest companion, and his only life-long relation to never look at him with an element of fear. He knew he should be pleased at these feelings of affection and tenderness. He knew here and now should make him happy.

So what's wrong with me?

This existence didn't fulfill him as he had hoped. That damn itch, that rumble was always with him. He struggled to choose Brynn over the rest of him. The competition was harder than he thought.

He caught his reflection in the mirror above the dresser. His eyes accused him.

You know you can't have it both ways.

Connor turned his head away.

Since he woke this morning, the itch had grown strong. Connor knew he needed to feed it, to keep it at bay. So the mountains beyond their window tempted him. Further still, it taunted him. The peak only looked like a fifteen-hundred- or two-thousand-foot rise in elevation, although harshly vertical. But that didn't matter to him. He must rise. His hand shook.

An electric feeling came over him as he slipped out of bed, leaving Brynn to her dreams. Water would be a good idea, and some food, but anyone could make it to the top with water and food. Connor would go now. He needed to go when he didn't quite want to, to make sure his body would perform when it didn't want to. He would tell it when to go and force it to obey him. So he opened the door and let the outside air wash away the comfort of their nest. In bare feet he charged towards the slope.

The rocks chewed at his feet, but he ignored them. "I like my odds."

The gradual rise shot skyward. Often, he had to crawl on all fours to take the steep ground. Thin air left his lungs unsatisfied and his head dizzy. The wind whistled as it wound through gullies and cliffs. His mind whispered for him to slow down and catch his breath, so he pushed harder.

"This mountain never counted on someone like me," he

said aloud.

An hour later, he reached the top and looked out over the vast wilderness. Connor knew he'd only use the view as an excuse to take a break and catch his breath.

"No, no. Come on, go." He turned and raced down the mountain.

A slick rock sent him to the ground with a crash. Stones stabbed at his side. He stood and kept going.

As he neared the motel, he noticed a large pond on the property. The water looked cold and uninviting, just the kind of thing he didn't want to do at that moment. He accepted the challenge.

"Just go," he said under his breath. Diving in, his body wanted to seize up in the cold water. But he made himself acclimate to the temperature before allowing himself to get out.

When he stepped back into their room, Brynn sat in a corner chair, reading with a cup of tea. She looked him over. "Should I ask?"

After pausing a moment, he said, "Exercising." The intensity in him waned and he produced a smile. He knew the fix wouldn't last long.

She made no reaction to the absurdity of his appearance. "How'd it go?"

"Fine," he said. "Where shall we go today?"

"How about Helena? I've never been there."

"Anywhere you wish."

"Anywhere I wish? That's quite an offer." She smiled at him over the rim of her cup. Sometimes in the looks she gave him, she was as exciting as a battlefield. But it just wasn't the same.

A shower and hour later, Connor's seat shook with the strong vibration of the V-8 in his '79 Trans Am. State Highway

200 across Montana afforded them views most would never see, rock and snow rising above crystal lakes. Both lanes were empty, creating a world of just them. The mountains glowed in the sun.

Brynn glanced over at him. "Have you thought more about what you'll do when you come back to Houston?"

Damn. How to tell her? How to let her know? Coming back to Houston seemed unfathomable. To see beyond the making of war was impossible. The thing inside him wouldn't let it happen. He'd die without the fight, and probably die because of the fight. There'd always be a need for men like him, willing to be violent and needing the violence. Dying in the desert or in some lost ocean was an end he relied on. It suited him.

STOP IT, CONNOR! Stop. I can't let this control me. I CAN be there for her.

He didn't believe his own inner voice.

Looking into her frosty blues, he didn't want to cause them pain. "That depends on the influx of new recruits and what the current stop-loss is. Could be a year. Could be three," he said.

"We can handle that." Brynn closed her hand around his, which he perched on the standard shift.

She spoke of the future. But there was no future. For the moment he had the wildness at bay, although it wouldn't last. Connor couldn't leave her and he couldn't stay. Loving her, he hated the thought of causing her pain. The razor's edge he walked grew shaky. He felt the control slip away from him.

Why can't I have both? Damn me.

He looked at his sweet girl making plans for the future and dreaded letting her down. He had to fight it.

"Well, now for the rest of our lives, we can say we've been to Helena." Brynn gazed in the direction of the welcome sign along the highway. "I think the University of Montana is here.

There's probably some nice little restaurant around there where we could eat lunch."

Signs along the simple and aged streets of Helena led them to such a restaurant. Before long they sat at a table for two looking out on the city. They ordered food and people-watched. Connor looked at a bowl of matchbooks with the restaurant's name inscribed on them: "Creek Don't Rise."

Brynn picked one up, passed it through her fingers, smiled, and put it in her purse.

"It's been crazy, but in the last few years they've been gentrifying Houston. People love living there, up-and-coming young professionals. You should drive around there when we get back and give it a look," Brynn said, taking a bite of her salad. A vibrant yellow daisy in a vase served as the table's centerpiece. It paled compared to Brynn's face.

Connor shifted and fidgeted in his seat. He wanted to make her happy and deliver on all her dreams, but his hold on the matter slipped. He felt like he was riding a ticking clock. But he refused to give up.

But the longer they drove, the more time passed, and the itch grew worse. Not knowing what to do, he tried his best to hide it. A week later and somewhere in northern Minnesota, the interior of the car closed in on him while Brynn kept saying beautiful things. Moisture accumulated on his palms. He worried she might be catching on.

Every now and then she asked him, "Are you okay?"

But it didn't matter. He knew it would end when things blew up and he would wrap himself in chaos. He needed to be back where he belonged and let Brynn go.

Stop. Don't let her go. Choose her.

He searched roadside establishments for a place to stop. A

dingy bar offered the only sanctuary. Just in time, raindrops speckled his windshield.

"Let's stop here," Connor said.

"Here?"

"Yeah. We'll never be here again."

"Good point." Brynn smiled.

Don't fail her, Connor. Don't.

As Brynn and Connor ran inside, the drizzle turned into a downpour. They stepped through a door on which most of the paint had chipped off. The place buzzed with conversations supplemented with commentary from the sportscasters on televisions. Every step was sticky. The bar's atmosphere hung with the putrid odor of spilled liquor. They found a table against the wall. Through his madness, he still appreciated Brynn's ability to feel comfortable any and everywhere. She smiled at him in a way he didn't deserve.

He watched her talk but didn't listen.

Stop. You're strong enough for this.

Connor knew it was coming and there was nothing he could do to stop it. The need was stronger than floodwaters. It welled inside him. His blood raced and his jaw clenched. The beast roared, clawing away and destroying all threats of being tamed. Here came the thunder.

His senses pulsated. Every corner and person in the room came into clear focus. He took account of every element: the exits, neon lights, possible weapons, who looked like they'd intervene.

Stop, Connor. Stop. But he wouldn't listen to himself. He had to fight. He needed to struggle.

Scanning the bar, he knew he needed to find someone big with spirited-looking friends. A few old men gathered at a corner table, slapping down aces and kings. A few young-looking individuals laughed in a booth. Many groups of couples and two or three friends engaged in conversation over the music. They leaned in to hear each other. The bartender was no help to Connor, as he looked out-of-shape and past middle age.

Then Connor found what he was looking for. Leaning on the bar was a large man, probably around his age. The guy had an easy four inches and fifty pounds on Connor. Connor assumed from the Tapout shirt he wore that he had some fight training or at least an aggressive personality. He also kept jovially addressing three men gathered next to him, clearly his friends. A short-skirted woman sat on his other side and kept tugging at his arm. When he shrugged her away, she pouted.

Just what Connor needed.

His fingers trembled and his heart beat fast in an exhilarated burst before the storm. Consequences mattered less.

This is how it ends.

Don't, Connor. You're going to hurt Brynn. Sweet, precious Brynn.

Connor fixed his stare across the table at her and let his disguise down.

She carried on while reading from a menu. But when she looked up at him, her words ceased. The smile ran. Color drained from her face. She slowly tilted her head while her lip quivered.

"Oh no," she seemed to say to herself more than to Connor. "I've lost you."

He made no response but slipped out of the chair, walking across the bar like a mindless drone. She shouted out. But he couldn't hear a word.

I'm sorry, Brynn.

Stepping around chairs, he approached the big guy and the woman next to him. Connor grabbed the woman's arm. She turned with an annoyed look on her face. "Hey! What the—"

Connor took the back of her head and pulled her in, kissing her hard and deep, silencing her.

A large hand wrapped around Connor's shoulder and yanked him away. He looked up at the giant.

"What the hell are you doing?" The giant's eyes bulged and veins strained.

Connor noticed out of the corner of his eye that the woman wore a devious grin.

"I said, what are you doing, asshole?" the giant yelled. Nearby people turned their attention.

"Just kissing the girl." Connor said loudly so everyone could hear. "I don't want to fight!" Then, moving his lips as little as possible, he quietly whispered so only the giant could hear, "Come on, pussy. Hit me."

The giant's eyebrows unfurled and he drew back.

"Come on. Hit me, pussy." Connor muttered again before hollering. "Let's just talk about this!" He spread his hands, prostrate. Then under his breath again he said for only the giant. "Come on. Hit me, you dickless bitch. All I need is you to hit first. Hurry up, your mom is waiting for me."

The giant's eyes flared, apparently choosing anger over confusion, as he dropped his leg back.

Here it comes.

Twisting his torso and swinging wide, the giant sent his fist across Connor's face. The impact spun Connor away. His jaw throbbed and he spit blood.

The blood tasted so good. The pain. That sweet, sweet pain dashed through his being. It was time to scratch the itch.

The noise in the bar evaporated. The music stopped.

Connor wiped the blood away and turned back to the giant, grinning. "Now hit me like you mean it."

Connor's party started. The giant threw his second haymaker. Connor blocked it wide with his forearm. The he jumped inside the giant's wingspan and hit the man's stomach, side, and chin in three quick, vicious strikes.

Damn, that felt good.

He had missed the misery. The giant stumbled back, clutching his abdomen.

Connor squared off with him but caught a flinch in the giant's eye. He ducked as a pool cue swung over his head, narrowly missing him. He turned around as his assailant swung the cue back again. Connor trapped it and broke it. Then he slammed the cue-wielder's head into the bar.

A beer bottle slammed over the back of his head, glass crashing. It stung and made Connor dizzy.

"Overcome," Connor said to himself, shaking it off as someone came in throwing hectic punches. Connor blocked and dodged them before seizing the man's arm and punching the outside of his elbow, dislocating the joint.

Connor felt alive again.

Two of the others managed to get their hands on him and grab him from behind. He struggled while a third came at him from the front. Connor threw two rapid kicks to the outside of the approaching man's knee. Then he put both feet on the bar and shoved back with all his might, until the men holding him stumbled backwards and crashed through the door. As a mass, they fell out into the pouring rain.

The three of them hit pavement. Rain pounded deafeningly on the blacktop around them. Cold water soaked their clothes as Connor breathed in wet air.

In the confusion, Connor rolled over and kneeled on top of one of his opponents. He threw fierce elbows at the man's face, using all his core strength and hammered him into the pavement. Certain that he was down and out, Connor stood and backed away. He wiped the rain from his eyes. The two inside the bar ran out and joined the one who rose from the ground.

Connor stood, facing them. "This will be more fun if you all come at once."

A pause. A breath. A beat.

They charged him, grabbing, punching, and hitting. Connor took the pounding and returned the favor, unleashing a melee of strikes; methodically, systematically, resolutely. He chopped them down. No matter how bad it hurt, he just kept going. The pain was irrelevant, an afterthought. All that mattered in the moment was victory. With fists, elbows, legs, and knees, he left his mark on them.

In the end, Connor stood over moaning bodies, savoring the moment he conquered. He felt drunk on his own ferocity. Once again, the world had dared to underestimate him. And he triumphed.

Tilting his head back, he tasted the rain that ran down his face, and inhaled deeply. Drops trickled over his skin and dripped off his fingertips. The high was so extreme. He let the menace out and it felt so right.

"Why?" A still, small voice cut through the rain.

Connor turned slowly.

Oh, no. Brynn.

There she was, looking so small and out of place in the pouring rain, outside a forsaken bar in the middle of nowhere.

The few feet between them was miles and galaxies wide.

Brynn looked down at his fallen adversaries, with pity on her face. Her soaked dark locks clung to her face. Her joy gone, she now seemed so frail. The moisture glistened on her skin.

She looked at him, bewildered. He watched her realize he was no good and never was.

Words failed.

Tears melded with rain. Her brow crinkled. She threw her hands down at her side. "Why, Connor! Why!" she yelled. "Why did you have to do this?" Her face burned with anger and sadness. "Why do you have to ruin everything?" She pressed her palm to her forehead, glancing back at the victims. "I was over you! You know? I survived you. I was living again!" She pleaded with him. "I can't keep doing this!"

Her pain was desolation to him. "I'm sorry—"

"*Sorry!* What's that supposed to be to me? Why do you do this? Break all this?"

"I don't—"

"I can't, Connor! I'm only human. I'm not like you. I feel pain. I hurt. I bleed, Connor! I bleed!"

He stared at the ground.

Without warning she shoved him with both hands. "What's this in you, Connor? What makes you do this?" She wept.

"I… I don't know."

"No! Tell me! What is it? Is it anger… hate? Ego? Is it passion or love? Is it fear?" She shoved him again. "Tell me! TELL ME WHAT MAKES YOU LIKE THIS!"

The forces within him welled up and erupted. "I DON'T KNOW!" He begged her. "I don't know! But it owns me!"

He wanted her to understand so badly. Though he'd never cried, something similar filled his eyes. "It's always there! I just…

I just have to. I have to fight! I have to war!"

"Then why can't you war for my heart like you war for everything else!" She turned and walked away.

Connor reached out and touched her shoulder. "Brynn—"

She spun like a viper, her eyes flared with anger and hurt. "NO!" She jabbed a finger hard into his chest. "You know what, Connor? I DON'T LOVE YOU! I'm through hoping for you. I'm done. Stay away from me!" Brynn stormed off through the rain, beyond the light of the street lamp that flickered above. The dark took her and she was gone.

Connor wanted to chase her, to apologize. He wanted to say he was sorry and promise her so many things. He wanted to be someone else, someone capable. But he wasn't.

Through the night, rotating red and blue lights approached with the growing sound of sirens. Connor thought the cops would be faster. He took one last look in the direction she disappeared. Then he swallowed his emotion and knelt on the soaked pavement. He interlaced his fingers behind his head and waited stone-faced as the police pulled up, illuminating him in their headlights while onlookers watched the wildman be arrested. The rain poured.

TWELVE HOURS LATER, THE sound of footsteps came down the hallway. Connor took his eyes off the fluorescent light that flickered and sat up on the concrete bench.

A deputy came around the corner and slipped keys into the cell door. "Let's go. You're being released."

Connor followed him across dirty floors down the sterile,

bland halls of the jail. The deputy led him through a door. In the office, a police officer sat at a desk while a civilian stood with his arms crossed.

"Hello, David." Connor greeted his father's aid.

David didn't respond. "So is there any else you need, officers?"

"No, you may go. Judging by the phone call I got, you must be pretty well connected. Just don't stick around."

"Yes, sir." David gestured for Connor to precede him.

Connor's steady, strong gate juxtaposed with David's quick little shuffle. The two pushed through double doors.

David looked around. "Do you realize what you've done?" He spoke quietly but aggressively. "I can't even count how many favors your father had to call in! Favors he could have used in the election!"

"He doesn't need favors, he's got you." Connor smirked.

"Yeah, *real* cute." David said. "I just don't understand how you can be so selfish. The world doesn't revolve around you. Your father has been bailing you out your whole life! Politically, you cost more than you're worth. But that doesn't matter to you, does it? You've never had to deal with the consequences of your actions. Thank God, the witnesses described it as self-defense."

"Calm down, Dave," Connor said. "Save it for the campaign. Where are we going?"

"Well, you're on the first plane back to Afghanistan. Hopefully no one will be able to inquire about you if you're on the other side of the world. And seriously, for your dad's sake, try not to cause any more trouble."

So, back to Afghanistan. Good. At least things made sense there and he couldn't hurt Brynn anymore.

Part 2

THOSE BROKEN ONES

CHAPTER 9

Twine was red and the hanging lights, warm. The bride spun in swirls of white as a jazz band provided the melody: their rendition of Etta James' "At Last."

Brynn sat with her hands folded on a clothed-draped table. Three hundred people gathered at the starlit wedding reception. Fair weather provided a comfortable temperature for the evening while the moon smiled down on the celebration. Conversation hummed among the guests. Centerpieces lent a floral scent to the air.

The wedding party's table sat elevated above the rest. Waiting alone in her chair, Brynn felt on display. She adjusted her burgundy bridesmaid's dress. The bride was a co-worker Brynn met while working at her new job in Austin. They'd only known each other briefly, yet the bride still asked Brynn to participate. And now, eight months after her move to Austin, Brynn found herself with wedding duties.

Brynn searched the crowd for a face she recognized but found none. On the dance floor, the bride laughed after the groom whispered something in her ear. The rest of the wedding party managed to find their significant others and also enjoy the band's music. Brynn felt lonely watching, instead of participating in, the party. She missed the flood of weddings immediately following college where she knew everyone. Only forty-five minutes remained until she could sneak out.

"Everyone left you here?"

Brynn looked up. An unassuming tall man with a pleasant and confident demeanor stood before her. Strong cheekbones positioned above a rigid jaw line. That, plus the fact he sported a pair of thick-brimmed, retro glasses reminded her of Clark Kent. Somehow he seemed more wholesome and innocent than Superman ever was.

"Someone had to guard the table," Brynn said. She could tell he wanted to engage her and was torn between wallowing and flirting.

"Yes, I've heard of you." He smiled. "I hear you're great at guarding tables. Nevertheless, I'll risk it." He sat down across from her. "I'm Kyle."

"I'm Brynn." She let her mouth twist halfway into a smile.

"So Brynn, besides guarding her tables, how do you know the bride?"

"She and I work together at *Texas Weekly*."

"Well! I'm a subscriber. Big fan. I'll tell your boss they should keep you around."

Brynn laughed despite her hesitance. "Oh, thank you. How do you know the couple?"

"Cal and I went to college together. I remember when he lived down the hall from me. Just a pasty kid that always stayed in his towel too long after a shower." He nodded toward the groom. "And now it's years later and he's getting married. They grow up so fast, don't they?" He wiped away a pretend tear.

"They do." Brynn smirked. "Eventually all you can do is let them go and hope you did your best."

Kyle chuckled. "It's not easy being a parent." Then he paused and looked upward, tilting his head and turning his ear.

"Do you hear this song, Brynn? There's something interesting about this song." His tone was playful.

"What's that?" She found herself excited about their exchange, wondering what he might say next.

"This song isn't going to dance to itself." He stood and extended a hand to her. "So we'd better."

Brynn felt herself blush. "I'm not much of a dancer."

"Neither am I. So we'll go slow. You'll trust me and we'll see if we can't figure something out." He smiled with kind eyes.

Intrepidly, Brynn reached her hand across the table and met his. She stood and followed him to the dance floor.

Who is this guy?

As he led her out, he turned and said, "Don't worry. I paid a kid to guard the table while you're gone. He seemed trustworthy. Said his name was 'Shady'."

She laughed again.

Before long, they spun to and fro. Her smile got away from her, and she found herself very much enjoying the evening.

He pulled her close. "Everyone out here is going to think I'm some sort of cool guy, getting to dance with a girl like you."

She blushed, and when the song ended Kyle said, "Let's take another lap."

Throughout the night, Kyle found Brynn again and again, song after song. And when the party was over, they cheered and waved sparklers with the others as the departing couple made their way to the getaway vehicle. Then the pandemonium passed. Brynn found her coat and prepared to leave.

"I should probably walk you to your car in case someone tries to mug you," Kyle said.

"Oh, yeah?"

"Yeah. I have a move, just in case. Honestly, it's not a very good move 'cause everybody dies, but at least we'll get the mugger. The way I see it, we'll either all make it, or none of us will. And be warned, I'm a screamer."

Brynn laughed longer and louder than she meant to.

He opened her car door. "You know, Brynn, I'd really feel like my night was complete if I got a number from you. I'd like it even more if I got all seven."

Brynn laughed, but paused for a moment. *Am I ready for this?*

But looking at him smile, simple and soft, she did not want to stop herself. "Fine," she smiled. "All seven."

"Jackpot!" Kyle pulled out his phone. "Go slow, I don't want to miss a single digit." After her recitation, they said goodnight and Brynn drove away.

BRYNN WOKE UP THE following Monday still riding the buzz of curiosity from the wedding reception. All day long, waves of anticipation, worry, and excitement fought for prominence. Anticipation: based on sheer curiosity. Worry: perhaps Saturday night never really happened. And excitement: he might call. But if it did happen, would anything come of it? Would she allow it to? But she checked herself. He was just some guy. Staying guarded was her number one priority.

At the office, she stared at her computer screen returning emails when her phone rang. Checking the caller ID, she saw a number she did not recognize. "Hello?"

"Well I'm certainly happy you gave me your real number. I bet guys must ask a girl like you for your number all the time. I wouldn't blame you if you passed out decoys."

Brynn recognized the voice. "I guess you caught me on an off day."

Kyle laughed. "Brynn, how's your Monday? Do you have everything under control over at the magazine?"

"I'm doing my best."

"I don't doubt it. Before long, you'll be running things."

Brynn laughed.

"I got an idea for your next article," he said.

"Really? What's that?"

"An investigatory piece about a night on the town with some dude you met at a wedding."

"Think so?" She found a strand of her hair and twisted it in her fingers.

"I do. I think it should take place on Friday."

"Oh, should it?"

"Yeah, let's see if we can't find some fun and maybe a little trouble."

"What did you have in mind?"

"Now, now, Brynn. Don't you worry yourself about details. That's my job. But if you were to say 'yes', what time should a guy pick you up?"

"Probably around 7."

"Let's make it 7:01, I don't think I can be there by 7."

Brynn laughed again. "Fine, 7:01."

"Good. All right, I'll see you on Friday at 7:01. I'm excited, get excited."

"I will." She said.

"All right. Have a good Monday, Brynn."

"You, too!"

Brynn clicked her phone off and set it on the desk. She

swiveled in her chair and looked out the window. Maybe she was moving too fast. She didn't know what she thought of Kyle. But she decided then and there to put her best foot forward.

And then Friday was upon her. She finished blow-drying her hair and looked at the clock. It was 6:30. The forecast pleased her, as it was cool enough for a light jacket and scarf. Wondering where the scarf was, she began her search. Elbow deep in her dressers, she rifled through drawers. Finding none, she knelt and turned to one of the drawers at the bottom where she stored items she never wore.

A brightly colored garment met her as she pulled the drawer open. Brynn removed and let it unfold. The never-worn Greene Family Reunion shirt brought back memories of the summer gathering with distant relatives on Lake Livingston. She next found a mess of tangled necklaces that fused together in a ball of insurmountable knots.

Brynn smiled when she found the coffee table book of French Impressionists she thought she had lost. She took it from the drawer. Pulling it away, it revealed a dark garment beneath she did not recognize. She lifted it out.

The black fleece unfurled in a wave of mustiness. Brynn jolted through time and space as she recognized it as the fleece Connor West loaned her on the night she was rescued in Afghanistan.

She passed the soft woven fabric between her fingers, staring deeply into it. That day was so miserable. Her tongue remembered the salty taste of countless tears. Then he had come.

The feel and smell of him enveloped her senses. Where was he? Was he okay? But Brynn knew better. Connor was always okay. He didn't break. He was somewhere else, leaving scars.

Still, what if he came back? He might come back. Maybe

he'd come back. Maybe he'd come in, bursting through her door. He'd tell her how sorry he was and that he'd change. He'd take her away. She'd know everything would be—

NO! she thought. You've wasted enough time on him. You're better and he doesn't deserve you. He was born to let you down.

She clenched her fist around the fleece and stood, to cross to her back door. When she stepped onto the porch, Brynn pulled the cover off the garbage can. She held the fleece over the bin and paused. But she furrowed her brow and summoned resolve. As it fell, the fleece crinkled against the garbage bag, winding its way to the bottom of the can.

She stomped inside, refusing to look back and decided on her fire engine red scarf.

The doorbell rang at 7:01. Brynn opened it.

Kyle's calm smile met her from where he stood a few steps down her front walk. "Whoa, Brynn! You look fantastic! I can't believe I get to walk around Austin with you."

She laughed. "You look nice, too."

"You better take these." He held out some flowers. "They're not really my color."

"Wow, they're beautiful. Thank you." She accepted them. "I'll go put them in some water."

When she finished arranging them, she set the vase on the coffee table in the living room.

"All right, let's get outta here." He beckoned her after him and led her to his car. After he opened the door for her, Brynn slid inside.

Kyle climbed in on the far side. "So, bad news—"

"What's that?" Brynn's excitement faulted for a moment.

"The private jet I chartered to Paris has a flat tire, so we'll have to do something else tonight," Kyle said. "It's a real bummer because I had Peter Frampton waiting to give us a private concert."

"That's the worst! Although, I'll bet Peter Frampton had something to do with the flat tire."

At the very least, he's funny.

They drove for a few minutes while Kyle commented on things they passed. Brynn laughed along. They pulled up to Moonshine Restaurant and left the car with the valet. Kyle let her walk through the doors first.

She enjoyed the way he interacted with people, asking the host his name and addressing him by it. For every service offered, Kyle responded with, "Thank you" or "I appreciate you."

The restaurant was a blend of wood floors and rafters combined with limestone walls. Garlic and spice aromas teased her appetite. The waiter handed them menus and departed with their drink order.

"So Brynn, how did a girl who grew up in Houston, went to Baylor, wrote for a New York paper, end up working for a magazine in Austin?" Kyle said. "Did you always plan on this?"

"Well, I had a change of plans at the end of my senior year at Baylor. I guess I needed a change of plans. So I took a job in New York."

"How'd you like living there?"

"I liked some of it and I didn't like some of it. It's fun being around all the glamour, but it's hard never having a moment to yourself. It's so crowded."

"Yeah, I'd guess. Living on an island surrounded by people," Kyle said.

"Exactly. Then after a few years I was on assignment covering the war over in Afghanistan," Brynn said. "It wasn't really my thing, so that was my last foreign assignment."

"The traveling must have been hard."

"It was."

Will I ever tell you the story?

"Did you come here next?"

"No, I went back to Houston for while. But, you know, I grew up there. I needed a change." Brynn fiddled with her napkin.

"So you moved to Austin."

"So I moved to Austin."

"Well, I think I speak for all of Austin when I say we're happy to have you. We're excited you're on the team."

Brynn laughed. "I'm glad I'm welcome. It's nice to know if I made the cut."

"It's strictly probationary of course," Kyle grinned. "But I've got some pull with the board."

"Okay, I'll be on my best behavior. Just put in a good word for me."

"Deal." He drank some of his iced tea.

"But where are you from?" she said.

"I grew up in Nebraska." Kyle shifted in his seat. "I came to A&M for their engineering program. When I graduated, I got a job at a firm northwest of town."

"Do you like it?"

"Sure. I'm also happy I got to move to Austin. I love it here."

"What's your family do in Nebraska?"

"Dad's a county judge, Mom teaches third grade."

"Do you see them much?" Brynn sipped her water.

"I'd say every three months." He cracked a smile. "Or four times a year, as a normal person would say."

They laughed.

The waiter approached. "Have you made your selections

yet?"

Brynn shook her head slightly toward Kyle.

"We're going to need a few more minutes. I just can't make up my mind." He winked at her.

"I'll be right back." The waiter left.

"We better get on our game before he throws us out of here," Kyle said. The two buried their noses in the menus.

After dinner, Kyle surprised her with tickets to Revello, a local Austin band she enjoyed. Kyle pulled her through the dark venue, navigating the crowd and thoughtfully asking attendees for permission to pass. Before heading to the front, they swung by the bar and ordered some beverages. Kyle carried hers and his. They continued and found room near the stage.

"Wow, we're close," Brynn said over the crowd.

"Yeah. Well, I want easy access in case they call me on stage for a solo." He smiled. "I keep telling them that I'm retired—" He lurched forward as someone stumbled into him. A splash of Kyle's beverage fell to the floor. Kyle turned.

"I'm sorry, man," a college kid said.

"Oh, no worries." Kyle nodded. "I've bumped into people before."

Brynn smiled. What a great guy. She was happy she said yes to the date.

★ ★ ★

THREE WEEKS LATER, BRYNN sat at her desk, editing one of her columns. Her fingers played the keyboard and the clicking drummed non-stop until she took a sip of hot tea. The flavor for the day was vanilla-citrus, the latest combination from the gift basket of teas Kyle had sent her.

"Brynn?" Her editor, Jerry, stepped into the room.

"Yes?"

He adjusted his skinny tie and messed with his cuff links. He cocked his eyebrow, eying the basket. "New boyfriend?"

"Just a boy I've been on a few dates with."

"Ah, nice." He nodded. "You grew up in Houston, right?"

"I did."

"Word on the street is that you're friends with Senator Benjamin West." Jerry leaned against her doorframe.

The mention of the name "West" seemed shouted in her tiny office. It was the loudest word she could fathom.

Please no.

"Friends of the family, sure." She found a hair tie and pulled her locks back into a ponytail. "But I haven't seen the Wests in quite some time."

"Well, get reacquainted." Jerry rubbed his hands together. "He's in Austin today discussing oil fracking's environmental impact. And it seems to me that would be the perfect topic for your next column."

Meeting with the Senator was one of the last things on earth Brynn wanted to do. She assumed forgetting his son meant she should avoid the father as well.

"I really don't know if I can—"

"Brynn." Jerry raised his hand. "You're so smart. I have no doubt you'll figure it out and I can't wait to read it." He left.

"But..."

He didn't turn around.

She adjusted her monitor. "Great."

Arguing with herself for an hour, Brynn finally picked up the phone and called her mom. She talked her mom into reaching Mrs. West and then the Senator so Brynn would not have to make small talk with Mrs. West.

A half hour later, Brynn received a phone call telling her when and where to be. She left her office and drove a few blocks to the state Capitol.

The dome along with the Grecian columns sat on one of her many jogging routes. The entrance was a guarded gate she ran past many times, never having given it a second thought.

"Welcome to the Capitol," a state police officer said. "May I have your name?"

"Brynn Greene. I'm with *Texas Weekly*."

The officer perused a list. "Ah, yes. Feel free to park anywhere on the second level."

The gate lifted and Brynn pulled her car ahead. She found a spot and entered the main door. Having only been in the public part where tourists and visitors go, she now visited halls that allowed access to different offices. She looked up and down at passing employees and legislatures.

"Ms. Greene?"

Brynn turned and found a gangly, young man and a petite exotic-looking girl. "Yes?"

"Hi, Ms. Greene. I'm Burton and this is my associate, Laila. We're interning with the Senator this semester. Please follow us. A room has been set up for your interview."

"Thank you."

Brynn walked behind them across the government-issued carpet that absorbed their steps. Equipment buzzed and phones rang.

"Through here." Burton indicated.

It was a buried space, with no windows and one entrance. The walls were a warm greenish tone. Brass-buttoned leather high-back chairs faced each other. Lamps produced a soft glow. The air smelled of stale popery.

"The Senator should be along shortly," Laila said as she and Burton left.

Brynn sat back in one of the chairs and found her voice recorder and laptop. She thought she should feel more professional, but her stomach churned in knots.

As she waited, the silence was deafening. She'd always seen the Senator as a character almost as unique as his son. All spoke of the brilliance of his policies and his ability to read people. He also seemed a sincere man. Everything he said struck her as heartfelt.

Her phone buzzed. She opened the text message, a picture from Kyle. The image showed a baby monkey riding a Great Dane with a caption that read, "New supervisor is shaking things up."

She chuckled.

A knock on the door pulled her from amusement. "Yes?"

"Brynn?" The door opened as Senator West stuck his head through. He looked at her and smiled. "Hello!"

"Hello. I really appreciate you doing this," she said.

"Of course, Brynn." He entered, leaning on his cane. "You're practically family." He closed the door behind him and crossed to his chair. "I was so excited when my wife called and told me you needed a meeting."

He sat and regarded her with fatherly affection. "Look at you. All grown up and interviewing senators. I'm really proud of you, Brynn. You've grown into such an impressive young woman." His look of political distance melted into familial relation. And in it all, something made Brynn sense he held back sadness.

"And you're so strong, Brynn. So strong." He put his elbow on the armrest and braced the side of his face with his fist, like he really wanted to vent. "After what you went through in Afghanistan and how you didn't let it stop you." He sat up straighter. "Oh, I'm sorry to bring it up. I don't want to cause you pain. I haven't shared it with anyone. I'm just privy to the information. It's how I check in on my son."

"That's very kind of you," Brynn said, truly appreciating the compliment.

He glowed at her.

"Are you ready for the interview now?" Brynn said.

"Actually, Brynn. There's one more thing I'd like to say; off the record." His smile withered and his eyes drooped. He, a bastion of fortitude and charisma, aged a decade in seconds. He looked very tired. Loosening his tie and undoing his top button, he said, "Brynn, I need to apologize to you."

She didn't say anything, only watched him as the air in the room suddenly felt very heavy.

He glanced around. "I didn't realize what would happen, you know."

Brynn felt like his peer.

"All my life, I always felt held back. Like I was missing out on so much because of this." He waved his cane. "I spent a lot of time judging those with two legs. I was always so bitter, so hateful, if I felt they weren't living big enough. I would have killed to be them. I always thought I'd be unstoppable if I just had two legs that worked properly."

He shook his head, laying a hand on his thigh. "Then Connor was born." The Senator's eyes twinkled. "And he was small for a baby. But he was strong. And I thought, this kid has a chance to be such a human. He can be ten times the man I am.'"

The Senator seemed to be talking to himself more than to her, as he blankly stared at the floor. "I thought I was teaching him to never give up, to achieve. I didn't want him to be held back by the things that hold others back."

The last thing Brynn wanted to talk about was Connor, but as the Senator bared his soul, she felt she needed to participate. "He certainly doesn't let anything hold him back."

The Senator chortled. "It seems that way, doesn't it? That kid's got more grit and gravel than I could have ever hoped. But…"

His sigh was laden with guilt. "I fear I've robbed him of the good things in life, of the chance to be happy." He looked up at her. "I'm afraid he'll never find peace. I worry that I've killed my son's future… so much wreckage follows him, I don't know how to apologize to the world… or to him." Senator West rubbed his eyes.

Brynn didn't know what to say. But she felt weight lifting from her soul as the Senator spoke.

"And Brynn, I've watched you chase him around since you were eight. I know so much of what I instilled in him has fallen on you. For that I am truly, truly sorry." The Senator's eyes held the hint of moisture, while Brynn felt tears well up in her own.

"Now I don't know what your current relationship to my son is, although I believe you've always truly cared for him in some way. I just want to tell you…" He straightened up and cleared his throat. "Stop wasting your time on him. It will only end in heartache. His life may be ruined. Yours doesn't have to be as well." He tilted his head sideways and let out a slow exhale.

They sat in silence for a long time. She felt closer to him than she ever imagined. She nodded slightly to let him know she understood.

Then she took a breath, turned her recorder on, and sat up straight. "Senator, thank you for sitting down with me. Could we please discuss what you hope to accomplish in the Capitol today in regards to fracking?"

Senator West smiled, his haggardness disappearing. Once again, he sat a regal statesman. "Certainly, Miss Greene. And it's my pleasure to meet with you today."

CHAPTER 10

The first bullet was the loudest and the first muzzle flash, the brightest. Early dawn shook. Connor thought he might be dreaming as blood erupted from Riley's chest, splashing red droplets into the air. His friend spun away and snapped back like a rag doll. His face twisted in pain. And as Riley collided with the ground, Connor was sure the earth quaked beneath the titan's fall.

"CONTACT!"

So many guns fired at once, it sounded as though the planet fractured. A million fireflies flickered on the hills. The slope in front of them came alive as Taliban fighters materialized from the rocks. Bullets ricocheted off every surface. The twelve-man team found no safe directions to move, so they scattered and dived for cover around the dry riverbed.

Connor squeezed the butt of his gun in his armpit and fired the weapon one-handed. With his left, he reached down and seized Riley's vest, and dragged him towards the cover of a low boulder. Riley took another round in the thigh. He grabbed at his leg and swore at the night. Connor pulled him behind the boulder.

"How the hell did they know we're here?" Bison yelled over the deafening gunfire, repeated explosions, and splintering rock.

"That little prick!" Lt. Ryan slid across the gravel and took cover behind another boulder, close to Connor. "Chalabi must've sold us out!"

Connor emptied a clip and dropped down to switch magazines. He closed his eyes and took a deep breath. His ears rang with the sound of bullets, his nose filled with the scent of gunpowder, and his fingers itched with instinct.

"I am the very worst thing on earth," he whispered. "A walking nightmare."

He gritted his teeth and came back over the top of the rock and laid the red dot on one insurgent after the other, signing their death warrants with his trigger. But there were so many. Now, his only job was ignoring enemy fire and making his shots count. A burst of rounds ricocheted off the rock next to him.

"Baker's down!" someone yelled.

"CONNOR!"

He looked down at Riley sitting in a pool of his own blood, clutching his gun and three magazines. "Prop me up!"

Connor tucked his gun and wrapped his arms around Riley, then hoisted him over the edge of the boulder. Riley clung to the rock with his elbows and started picking targets, 70 yards away.

Enemies made desperate runs, AK-47s held above their head and screaming. They bore their chests and dared the SEALs. Connor obliged.

Shockwaves from an explosion next to Lt. Ryan flung earth everywhere and concussed against Connor. Lt. Ryan flew back hard, his body bending in the air like a limp sack. Before Connor could turn to him, he was up on his knees. He bared his teeth and grunted.

"COME ON!" he yelled, spitting blood. Debris tangled in his jet-black hair.

Connor jumped and slid in next to him. "You'll be fine!"

"Of course I'll be fine!" He looked at Connor. Mutilated flesh replaced his left ocular socket while the tip of his ear was blown off. The bloody mess glistened in the orange light from a sliver of sun reaching over the horizon. Wetness and dirt mixed. Lt. Ryan snatched his rifle off the ground and kept shooting.

Connor rolled back to his position by Riley, stood, and fought as fast as his finger could pull the trigger.

Riley slowed. He fired a few rounds then his head bobbed down. Then he jolted back and fired a few more. But his head stayed down longer and longer until it didn't come back. Connor peeked sideways to find Riley slumped over on the rock. Blood seeped from his chest and formed a crimson puddle, half his face submerged in it.

Connor wanted to go to Riley, to hold his dead body, and cradle him. He wanted to close Riley's open eyes. But this was not the time for that. So Connor kept fighting.

"RILEY'S DOWN!"

"Air support inbound! Twenty minutes!" Lt. Ryan yelled.

Connor turned his head slightly. "I don't think we have—"

A wave of heat seared over Connor's left hand as the rock splintered. Connor pulled his arm back. The hurt dashed through him.

"Oh hell!" Connor said as he looked down. His little finger was gone, ripped off by a bullet above the second knuckle. The appendage trembled.

As it drained blood, Connor marveled. It had been there only a moment before and now was gone. *How could such a thing happen?* One brief moment and now every day for the rest of his life, he would no longer have that finger. The pain was great. Bullets were so incredibly powerful.

But pain didn't matter now. That was something else, something for later, something for the back of his mind. Now, he needed to rise. He needed to keep going, never stopping.

"Pain isn't a good enough reason." Connor said as he pulled a quick-clot pack from his vest, ripped it open with his teeth, and doused his finger with it. He shook his head. Then he came over the rock and started shooting again, his sleeve now damp with blood.

Connor shot an insurgent aiming a rocket launcher.

"SHIT! They're coming down the ledge!" Bison yelled. "There's so many! Is half the damn country here?"

From cover sixty yards away, a group of eight ran towards Connor's end of the line. With smooth leaps and bounds, they flew over the rocks. Connor started with the farthest one away and dropped them man by man. The last and nearest fighter was jumping over the boulder when Connor shot him through the chest. The dead body landed on Connor. He shoved him away.

"MIKE'S DOWN!"

"DAMN IT!"

Connor gunned down two insurgents who came over a ledge high and to the left. Their bodies crumpled and fell to the rocks below. But more replaced them.

"Connor! Remo!" Lt. Ryan waved them over.

Connor jumped and slid over, until he was shoulder to shoulder with Lt. Ryan. They fired waves of lead down range. Remo slid in on the other side. They never looked at each other while they spoke.

"You two, take the high ground to the right! Otherwise we can't stop them!"

"But, Chief! The cliff's too steep!"

"DOUBLE BACK AROUND AND TAKE THE SLOPE!"

He changed magazines.

"WE'RE NOT LEAVING YOU HERE!"

"DAMN IT! It's an order! We need to buy time until air support arrives! WE CAN'T HOLD THIS POSITION!" Lt. Ryan pointed up the ridge. "Take extra mags! And Connor," he turned to him. "Use that speed I'm always hearing about!"

Connor hated this plan. The last thing he wanted to do was leave the team behind. But it was orders, and besides, the lieutenant was right.

Connor yanked extra ammo from his fallen comrade's vests and loaded his own. For a moment, he studied the enemy in front of them. They scurried over the rocks like a plague, not cowering as much as they should. Connor guessed they had gotten confident, assuming their victory. Then he glanced behind and his mind marked the path he must run. The longer he took, the more his team would die.

"Hey, Connor West! I hear you're pretty fast!" Remo checked his gear over.

"I just fake it well!" Connor yelled. "COME ON!"

The two exploded from their cover and charged. Bullets sang in the air as they whipped past Connor's head. His body entered the well-exercised and rhythmic motion of running while cradling his weapon. The gravel crunched under their feet as they propelled back around the bend of the dry riverbed, past where the sheer cliff ended to a manageable slope. Their boots sank into the loose shale that slipped away as they ascended. Every step was double effort.

"You know what the trick is? It's not about being fast." Connor leaned in and pumped his legs. "The trick is to keep running when everyone else stops!"

The hill was steep and the ridge above seemed far. Connor's

thighs burned. He might have considered stopping but he knew that many men before him had run up similar hills, and he was by no means least among these.

At the top, he and Remo crested the ridge. "EYES UP!" They did not know what was on the other side. They emerged from the shadows into abrupt sunlight.

One hundred yards away, three insurgents crept along on the ridge above the rest of the SEAL team and down slope of Remo and Connor.

The two hunters slowed, steadied, and weighed the insurgents down with enough lead to ensure the group would not be getting up again.

Remo looked over at Connor. "I love our job—"

Remo's shoulder ripped open. Connor watched his teammate tumble, the friend at his side for his entire wartime baptism. Remo's body jerked and his head twisted as flecks of sweat fell from his soaked hair. Eyes closed, gravity pulled Connor's friend to the ground, slowly.

How can such a man fall?

"I'LL KILL YOU!" Connor's shouted to the landscape. His eyes raced everywhere trying to identify the sniper. A muzzle flash and a bullet whizzing past Connor let him know his assailant's position. Unlike the sniper, Connor didn't miss.

"Remo! Can you hear me?" He checked and found a pulse. "Remo!" He slapped his friend's face. "Come on, man!"

"Oh, damn!" Remo's eyes burst wide open and searched wildly before they found Connor. He tried to sit, then winced and ceased. His eyes glistened, seeping with pain. He pounded on the dirt. "It's bad, Connor, real bad!"

"It's all right, we'll be back at base soon. You'll just have a badass scar!" Connor looked down the ridge where the rest of the team still needed their cover.

"It's so bad, man!" Remo coughed.

Connor seized a handful of Remo's collar and pulled him in, trying not to show his concern. "We're never out of the fight! Do you hear me? NEVER!"

Remo looked back at Connor. His agony retreated before a look of resolution, of courage, of immortality and a little crazy. He took a deep breath. "You're damn fucking right." He stuck out his hand. "Get me to that ridge!"

Connor grabbed him, lifting Remo from the dirt. Then he heaved his friend over his shoulder and scanned the final 200 yards. He ran, one step after the other. It was hard and hurt, but his team needed him to be fast. So he was fast. Remo's warm blood ran down the side of Connor's face and neck.

Connor hit the dirt and set Remo down. Crawling, he dragged his friend up a ledge where they could flank the enemy. Then the two let it rip.

Connor dropped 14 insurgents before they realized gunfire was coming from their flank. As the insurgents scrambled, Connor put down a group setting up a heavy machine gun. Together Connor and Remo went through clip after clip as the enemy returned a swarm of bullets.

With the cover fire, the team below advanced on the enemy position. Connor started to believe there might be hope for the day.

Another splash of blood sprayed across Connor's face. A bullet had ripped through the side of Remo's neck. His friend closed his eyes, took a strained breath, then opened them, and continued to fight. The ground glimmered with their empty brass casings.

Then came the thunder at long last. Out of the clouds

dropped two F-15s and let their armaments go. The hills before Connor vaporized, blanketed in an inferno, complete and total desolation. Then the death angels disappeared as swiftly as they came. And the land burned.

Connor panted as he hugged the ground. An eerie calm followed as the giant dust clouds settled. No more shots fired. In the distance, a few insurgents scrambled away over the ridge. The hurricane of bullets and all their death, ceased. The landscape quieted.

The tension in his shoulders eased as Connor exhaled.

It's over.

Down the ledge, one of his teammates cheered.

Remo!

Connor turned to help his brother, but motion 30 yards to their right caught Connor's attention. Insurgents came charging around a rock pile, firing wildly. A bullet crashed into the side of Connor's M-4. He spun on his knees towards them, but the gun wouldn't fire.

Under a barrage of automatic fire, Connor jerked his pistol and sent lead in an instant. White hot, searing pain flashed across his eyes and venom tore through his stomach. His insides sizzled. He fell away and crashed into the ground, clutching his gut. The AK-47 round was a vicious and furious tempest. Connor knew he should be seeing, but he couldn't see. And he knew he should be hearing, but he couldn't hear. And he couldn't move.

Come on, Connor. It's just pain. You need to fight. Get up! Get up, you pussy! Be better! Be bigger!

With all he had, Connor rose, tightly closing his eyes trying to get them to refocus. Slowly, the world cleared up. Sound became unmufffled. Colors, light, returned. And their were more to fight.

I need a weapon.

But as he searched, he saw two Taliban fighters standing over him, just feet away. The barrels of their AK's were pointed at his chest.

Remo stay motionless.

Connor looked at them through the one eye he could open, his blood-ridden hair matted to his forehead. They stared back, their eyes full of a hesitant confidence, like when big game hunters approach their fallen prey, unsure if the animal is truly dead.

This is the end.

Connor smiled and softly nodded, letting out a laugh full of pain. He slowly rolled over and rose to his knees, looking up into the eyes of those before him. With a calm hand, he eased the knife from his vest and held it before the insurgents.

"Before we do this," he said to them, "you should know I won't stop until I put you in the ground, so do the same. Because, you see, I get up every time."

The insurgents stared at him and then glanced at each other, raising their eyebrows. One of them shrugged, then they faced him and raised their weapons.

Connor summoned all he had, preparing to jump, one last burst of strength. This was it… his death…

Gunfire littered the insurgents' chests with bullet holes. They flew back and slammed into the ground. Connor turned and saw Lt. Ryan coming down the ridge with Bison.

His friend, death, waited, paused in the shadows.

Then the world faded to him. He crawled over to Remo. He talked to his buddy but Remo didn't respond. Try as he might, he couldn't find a pulse from the lion's heart in his friend's chest.

So Connor cradled the warrior's head and looked across a crisp dawn. The otherse tried in vain to resuscitate.

The silhouettes of two black hawk helicopters approached against a blood soaked sunrise. And Connor felt himself tiring. He crawled away.

On the lonely mountainside, he reached into his vest. His fingers closed around his prized possession. Connor unfolded the photograph, part of the image tainted crimson. But still her smile, her eyes came through. Those forever-blue eyes reached from the photograph and warmed him. He could almost feel her touch.

"I'm sorry, Brynn," Connor said to the dawn. Then everything faded to black.

★ ★ ★

TWO WEEKS LATER, CONNOR sat in a hospital bed. Cool gray walls reflected the fluorescent ceiling lights. Heart monitors and the nurses' station beeped steadily.

Admiral Scott Harley, high commander of S.P.E.C.O.P.S for the war in Afghanistan, sat by Connor's bed. He was a man Connor respected. His weathered eyes had seen enough to grow fearless. Two other high-ranking SEALs stood behind him.

"I know it means little in light of your friends we've lost, but I'm sorry. I should have insisted Omar Chalabi fall under greater scrutiny. Turns out, he was playing both sides. He owed a sizable debt to a tribal leader, and…"

The Admiral rubbed his brow. "You know how revered and legendary we are in this part of the world. It seems offering up an entire team was his payment."

"What happens to him now?" Connor said.

"I'll fight for him to be punished, executed, but..." The Admiral closed his eyes and clenched his fist. "Half his information has proved good. So some bureaucratics will allow the C.I.A. to protect him."

Connor leaned back in his bed and stared out the window.

"It doesn't feel right, does it?" The Admiral said. "When such men die at the workings of a wretch. The world's so full of cowards and the fearful that it seems like mankind can't afford the death of so many brave men."

Connor nodded.

The Admiral stood and approached Connor. He opened two small boxes and set them on Connor's bedside table. "Another purple heart and Navy Cross." He saluted Connor. "Maybe someday they'll mean something to you."

Then the men left the room. And the heart in Connor rumbled.

TWO DAYS LATER, CONNOR turned the handle as the door opened. A dirty, white room seemed even more barren in its harsh lighting. The space was a different world from the arid desert, just beyond the walls.

The man sitting in a metal folding chair at the table looked towards Connor with a tilted head and wrinkled brow. Connor closed the door behind him.

"Who are you?" the man said.

Connor pulled a chair from the corner and braced it under the door handle, creating a barricade. "My name doesn't matter.

Just know that you're going to die soon." Connor turned to him and said calmly, "You see, you betrayed my team and I'm going to kill you today."

Chalabi's squinted eyes opened wide and he tilted his head back. "Oh. Yes, of course." He leaned back in his chair with a confident little sneer. "You're the one the United States sent after Yasin." His mouth opened into a wider grin. "What's the problem? Have trouble finding—"

"I understand why you're laughing." Connor sat down across from Chalabi. "You think you're untouchable. We salivate at the information you provide and now you're under the impression you could betray thousands more and we'd still welcome you with open arms. You're just worth too damn much to us."

"Yes!" Chalabi snapped back. "And you're just a foot soldier, an expendable piece of equipment. It must hurt to have your government care more about me than you and your dead—"

"Hurt is what I live for," Connor said through clenched teeth, gravel in his voice.

Chalabi paused and watched him for a moment. "*And* of course you realize that if you kill me, it would only end in your death or life imprisonment."

"You know, you're right." Connor bore into his eyes. "And I consider the worst to be worth it: life in prison is worth killing you."

A touch of uncertainty passed over Al Chalabi's face. "Don't forget execution."

"It's *only* death." Connor stood and drew his pistol, slowly racking the slide.

The uncertainty on Chalabi's face gave way to a hint of fear. But he seemed determined to look defiant.

With icy composure, Connor stepped to the side. Grabbing

the table with one hand, he flung it end over end across the room. The sharp crashing noise seemed so much louder in the tight space.

Chalabi twitched.

Just then, a loud thump emitted from the door. The handle rattled. Muffled shouts came from the other side.

Chalabi lost his sneer. Sweat beaded and poured from his temples.

Connor stood over him. "I'm going to shoot you four times. First in your knee, then in your arm. Then I'll shoot you in your stomach, where it won't kill you, before finally shooting you in the head. My hope, of course, is that before you die, you'll believe me when I say 'I'm going to kill you.' This is going to happen over the next ten seconds."

Chalabi looked bewildered. "What—"

"One..."

BANG! Connor put a bullet in Chalabi's knee. Blood spattered across the floor.

The man let out a high-pitched squeal. He clutched his leg. Tears and snot dripped from his face. "AHHHHHH!" he bellowed, looking up at Connor

"Two, three, four..."

BANG!

The second bullet entered and exited Chalabi's arm.

"AHH!" Chalabi fell out of his chair to the floor. "YOU BASTARD!"

"Five, six, seven..."

BANG!

Chalabi folded over as he clutched his abdomen. "Ah, ah, ah," he gasped. He raised a feeble head towards Connor as he towered over him. "No, please! Ah... I believe you! I believe you! I'm sorry! Please don't—"

"…10."

BANG!

The man's writhing ceased.

Connor took the clip from his gun and set the weapon on the ground. As he stood over the exterminated rat, the storm inside him churned, unsatisfied he couldn't do more. And still heroes stayed fallen.

He crossed the room and sat down in a chair. Then Connor watched as the door came crashing open and a horde of people charged into the room.

CHAPTER 11

"All right folks, good meeting," Jerry said from his end of the conference room table. He scratched his head and ruffled his hair. "I can't wait to be blown away by your articles."

Brynn and ten of her colleagues stood, rolling chairs every direction while gathering their laptops. They left the glass-encased room and filtered into the rest of the office.

Marty, a red-haired girl with ironic pigtails, walked next to Brynn. "One hour left." They strolled down a hallway.

"Yeah, we're almost there," Brynn said. "Are you and Andrew doing anything this weekend?"

"His parents are coming to town so we're taking them on a winery tour out by Fredricksburg. Hopefully make it to the HillTop Café."

The pair rounded a corner. "What about you and Kyle?"

"He's taking me to his office party tonight," Brynn said.

"Ooooh, *trophy girlfriend*." Marty nudged Brynn. "Wear something sassy!"

Brynn rolled her eyes at her friend. "See you Monday."

Parting ways with Marty, she went into her office and surveyed the stack of new papers on her desk. She sat down and pondered the evening. What should she wear tonight? Was a dress too formal? What about a skirt? It might get difficult standing for hours in heels. She popped the lid off her iced tea and let the floral aroma waft through the room.

"Brynn!" A voice called from down the hall.

"Yes?"

"Come in here and take a look at something."

Brynn sighed and set aside her work. She stood and left the room. A few doors down, her peers gathered in Alan's office. All eyes transfixed on the television.

"Alan, can I help—"

"Look at this." He pointed to the screen.

Brynn felt annoyed she was summoned to see something on TV. She turned to leave, but a close-up of a familiar face grabbed her attention.

The handsome smile and caring eyes had been familiar to her since she was a child. The camera captured security surrounding Senator West as they led him from a vehicle to a government building. He nodded towards a crowd. Next, a picture of five Navy SEALs on a mountaintop flashed across the screen.

Even through the TV, his aura still overwhelmed. The image was of Connor West standing alongside other fierce men, emotionless face and rigid posture.

She gasped.

I can't believe he's dead. God please…

Brynn shook her head and blinked, forcing her hand not to shake. She watched the reporter's lips move.

"Chairman of the Senate Arms Committee, Senator Ben West arrived in Bethesda today to greet his son, Lt. Connor West. The Senator's son served as part of an elite tactical unit. We have recently received word that the Senator's son has been dishonorably discharged, although no reason has yet been given."

He isn't dead? Then what happened to Connor?

"Brynn?"

The voice shook her back to attention.

"What's going on there?" Alan nodded towards Brynn's hand that clenched the back of a chair.

She eased her grip. "Nothing."

"Don't you know Senator West?"

"I, uh…" She cleared her throat and stood up straighter, forcing eye contact. "Yes. Kind of. We lived in the same neighborhood."

"Do you know what this is about?" Alan said.

"No." Brynn shook her head. "No, I don't. Interesting, though. All right, everyone have a good weekend." Her thoughts raced uncontrollably. She hoped her forced poise was believable.

Back in her office, she stared out the window and tapped her fingertips against her forehead.

Just be over him… but what happened?

She sighed as, with effort, she lifted the phone to her ear. She heard the dial tone on the other end.

Why are you doing this?

"I feel so cool when a pretty girl calls me," Kyle said on the other end of the line. "What's going on, Slick?"

"Hey, I'm *really* sorry. I can't make it to your office party tonight. Something has come up, a family issue. I need to drive to Houston right now."

"Oh, no! Is everything ok? Do you need any help? Should I come to Houston with you? What can I do?"

"Oh, you're sweet," Brynn said. "It's not that big a deal, but I need to head there. I just feel bad I'm missing the party."

"Don't worry, there'll be plenty more. But are you sure I can't help?"

"I promise you, I'm fine. I'll make it up to you. "

"All right, let me know when you make it to Houston."

"Sure," Brynn said. "Bye."

"Bye, Brynn."

She hung up the phone. As she departed, she didn't look in the mirror to avoid the self-loathing. In the parking lot, she climbed into her car and began the two-hour drive.

"What am I doing?" she said out loud. "Leave him in the past! What do you think will happen anyways?" She rolled down her window. "Be stronger than this!"

But Connor might be in trouble.

She argued with herself every last mile until she reached the exit ramp for her street. Unsure what to do, she went to her parent's. Driving through the neighborhood, she passed Connor's street, afraid to turn.

Her parents' cars sat parked in the driveway and the curtains were open. The shrubberies lining the porch looked healthy. Moisture from the sprinklers clung to the flowers and filled the air with a sweet scent.

Brynn pushed the front door open. Sunlight followed her into the darker interior. Her eyes took a second to adjust. As the room came into focus, her mother stood behind the couch in the living room. The woman's expression went from puzzlement to frustration in a heartbeat.

"No! Brynn, no!" Her mother tossed her hands in the air. "You get right back in your car and go back to Austin." She shook her head and marched toward Brynn. "There's nothing you can do for him. So just leave!"

"What are you talking about?" Brynn crinkled her forehead.

"You know *exactly* what I'm talking about. That business with Connor in the news. Kyle is a nice young man." Her mother put her hand on Brynn's shoulder and spun her towards the door, pushing her out. "You spent too long chasing that wrecking ball of a human and I won't let you waste any more. Whatever happened, there's nothing you can do for him. Go!"

"Brynn?" Her father appeared around the hallway corner. "What are you doing here?" He pulled his glasses off.

"She's here because of *him!*" Brynn's mother said.

"Oh, that business on the news? I was curious... do you know anything about it?"

"No! She doesn't and doesn't need to.," Her mother tugged at Brynn. "Quick, Eric. Help me get her to her car."

Her father's warm chuckle resonated through the entryway. "Can she at least stay for dinner?"

Brynn's mother shot her gaze from her husband to her daughter. Her grip on Brynn loosened. "All right, but then it's straight back to Austin!"

Brynn smiled. Her father knew she couldn't resist feeding Brynn. Her mother stormed off to the kitchen.

"Hey, pumpkin." Her father eased his arms around her.

"Hey, Dad." Brynn hugged him back.

"We just don't want you to get hurt." He rubbed her back. "And for some reason, Connor seems really good at it."

Dinner was full of dichotomy and juxtapositions. Her mother ranted herself tired. Then her father carried on and on about his new biking hobby, interrupted every couple of minutes by another charge of her mother. Afterward, Brynn helped her mother with the dishes.

Later, they settled into the living room couches. They agreed on a movie.

Brynn knew her mother never lasted long when the lights were low, and sure enough, she fell asleep on her father's shoulder. Brynn stood, careful not to make noise.

"Brynn," her father said.

She turned to face him.

"For the record, I agree with your mother on this one."

Brynn nodded slowly. "Bye, Dad."

Without making any noise, Brynn closed the door behind her. She wished she knew what she were doing as she started her car and put it in reverse. And no answers came to her as she drove down the block.

Vehicles filled the driveway and street in front of the Wests' home. She parked near the corner down the lane. For twenty minutes, she sat in her vehicle without moving.

"Why are you doing this, Brynn?" she said to herself. "There's nothing to accomplish here. Plus, you hate Connor."

But what if he needs my help?

Finally she pushed her door open and stepped out into the night. As she walked towards the house, she whispered, "You're being so stupid."

Her feet seemed determined to carry her to the front door, try as she might to turn them. Two black-suited gentlemen stood on either side of the door, standing sentry. One of the secret servicemen held his hand up to her. "May I help you, miss?"

"Jack, it's okay."

Brynn turned as Agent Petty approached, a man she'd encountered before. He'd been on the senator's staff for years.

"She's a long-time friend of the family." He smiled. "Go right in, Miss Greene."

"Thank you, Agent Petty."

The agent named Jack opened the door for her. She stepped inside.

The house was packed, with so many stacks of papers, computers, and dry erase boards that the home seemed more like an office or a beehive. People with dark bags under their eyes buzzed to and fro. Phones rang constantly. However, as she looked the group over, no one in the crowd was the man of thunder.

Regretting her decision and feeling dumber by the minute, she realized she had nothing to say if she spoke with any of the Wests. Connor probably hadn't told his parents of their falling out.

I should leave.

But she moved forward anyway. She did her best to go unnoticed, staying by the wall where people zoomed past her.

Sweet, little Mrs. West came out of a room at the far end of the long hallway. She stood with her back to Brynn. "Come on, y'all. There's no way all these people are going to work in my house this long and hard without getting fed." She waved employees carrying trays of food to the next room. "Let's set up in here."

Brynn didn't want to shout for her so she watched as Mrs. West disappeared.

"Don, I'm telling you, if he broke the law, wouldn't he be in jail?"

Brynn recognized Senator West's voice. She followed it down the hall and approached the library. She peeked around the corner.

The Senator stood, looking through the big bay window out to his darkened lawn. He leaned on his cane with one hand and held a phone to his ear with the other. Both sleeves rolled above his elbows.

"No, Don… I understand that, but… well I'm not exactly

sure what I'm allowed to tell and what I can't tell you... Don, you know how these things work... No, he didn't kill any Americans!"

The Senator laughed. "You might have to accept that this is just a boring story, Don... what if this is just between him and his superiors?" The Senator straightened up. He switched his phone and cane hands while shifting his weight. "I know America cares, but it doesn't care *that* much... it's just a story on some random senator's son... fine, Don, you want a statement, here it is: 'Due to unforeseen circumstances, our son is no longer able to participate in his service with the United States Military. I know I speak for Connor when I say his years with the Teams have been some of the most fulfilling years of his life. Our country has, does, and always will owe a debt of gratitude to my son, Connor West, for his unceasing efforts and sacrifice protecting our freedoms. We are now, and always will be, proud of our son.'"

Senator West looked at the ceiling and sighed. "Dishonorable discharge? Being with the Teams is so honorable, I'm not sure it's possible to be dishonorably discharged... yeah..." The Senator laughed. "All right, deal. Thanks, Don." He pulled the phone from his ear and clicked it off.

Fearful of being perceived as nosey, Brynn drew back. After their talk, she also felt like she was letting the Senator down by being at the Wests' house. She turned and walked down the hall. As she re-entered the main living room, she recognized a small-statured man. David, the Senator's long-time aid, marched across the room and out the back patio doors.

Stepping around the crowd, Brynn made her way to the patio doors as well. She watched David through the panes of glass. He paced back and forth, one arm crossed and the other cradling a smoldered cigarette. He kept closing his eyes and shaking his head.

Brynn gripped the handle and pushed the door open. After stepping through, she closed it behind her. "David?"

"What!" He snapped the words out, then looked at her. "Oh, sorry. Hi, Brynn."

"What's going on?"

"*What's going on?* I'll tell you what's going on. Once again, Connor caused a huge mess for the Senator to clean up. He's just, so, selfish! And *of course* he can do no wrong in the Senator's eyes."

"What happened?"

"Seems like the golden boy killed a terrorist who was in the custody of the United States Government."

"Why?"

He drew a quick pull from his cigarette. "*Why?* Oh, I don't know *why.* He's just hell bent on making everyone else's lives miserable. He should have been way more than just discharged. Should have stood before a military tribunal, get death or a life sentence. The Senator called in so many favors keeping Connor out of jail, it's going to cost him his presidential bid! He'll never get the chance again. Ben threw away his whole life. But of course, it's nothing to him! Just as long as Connor gets everything he wants."

"I'm sure it's not that bad."

"Trust me, *it is.*" He turned back towards the veranda. "Of all the selfish, dumb things to do! And to think of all the Senator could have accomplished…" David ditched his cigarette. "Sorry, Brynn, I have to get back."

He opened the door and waited for her to walk ahead. She slipped back into the crowded space.

"Brynn!" The room fell silent. The Senator's voice seemed one of the few able to silence the bustle. He stood on the landing, smiling.

"Hello, Senator West." She forced a smile and gave a little wave, feeling caught. "How are you?"

His eyes masked any disappointment he might have in her. "Oh, fine. Just managing a little issue—"

"A *little issue!*" David hollered.

"Easy there, David." The Senator chuckled as David fell silent. "He's not happy unless he's stressing out. How's Austin? I've enjoyed your article in *Texas Weekly* about me."

"Thank you."

"Yeah, did you hear that everyone? We've got a famous person here. That's Brynn Greene of *Texas Weekly.*"

Brynn laughed, understanding exactly why people voted for him.

"Did you come by to see Connor?" The Senator tilted his head and put his hand on his waist.

"I, uh—"

"I'm pretty sure he's around here somewhere. But if you're in a hurry, feel free to come back another—"

"Excuse me, Senator." An aid approached him with a cordless phone. "You have a call. It's Congressman Gaus."

The Senator glanced back at Brynn. "I'm sorry, my dear, I have to take this." He smiled at her and took the phone. "Representative Gaus?"

He walked off. David chased after him.

Brynn stood feeling awkward for a few minutes as her confidence deteriorated. The people near her probably pitied her, the silly girl who chased Connor around. Though she had nobly parted ways, the moment something dreadful happened, she came running back.

Her phone rang in her purse. Digging through the mess, she retrieved it from the depths. The screen flashed the message: Kyle Davis calling. Intending to answer it, she gripped the phone and turned to head out the front door.

"Brynn?"

Her soul caught fire at the familiar voice. She knew only one voice with that much gravel. Every other thought faded as she found herself captivated. She turned and fell into his green eyes, the same eyes that dared the world.

"Hi, Connor." She tried to read his reaction, but he was a stone. If he had anything to give away, he wasn't.

How can he look so calm after all he's been through?

Once convinced that no one on earth was as close to him as she was, her soul questioned how he could look at her so cooly.

"It's been a long time," he said.

"It has."

"What brings you here?"

"Oh, just checking in on your family. I was in town." She hoped to match his lack of readability. Something told her she had failed. Then she noticed his hand. "Connor! What happened to your finger?"

Connor withdrew his injured hand. "Oh, nothing, just left it in the desert somewhere."

"Oh, Connor." She hurt for him. "I'm so sorry!"

"That's very kind of you." He smiled and swept his arm towards the rest of the house. "Make yourself at home. Mom is in the kitchen. I believe dinner just arrived." He patted her shoulder. "It's good to see you, Brynn." He smiled and walked away, leaving her there, drowning in the buzz of the crowd.

She couldn't believe that was it, that was all she was getting from him. *How could he look on her as such a stranger? How could he not give her more?*

But she should have known. He didn't change and never would.

I'm so dumb.

And standing on the precipice where she had fallen before, a still and gentle voice whispered in her head to call Kyle. She ran outside and redialed as fast as she could.

"Well, if it isn't that pretty girl who was supposed to let me know she made it to Houston safely," Kyle said from his end.

"Hi, sorry. I got distracted."

"Not even an issue. Just glad you're safe. How's the crisis?"

"It turned out to be nothing."

"Oh, that's good!"

"Yes, it is. I'm actually about to head back to Austin."

"You sure? It's getting kind of late. Maybe you should sleep at your parents' house."

"It's fine. I'm anxious to get back."

"Well, you're an adult. You know what you're doing. Just promise me you'll be careful."

"I promise."

"All right, goodnight, Brynn."

"Goodnight."

Brynn hung up and hurried back to her car.

"Good night, Miss Greene." Agent Petty called from a corner of the porch.

"Oh... good night. Thanks." She slid into her driver seat. She had been more than stupid to come here. What was she thinking? What was she expecting?

I'm an idiot. She pounded on the steering wheel.

Shame and embarrassment rode in her passenger seat all

the way back to Austin. She pulled in at 2:30 am, and by 2:40 climbed into bed.

But she rolled over in her bed a few more times, with fitful tossing and turning. Not only had she wasted her time chasing a phantom, but she also had let down Kyle. While her legs passed over silk sheets and her ponytail rested high on the pillow, she made a resolution to be the girl who Kyle, in all his kindness, deserved. Fighting her thoughts and craving rest from her wanderings, she hoped for sleep until sleep found her.

THE NEXT MORNING, SUNLIGHT filled her house. The clean smell of air fresheners greeted her nose. She rubbed the sand from her eyes and pulled her covers back, then slid her feet into slippers. The aged wood floors creaked under her shuffled steps. The warm shade of yellow she had painted her halls glowed in the morning light.

A familiar sound of heavy equipment came from outside. Brynn panicked, knowing she forgot to put the trash bin by the road. But when she looked out the window, the garbage man already had lifted her trash receptacle. She wondered how it had made its way to the curb.

Then she strolled into her sky blue kitchen, only to find a cup of coffee from her favorite shop and two of her favorite muffins. And a glorious bouquet of sunflowers smiled at her from her kitchen counter. She found a note scribbled in crayon: "Good morning, beautiful! I didn't want to wake you (you shouldn't have shown me where the secret key is, sucker!). Enjoy these and give me a call when you wake up. I can't wait to spend the day with you! –Kyle"

A man like that deserves for me to try harder.

Brynn picked up her phone and dialed. He answered after the first ring.

"Hey, handsome! What should we do first?"

CHAPTER 12

Connor mourned his lost identity. They said he couldn't be himself anymore. They took away the first thing in his life that ever made complete sense to him. There was no way around it: no one to fight, nothing to overcome.

His whole life, he'd risen above. But no longer. Now he existed in a void. He was a peel of thunder without a voice. And both his worlds had crashed.

Two things stimulated him, harnessed him. One was being a fighter. It embraced the force inside him.

The other was *Brynn*, the girl with eyes of blue infinity. He'd fallen through the dawn skies and seen limitless, indescribable blue on the horizon. The kind of blue that burned, equal parts rain and fire. And those shades paled in comparison. Being around her thrilled him.

But how could it be worth the cost she bore? She deserved more than being a hopeful ship, tattered on the rocks of the thing inside him. He let her go for her own good. The storm inside him always came back to destroy. That's why he had to let her go. And that's why it hurt so much to watch her leave.

He hated being short and curt with her. She deserved more and he wanted to give it. But he needed her to stop believing in any sort of hope for them, for her own good.

Connor watched her from an upstairs window. Brynn

walked away from his parent's house, across his lawn, and towards the car. He knew he hurt her again, but what else was new?

As she climbed into her vehicle, he fought the urge to run after her. He was fast. Maybe he could catch her. But he was pain to her and always would be.

Connor walked downstairs. Three steps from the bottom, he paused to survey the many who shuffled to and fro. They worked to overcome what he had done.

When he made the choice to kill that vermin in Afghanistan, he believed death or life in prison was his end. Death didn't scare him. And life in prison would have been a wonderful, lifelong fight. Being excused, discharged, was out of his realm of expectation. Condemned to ordinary life was a worse fate than any other he could imagine.

The people in his living room yawned repeatedly and followed their own bloodshot eyes. None looked at him, but he knew they blamed him.

"Oh, *Connor*." David approached from the corner. "So nice of you to join us. I hope you're happy. You did all this." David sneered.

"I didn't expect him to do this," Connor said.

David looked at Connor in a confused way, then furrowed his brow. "Maybe not, but you should have anticipated it. And now it's happened." When his phone rang, he answered it and walked away.

Connor wanted—*needed*—to leave. The thing inside him had no outlet. He wandered down the hall, those around him blending into a haze as his heart sped. He stayed in the dark. He needed to say something. Connor peered through the library doors where his father conducted the madness.

Standing against the backdrop of rich wooden bookshelves lined with countless leather-bound volumes, the Senator glanced up between directions to his staff and papers read. Even Connor had to admit how stately, how regal, his father appeared. The man paced back and fourth, speaking soothing words into the phone.

His father, Hrothgar, and he, the dragon. The man could such do great things, build so much. All Connor could do was destroy.

Mid-stride, his father looked up and locked eyes with Connor. The man's air of business acumen and determination faded as a sorrowful, almost pitying expression came over his face. He searched his son as his staffers continued to pelt him with questions.

Connor and his father spoke without a word. The man let out a slow sigh, shrugging his shoulders. Then his dad nodded towards him, as if to say, "Go. I understand."

The staff looked back and forth between Connor and the Senator. They didn't understand and didn't need to. They'd probably feel relieved when he left.

Connor slipped out the back door, exiting the warmth and comfort of the house for the slightly chilled night. Staffers' cars filled the driveway and blocked in his Trans Am. Connor entered their free-standing garage. Through glass panes, light from the moon lit the inside. The smell of oil and cut grass perfumed the space. He rifled though a drawer and withdrew a set of keys.

His father's old Triumph motorcycle sat under a dust-coated tarp. The matte black finish two-wheeler was salvation for him. It didn't take much for Connor to steal the bike. After he lifted open the garage door, he settled into the old, leather seat of the bike. A firm kick fired the engine. Dropping it to first gear, he passed over the thin strip of grass between the driveway and fence and bounced over the curb.

The street emerged and not long after that, the highway. Connor's breaths were deep and rich, something like freedom. Freedom from everything the world behind him meant. He twisted the throttle back, becoming fluid steel with the machine. As he zipped between cars until their red taillights blended and blurred, Connor rode through time and space. Distance was good and sweet. And the unknown: the next conquerable endeavor.

TWO MONTHS LATER, CONNOR stood under a hot Nevada sun. The desert heat beat down, unmerciful and unrelenting. For miles in every direction, there were only more miles and miles. Anywhere he looked, the horizon was traced in mirages.

He fired up the welder and sprayed sparks everywhere, meshing metal together. When the task was done, he pulled off the welding helmet and wiped his dripping forehead.

"Cole, what the hell are you doing?" A voice behind him yelled the name by which Connor chose to go. He turned to see the oil field foreman, Gentry.

"You told me to install the joint," Connor said.

"Well, yeah..." Gentry said, a sandy-haired roughneck, broader in his belt than his chest. "But how did you get it in place?"

"I lifted it."

"You lifted it by yourself?" Gentry looked slightly annoyed. "You should have gotten help!"

"Didn't need the help." Connor drank from a water bottle. "Just trying to stay productive."

Gentry's gaze passed between Connor and the joint piece. "Well, okay. Just remember, don't try more than you can safely do. 'Cause if you ever cost more than you're worth, I'll beat your ass."

Connor nodded and turned away. "Wouldn't dream of it." He spun and headed down the stairs off the oil platform. His boots hit the hard, dry earth. The smell of machinery followed him.

Next to the trailer he shared with three other roughnecks, he found a hose and cranked the handle. The cool, crisp water flowed around his body and chased his sweat away. Standing in the shade, he leaned against a wall and looked out over the desolate landscape.

But standing still was a mistake as it always was, for she materialized out of the wind. Or at least, her ghost did. He would spend his days somewhere in an oil field, calling out her name. So he cut his rest short and went back to work, trying to break himself. But the work was not strong enough and sixty days was just the beginning of a lifetime to forget her.

A cloud of dust lifted from the land beyond his view, rising from a truck. Ten minutes later, a white pickup rolled in.

"Hey, there," Andrew, their engineer called as he approached. "How's it going?"

"Living the dream," Gentry said as he stood next to Connor. "As always."

"Is that right, Cole?"

"Yep." Connor said. "Production is up. Costs are down. And morale is at an all-time high."

They laughed at his playful sarcasm.

"All right, all right. Let's see what mess you've made this time." Andrew pulled out his tools and went to work. Since many of his measurements and tasks took hours to materialize, the three would often find themselves shooting the breeze in the office trailer. Although he spent his days counting down until the weekend, Connor liked the work for the struggle, and the engineer brought him decent conversation.

On Thursday, after his fourth and final fifteen-hour shift of the week, he pointed his motorcycle towards Vegas. The first time he headed there, it was to get drunk on lights and distracted by sound. But fate had provided him with much more.

Casinos towered overhead, shining in all their colors as Connor cruised down the strip. Winnings and jackpots rang in the background. Characters dressed in every fashion imaginable paraded down the sidewalk. Cars fought for passage while the traffic moved in a clumsy fashion, riddled with limousines and distracted drivers.

Then, well away from the frequented blocks of Las Vegas, Connor found a broken strip of buildings. Individuals, too poorly dressed to be tourists, passed between the bars. Connor hopped the curb and parked his bike. After grabbing his bag, he headed inside.

A thick cloud of lost hope and cigarette smoke met him. Grime on the floor stuck to his shoes with every step. The bartender looked like a former redneck prom king.

Connor approached the bar and signaled the bartender. "Shot. Bourbon."

The aged bartender clenched a toothpick between tobacco-laced teeth as his bent hands seized the bottle of amber escape. The fluid flowed into the shot glass. Before passing it to Connor, he pulled it in and looked his customer over with a lazy eye.

Connor stared back at him, awaiting his beverage. "What?"

"I've seen that look before." The bartender passed the liquid promise to Connor. "Trust me. Whoever she is, she's just another girl."

Connor stared at the drink. "There's no such thing." He swallowed the whiskey hard and tossed the shot glass back.

He headed towards the back and a door marked 'Employees Only.' The roar of the crowd rumbled through the narrow passageway. He pushed the door open and passed down a dark hallway. The noise grew. He burst through a second door and reality shifted.

Several hundred people gathered in an old hanger. A waft of vomit and sweat lingered. Energy buzzed throughout as those gathered watched one of the most popular underground MMA facilities in the city. Music blared. Concessions passed over tattered folding tables. At the center of the space was a homemade octagon, complete with cage. The patter and thud of fighters navigating the arena was barely distinguishable. Inside it, two no-names tumbled to the ground, employing what method they could. Waves of people shoved towards the front and shouted.

Connor watched. This looked like a featherweight fight and the fighters couldn't have been more than 21 years old. One kid was Hispanic, covered in tattoos and sporting an orange Mohawk. The other was a pasty white kid with very dark hair. As they writhed on the ground, the Hispanic slipped inside the white kid's guard, hammering his abdomen with punches while the white kid struck the top of his head. Their hits grew slower and slower as perspiration dripped. Their panting increased. Then they rolled over one another trying to get submission holds.

Connor walked the parameter, searching the crowd, never giving the match another look.

An ogre leaned against the wall, broad in shoulder and chest. His gray hair suggested his years and he wore a track jacket and athletic shorts. He waved Connor over.

"Crowder." Connor nodded as he arrived.

"You got a good fight in you tonight?" Crowder said over the roar of the crowd.

"I'll see what I can manage."

"Okay, 'cause I got a new kid for you. They call him the Wrecker. He's taken a few amateur belts and I've been thinking of an exhibition fight between him and a pro next month. I'd like to put him against you. And heads up, he likes the ground and loves being off his feet."

"Sounds tough."

"Yeah, yeah," Crowder curled the corner of his lip, exposing a gold tooth. "You've said that before."

"Hey, Crowder!" Another man, wearing a three-piece suit and mischievous look, approached. "Is this the guy?" He stuck his thumb towards Connor.

"Yeah."

"Is he any good?" The man said, never looking at Connor.

"Not really," Crowder said. "But trust me, he's the guy you want. He's 7-0 around here. Hasn't lost since he first showed up."

"What do you mean 'he hasn't lost, but he's not good'?" The suited man finally looked at Connor.

"He fights sloppy and doesn't score points. It's just no one can knock him out before he knocks them out," Crowder said.

The suited man drew back slightly and raised an eyebrow. "You got a name?"

"No." Connor sneered.

"We just call him the punching bag," Crowder said. "He keeps taking hits."

"Well, hell." The suited man shook his head. "Go get dressed."

Connor dressed and taped his hands and feet in the locker room. Connor wore a tight t-shirt to hide his scars, trident, and BUDS tattoo. He knew chances were slim, but he didn't want to be recognized. When he was ready, he left the locker room.

Halfway through the crowd, someone cheered. Then the avalanche gained momentum as the group celebrated him. But Connor was deaf to it.

He entered the cage and lapped its circumference while staring at the mat. When he finished, he crouched in the corner, head between his hands, eyes down. He focused.

A distant announcer's words came out muffled and distorted. A slight breeze from rotating fans above cooled his back. His heart pounded. He took slow and steady breaths until the motion of the room seemed half speed. The murderous element inside him pushed at the gates.

Slowly Connor looked up and acknolwedged the challenge across from him. The fighter, the one they called the Wrecker, was built of layers and layers of thick muscle.

Somewhere else in the night, a count chimed.

"Fighting is *their* game but it's *your* life," Connor whispered. "It's what you sold yourself for, and why you can't be with her."

A toss of long black hair in the crowd distracted him. Connor let himself indulge the insane hope that *she* was there. But she wasn't. He couldn't have her and life would not be a story of them.

His teeth ground and his fist tightened. Someone else got to hear her speak and listen to her thoughts.

Stop. It's time to fight.

He'd blown it and ruined it. He was no good and never was.

A bell rang.

Then the man approached him. Every muscle flexed and Connor stood waiting. A lightning quick fist streaked through the air, striking Connor across his face. The force ricocheted through his body, a shock full of reality. The hit was so true.

Connor stumbled back. It was the strongest wallop Connor ever received in the cage. He shook his head... and then shook it again.

That was a hard hit.

Connor fired three quick kicks up the Wrecker's left side, starting outside his knee and ending on his shoulder. At the final strike, his opponent dropped his right guard so Connor sneaked in a hook.

Before Connor landed the hit, the Wrecker exploded forward inside Connor's swing and seized him. He couldn't let the kid take him to the mat so Connor launched himself backwards into the cage wall and spun outside. The Wrecker followed him around the parameter and they exchanged strikes.

Soon both of them wore their own blood. Connor felt thankful.

The Wrecker threw an uppercut and elbow. Connor blocked both with his forearms and put a fist in the Wrecker's side, before coming up and—

The Wrecker's speed got around Connor as he wrapped his left arm. When Connor yanked it away to avoid the mat, a vicious little pop came from inside his limb. The deadening pain blinded him.

He fell back. The Wrecker put a front kick in Connor's

chest. Only the floor stopped his fall.

That was bad.

Connor spat blood on the mat. Lights overhead swirled and spun. Getting up seemed so hard and far away. Goliath stood just steps from him.

Titanium doesn't break. So just be titanium.

Connor stood. Gasping, he focused on the one before him. He pulled his right arm up and instructed his left to do the same. But it would not obey. *Does it hurt?* He couldn't slow down to decide. All he knew was that his arm wasn't moving like it should. But he was never out of the fight.

His opponent huffed and puffed, visibly exhausted from hits thrown. The man stared wide-eyed at Connor. And it was the fighter's wide-eyed wonder that let Connor know all he needed to do to win was keep going.

So when the first desperate punch came around, Connor thought of everything in his life and unleashed a fountain of energy from his neverending storehouses. With one working arm and two working legs, he tore down the Wrecker's defenses.

The Wrecker had hit hard, very hard, many times. But now his strikes grew slow and soft. So Connor chopped the tree down, until at the end of it all, he stood over a very unconscious pile of human.

As every past fight, the ref hoisted Connor's hand into the air while the crowd roared. But before they quieted down, Connor pulled his hand away and exited the ring. The attendees crowded him and berated him, but he walked out, never looking to the left or right and charging through the crowd. He only acknowledged the bookie who slipped him the money.

Before nursing his wounds, Connor washed the blood away in the dingy locker room shower. He held his breath as he hammered his left shoulder into the wet tile wall and forced the joint back in place.

"Damn." Connor winced

He changed clothes and slipped through the crowd with a hat pulled low. Now that the struggle had passed, the pain set in. Connor had to give it to the Wrecker. He hit like a semi-truck. This fight was closer than Connor expected. But he drank in fulfillment, momentarily not haunted by the memory of her or the devil inside him. Connor refused painkillers.

The door between the arena hanger and the bar swung open before him. His pallet craved the crisp taste of hops before leaving. Connor draped his aching bones over the barstool.

"Survived again, eh?" The bartender smiled as he popped the cap off a long neck bottle.

Connor took it and sipped the cold brew.

The bartender leaned back and worked a rag over a glass. "Ain't enough fights in the world, son. She'll always be inside you."

Connor stared at the condensation on the bottle and said nothing.

The television hanging in the corner blended into the background. Images passed back and forward across the screen. Every second of it meant nothing to Connor. But then something flashed in the corner of his eye, something too familiar: a picture, a face, a memory.

Connor spun in the stool. His suspicions were confirmed. There, plain as day, his father's face filled the screen while the caption "Breaking News" ominously patrolled the bottom of the screen.

Connor pointed at the electric box. "Turn that up."

The bartender reached for the remote and the sound came

back.

"And sadly, today, Senator Benjamin West suffered a brain aneurism while on the campaign trail. The Senator is being treated at M.D. Anderson."

Connor damned his ears for hearing the wrong thing because he was sure there was no way what the reporter said was accurate. This could not happen.

"That guy kind of looks like you," the bartender said.

Connor dug through his bag until he retrieved the cell phone he hadn't turned on since he left Houston. As it blinked to life, it vibrated without ceasing.

One message from his mom's number said: "Call now. Dad in trouble."

"Not this!" Connor whispered.

He tore through the door as he raced from the bar to the motorcycle that awaited him, leaving his bag behind. He didn't wait for the bike to warm up before dropping gears and sinking spur into the night.

CHAPTER 13

The sun winked at Brynn through spread branches as leaves swayed back and forth in the tree above. They separated for moments at a time, sending shimmers of light for her to enjoy.

She lay back on the blanket, its soft fabric lifting her above the grass. Between glimpses at the beautiful day, she flipped the pages of her book. Kyle lay next to her.

Down the hill, college students threw a Frisbee. Elsewhere, someone played a guitar for onlookers.

"So Brynn, I have some big news." Kyle stroked her arm.

She put her book down and looked into his kind eyes. "What big news?"

"Well, it might be nothing. But you should probably hear about it." He rolled over and propped himself up on his elbow. "I got a call from Corporate. They say I am one, of what I'm sure are *many* candidates, they're considering for lead designer."

Brynn propped herself up as well. "That's exciting!"

"Sure, I guess. That step is months and months away. I probably won't even get offered it. Which is all the same, 'cause the job is in San Francisco." He stared at her, pausing.

"San Francisco?"

"It's pretty far." Kyle said. "And, not that I will get offered it, but if I did, I'd turn it down." He grinned. "You see, I've been dating this girl in Austin for a while now."

Brynn smiled, feeling her face go flush for a moment. "Oh, are you? Anyone I know?"

"You might have read her stuff. She's a pretty brilliant columnist down at *Texas Weekly*. And I mean *really* brilliant. There's talk of Pulitzer prizes." He nodded. "That's right. Prizes. As in, multiple."

"Where'd you meet this person?" Brynn said.

"Mail-order bride. I think she's Slovenian. Doesn't speak English, but I feel a real connection."

Brynn laughed. "Sounds like a classy dame."

"Oh, the classiest." Kyle paused for a moment, then his smiled waned. "Although, I'd consider going if she'd go with me. I mean, she and I aren't there yet. But someday, we might be."

Brynn looked at Kyle. He was so kind, thoughtful, and secure. "Sweep her away to California, eh?"

"It might not be worth going if she isn't there." Kyle said. "What about it? Could you see yourself there?"

The future? Brynn could see it: nice, quiet days with Kyle. The future was such a scary thing to think about: children, family, income, being loved and loving someone in return.

But it seemed less frightening and more exciting with the thought of *him*. He was a good, steady worker, great at his job. His parents were wonderful. Kyle was a joy to be around. Children were always drawn to him. Perhaps they sensed his kind heart.

Plus, Kyle took such good care of her that she forced herself not to become spoiled. Brynn worried she might actually start to believe she really *was* a princess. That future, those images, that idea felt to her as calming as an exhale. And it definitely felt easy.

"San Francisco?"

"Yeah, what do you think? I mean, you don't have to answer right now, but it might be kind of nice. Get out of town, go somewhere where no one knows your name. You saw the sunrise in New York, let's go watch some sunsets in California."

Never in her life did she think her story would go like this.

"That certainly sounds nice." She brushed some of his swooping bangs to the side. "And I could probably answer a question like that someday. Just, not yet."

He nodded with a twisted little smile. "Good enough for me." Then he rolled away from her, before standing. "Now, on to more important matters!" He nodded towards a food trailer a few hundred yards away. "What kind of snow cone do you want?"

She laughed. "Blueberry."

"Oooh, exotic! Nice." He turned and ran off, with a comedic stride she knew he did for her amusement.

She sat up and gazed out over the green slopes of Zilker Park as a gentle breeze brushed through her hair like the playful hand of a lover. The future could be full of more calm days like this. On paper, the idea seemed great.

A dog bolted across the ground, opening its teeth to snatch a tennis ball from where it rolled. The animal seemed to smile as it carried the retrieved item back to its master.

Is this what I want?

From somewhere in her mess of things, a vibration emitted. Brynn rifled through her purse until she found her phone. The screen flashed "Home."

She put it to her ear. "Hello?"

"Hi, Brynn, how are you?"

"Hey, Dad." She sensed a bothered tone in his voice. "What's going on?"

"Brynn, honey, do you have a minute? I need to tell you something."

His melancholy and cautious tone put a worry in her. Her heart pattered. "What happened?"

"Well, sweetie, there's no easy way to tell you this. Senator West passed away this morning."

Oh, no. Connor. Where was Connor? Was he okay? But she shook her head, not wanting the outlaw to be part of her thoughts.

"Uh... Brynn?"

"I'm here. That's awful. Is Mom with Mrs. West?"

"She is. They haven't made a public announcement yes, so we have to keep this to ourselves. The funeral is on Thursday."

"Ok, I'll probably come in tomorrow night... and, Dad, how's, uh, how's—"

"*Connor?*"

"Yeah."

"I don't know, Brynn. I haven't seen him."

"Well, okay. Thanks for telling me. I'll see you tomorrow. Love you."

"I love you, too." The phone clicked off.

As she sat staring across the way, she fought guilt over being more fearful of seeing Connor than feeling sympathy for the family.

Kyle came marching across the grass, brandishing two trophies in the form of snow cones. "Well, it wasn't easy. But I managed to get the last blueberry. I had to punch a 9-year-old." He settled in next to her. "Don't worry, she's much tougher than she seems. Despite what her crying implies."

He turned to her, his smile fading. "Brynn, what's wrong?"

"That was my dad on the phone." She set down the device. "Senator West just died."

"Oh, Brynn. I'm so sorry. I know your families are fairly close."

"The funeral is on Thursday. Mom's gone over to be with Mrs. West right now."

"So when do we need to leave for the funeral?"

What if I have to see Connor?

Brynn looked at him. This seemed an odd proposition to her: Kyle come to the funeral? Why would he? To comfort her? Did she need comfort? Yes.

This would be hard. She would need comfort from somewhere and this time it would come from him. That was his job now and she would have to rely on him. He deserved it. On Thursday, her universes would collide, but she must allow him to accompany her.

"We should probably leave tomorrow night. Can you do that?"

"Of course." He slipped his arm around her and hugged her. "How are you feeling?"

"I suppose it hasn't sunk in yet."

"Just know, I'm here if you need anything."

Nodding, she nestled in and watched the clouds draped behind the skyline. One thunderhead suggested a storm on the horizon. It carried with it dark shades of blue, like a cloak in the wind.

But what if Connor looked at her?

"It looks like a storm is coming," Kyle said.

★ ★ ★

TWO DAYS LATER, RAIN came down in thick drops on the cemetery. It fell without ceasing or apology. Row upon row of gravestones stood sentinel, with no visitors to speak of on this gloomy day. The precipitation pelted them and coated them in a glossy sheen.

All except one grave, a freshly dug one, intended for a servant of America: Senator Benjamin West.

Fewer people attended the graveside service than had come to the service at Memorial Presbyterian, most likely unwilling to brave the moisture and the cold. Still, hundreds gathered, clustered tightly under black umbrellas while assaulted by liquid torrents.

Uniformed military attendants stood guard over the coffin, rigid as the gravestones. A number of melancholy political officials loitered to one side. The governor of Texas, along with numerous members of Congress, waited with sincere or forced grief passing over their faces.

Brynn wanted to be in a mood to enjoy the fact that the President of the United States himself stood nearby with his wife, surrounded by Secret Service.

Senator West's siblings stood with their arms around their sister-in-law, uniformly fighting tears with handkerchiefs. Reverend Ward rattled off some beautiful words about eternity and dedication to the service of others. Soldiers conducted procedures involving the flag. David and other staffers of the Senator stood crying and seemingly bewildered as the futures they planned lay in the coffin with Ben West.

Brynn and her family stood alongside lifelong and dear friends. Her father had his arm around his wife, who wept for her friend. Kyle, her loving and attentive boyfriend, held an umbrella for the two of them.

And there, near the foot of the coffin, surrounded by people yet standing alone, was Connor West. He looked so lonely and apart in front of the crowd. He hadn't bothered with an umbrella. Rain drenched him, dripping from his hair and running off his face. The collar of his jacket folded up, shielding the back of his neck. He wore dark glasses under gray skies.

The way he slumped seemed so broken compared to the posture of the military personnel. Yet that same old explosiveness enclosed him. As he stood, transfixed on his father's coffin, he turned neither to the right nor the left. His lip was split and a bandage stretched over his forehead. The crowd pulled away from him as it always did.

"Who's that?" Kyle leaned in and whispered to Brynn's father. "The guy over there, by the casket?"

He didn't answer right away. Brynn knew he was treating the matter delicately.

"That's the Senator's son. Used to be a military man. But I don't know what he does these days."

Kyle turned to Brynn. "Did you know him growing up?"

"Yes."

Reverend Ward continued. But Brynn was not watching. Her attention was riveted to the warrior.

Connor turned his head down and held one side of his coat open, reaching inside with the other hand. He withdrew a full bottle of whiskey. Showing no emotion with the lines of his face, he twisted the top loose and held it out before him. With a tilted hand he emptied the entire bottle on the ground before his father's coffin, toasting the life of the man. One last drink shared with his father. The amber liquid fell, mixing with rain, soil, and memory.

Connor never flinched as the coffin was lowered into the ground. Brynn recognized a certain force, or will, that seemed to draw Connor to the grave, like he, too, belonged there. Nor did he stir as the pastor concluded and countless white-haired old men expressed their condolences to his mother. None approached Connor.

Brynn watched him, dancing on a knife-edge over what she'd do if he looked at her. But he never did.

Brynn and her family waited for their turn to speak with Mrs. West.

Close and within arm's reach, the President of the United States clutched Mrs. West's hand. "Not only was Ben a great Senator, but he was a truly great individual. I looked up to him. I am better off for having known him. Please, please, let me know if there's anything we can do to help you in the coming days."

"Thank you," she said.

Then Brynn and her family approached Mrs. West.

"I'm sorry, Juliet," Brynn's father said. "I'm going to miss him."

"Yes." Brynn stepped forward. "I'm so, so sorry." Rain crept through the space between umbrellas and decorated their held hands in a coat of moisture.

"Oh, Brynn." The woman cried beautiful tears. "Thank you so much for coming. It means so much to Connor and me."

Brynn truly felt grief for Mrs. West, yet cringed at the association of her and Connor before Kyle.

Then, as Brynn glanced back at the grave, Connor's face was turned directly at her. Although his sunglasses obscured his eyes, she trusted the chill down her spine, the flushness of her face, and the way her heart sped.

He gazed right at her, yet seemed so far away, miles and miles, years and years.

Her breath stopped while she waited. But as a mess of people passed between them, she lost sight. And when they were gone, Connor once again seemed unaware of anything on earth but himself and the casket in the ground.

Inwardly, Brynn cursed for allowing herself such reaction to Connor. She clung to Kyle out of penance and support as they walked the soft, saturated ground.

The Greenes journeyed back to the car. The smell of damp hair filled the vehicle as they climbed inside.

"That was truly sad," Kyle said. "I've never met him. But after that funeral, I feel like I knew the Senator my whole life. Seems like a good man."

"Yeah, and I'll tell you what, Kyle." Brynn's father looked into the rearview mirror from the driver's seat. "He'd come to neighborhood events or the kids' school stuff and act like he was just one of the parents. Very down to earth."

"And that was his son standing by himself? Looked like he had a shiner."

The car filled with silent energy. She cringed as she guessed the countless things her parents might say.

"Yes," Brynn's father said. "Yes, it did."

LATER, THEY PULLED INTO the Greene driveway and managed to have a decent evening. Brynn felt the interactions were natural.

The next morning, she and Kyle left for Austin. The long drive down 45th street made Brynn thankful for the richness and beauty of the hill country. Kyle parked his car in front of her house. It looked so lovely against the backdrop. Its Easter egg blue siding popped against the green grass. The flowerbed greeted her. Trees, thick and lush, acknowledged the slight wind.

She turned and waved goodbye to the handsome, kind man, the one with the wavy brown hair and confident smile. He said he'd see her the next day. She knew it to be true because he never, ever lied. As he pulled away, she found herself wishing he were still with her.

She walked up the stone steps of her home. She was conscious of feeling far away and different from the Houston reality she'd just encountered. The jovial feel of the house made her feel loved. In her domain, every cushion and pillow of the denim couch was still in place. Her coat hung exactly where she'd left it, stationary on the hook. The door closed behind her.

At the small table next to the entrance, her mail had piled up. Curiosity led her to shuffle through the envelopes, rifling them with her fingertips, until her phone rang.

"Hello?" She spoke into the receiver.

"Brynn?"

"Oh. Hi, boss."

"Are you back from the Senator's funeral?"

"Just walked through the door."

"Perfect."

"Why is that perfect?"

"I need you to write a report of his funeral and sort of an… homage to him. On my desk tomorrow morning. Okay?"

Brynn hesitated. "Okay."

He hung up.

Brynn stared across the room at her laptop that loomed like a burden, knowing she'd never find words adequate enough to describe the man, his life, or his son

CHAPTER 14

Rain struck his casket. Droplets drew near one another and formed beads on the dark wood. They grew and rolled down the curved edge of the box. Each splash seemed so massive and so final. The weight of his father's funeral fell on Connor.

Rain struck him as well. It clung to his hair and neck, and ran down the back of his collar until he was soaked. But it was only rain. And that was *his* father to be lowered into the ground.

Connor had buried friends in the desert. He'd seen them memorialized, with the barrel of their gun shoved into the ground and a helmet perched on the end. But those men had chased death down, pursued it, hunted it. They were Spartans and reapers.

To Connor, standing alongside the grave of the nonviolent seemed a thing so odd.

I should be buried in the desert.

Connor wasn't sure what he should be feeling. Normally, he moved too fast for feelings to catch him. From the day he chose never to cry until this moment, there was always a distraction or a fight to occupy him. But he was no longer a soldier. A piece of paper told him so. And that made him angry.

And steps away stood Brynn, the girl he loved. But he couldn't go to her. He couldn't hold her or fight off this rain, because he knew he'd only hurt her. For her sake, he must not flinch.

And who are these people?

As his eyes skimmed the crowd, Connor knew most of their faces, but had only met a few of them. Some had backed his father's policies, while others had spoken ill of the Senator. Now they were here, acting like his friends.

How dare they.

They all talked and smiled. They shook hands and played their various roles, no sincerity among them... sickening.

Connor recognized he needed to get out, get away. He turned his head and spun on his heel, leaving them all behind. Hands in his coat pockets, he marched passed the headstones of many who had fallen. The scent of wet grass accented his retreat.

Where am I going?

He knew the truth. He had no idea where to go.

Soon the slope ended. So did the graveyard, and he passed through the iron-gate. A sidewalk that lined a busy street replaced the haunted tranquility of the cemetery. He watched his feet as he crossed the street. They looked so far away. Car horns blasted and tires screeched but he didn't care.

What's left?

Connor wandered without paying attention to time. He missed Brynn. He missed his identity. His father was dead. And the fire burned without an outlet.

In the frustration, he jerked his head up violently. Rain flicked from his bangs. Searching wildly in every direction, he saw a worn down building with two garage bays. Motorcycles and old cars, in their entirety or broken down, sat about. Some gleamed, seemingly newer.

One bike looked fast. It waited under an overhang. A

protective gear-clad man stepped away from the vehicle and into the building.

Connor crossed the street and marched across the parking lot. No one approached him from within the building.

Without hesitating, he slung his leg over the bike. He took the helmet and pulled it over his head. With a flick of his ankle, he lifted the kickstand. He twisted the keys and turned the bike on, its rev deafening under the overhang.

"Hey!" a voice screamed behind him.

Connor never looked as he dropped gears and slipped away. "HEY!"

As he exited the parking lot, he turned onto the major street and found room in the left turn lane to blast past cars. Eventually he found the road he wanted and turned south away from traffic, the city, and his current existence. As he turned, the back wheel slid out, hydroplaning a touch. Connor corrected the bike and continued.

That could have been bad.

Connor slowed slightly, the rainy conditions seemed dangerous.

Wait. Are you scared? You're never supposed to be afraid.

"Damn it." Connor said under the roar of the engine.

Come on, you scared little boy. Go... GO!

He stared at the rain.

I don't care that it's raining. Overcome the rain.

"Come on." He pulled back on the throttle. The rocket between his legs roared. With a tap of his foot, Connor dropped a gear. Then he let the wild stallion loose.

He and his steed charged through walls of water, pushing it out of the way. The tears from the sky struck the exposed part of his neck, between his jacket and helmet, as if every hornet on earth stung him.

85 m.p.h.

Connor held the bike steady, charging down the center of the two-lane road, dashing across the yellow line.

What are you holding back for?

"Come on."

Connor pulled the throttle more; the vehicle screamed

100 m.p.h.

The bike beneath Connor danced between grounded and loose, a chaos to be harnessed. Trees and roadside markers were indistinguishable as they blew past him.

110 m.p.h.

"Come on."

Connor pulled more, clutching the handlebars with everything he could, trying to hold his body as still as possible. The sensation of fear made him angry. Not giving into fear was all he had left in life. And nature would not take that from him.

More.

115 m.p.h.

The nerves in his stomach begged him to stop. He clenched his teeth and narrowed his eyes. "Come on."

There seemed little contact with concrete as water shoved the tires away from the ground. "Come on!" Connor said louder.

The bike shook. "COME ON!" Conner screamed.

The unstable tornado under him shuddered. "COME ON!"

119 m.p.h.…

The rear tire slid far to the left, then to the right. The front of his bike no longer faced forward. Wobbling in a sickening fashion, the engine raced beyond the capacity of the gears.

Connor tried to react but it was too late. He stopped breathing as in slow motion he watched the back of the bike come along side him. The road pulled him down.

In the nanosecond Connor had to react, he slipped his leg out from the side of the bike going down, putting his weight on the upward side.

At tremendous speeds, Connor and the bike slid forward. The hard surface ate away at the body of the bike and Connor's side.

He held on with all he could as the world rushed by, too fast to focus on anything. Somewhere in his universe, a guardrail seemed to be approaching too fast. A heavy thunk followed and Connor was airborne. The world spun around him; his surroundings indistinguishable.

Although in the madness, one thing stood out.

Was that a tree—

Blackness.

Then white and far away sound.

AS CONNOR PULLED HIS heavy eyelids open, brightness assaulted his pupils. He cringed and closed them tight. Then he opened them again, this time, slowly.

His world lay covered in a bland, monochromatic film until the overwhelming light retreated and solidified into florescent rectangles above him. As it cleared, the shapes and designs of ceiling tile came into focus.

He needed to wipe the sleep from his eyes, so he lifted his right hand to his face.

A shot of pain jolted through him like a liter of espresso. Gasping, his senses fired, screaming at him to stop moving.

Why does my arm hurt?

A thick, white cast engulfed his limb, the whole assembly cradled in a sling. Now, the rest of the room came into focus. The tile floors and the mechanical bed on which he lay proved he was in a hospital. Wires attached at his chest and lead to machines kept him company.

Connor shook his head. "All this for a broken arm?"

He needed to go find someone to answer his questions. The first step was getting out of bed. Connor drew the sheets away and lifted his legs... except his legs did not come. Connor raised an eyebrow and moved them again. But still nothing happened.

"Work."

Again he climbed out of bed. And again, he didn't climb out of bed. He ground his teeth.

Where aren't they working?

His body always listened to him. He was the boss. Even when it wanted to give up, it would always obey him and do more. Connor felt insulted that it wouldn't listen to him. So he forced it to.

He rolled sideways. The action of twisting his torso sent his limbs over the side of the bed. Hanging on the edge of the bed, he leaned forward and pushed off with his left arm, ready for his feet to catch his weight.

But he never stopped. His ankles, knees, and hips folded, bending over themselves like paper. Connor crashed into the floor. His knees and elbows smacked the unforgiving surface.

"What's happening?" Connor looked in every direction for an answer.

"What's happening?" He hit his legs with his fist.

Why can't I feel my legs!

"WHAT'S HAPPENING?" Connor beat his legs and tried

using his good arm to right himself.

As he struggled against gravity, nurses, doctors, and orderlies gathered around him and grabbed at him. They were a haze as he gasped. His thrashing body pushed some of them away. Yet when the needle went into his neck, he calmed and stopped, closing his eyes under the same lights to which he woke.

AN HOUR LATER, A graven-faced doctor stood alongside Connor's bed. His shoulders slumped as he held a clipboard at his side. "I'm sorry, Connor. There's no easy way to say this."

The doctor sighed. "I'd like to wait for your mother to arrive before... but, well..." The doctor shifted his feet. "You broke your back, Connor. Three vertebrae in the lumbar with substantial damage to your nerves..."

Connor stared out the window.

"I'm not going to sugar coat it for you; chances are you'll never walk again. It's a little early, but it doesn't look good... in fact, don't expect to."

Connor never turned his head while the doctor talked at his ear.

"I know this is hard, it always is. I'd recommend speaking with one of the hospital councilors or the chaplain, and your mother is on her way here as well. She's been at your side the whole time before she finally went home for a few hours today... Connor?"

The doctor walked around the end of the bed. "Connor?" He put his hand in his pocket and sighed. "Connor, staring out that window isn't going to make this go away. It's easier if —"

"Thank you, doctor," Connor said curtly.

The doctor watched him for a moment and shook his head. Then he walked from the room.

Silence filled the space. Through the window, tremendous thunderheads approached on the horizon of Houston. Blue, gray, and white wisps folded over each other, creating the mighty whole.

So, I'm paralyzed.

Connor watched the clouds. Because if he turned his eyes to the room in which he sat, the results of his accident might prove themselves true.

I'll never fly again.

An unfamiliar liquid sensation ran down his cheek. He reached his hand up and touched the droplet. As he drew his hand away, he looked upon his glistening fingertip.

A tear?

The memory of the last time he cried ran through his mind. He was seven and had wept over a lost soccer game and the missed trophy.

Little Connor turned to his father as he sobbed, expecting his father, like the other fathers, to express how proud he was and that Connor deserved a trophy as well.

His father looked at him and said, "I see that you're crying. I'm guessing you're not happy you didn't get a trophy."

Connor nodded through his tears.

"So you're crying because you didn't win a trophy? Okay. Well, son, you can cry all you want, and that won't change anything. You'll still not have a trophy. I love you, kid. But the only way to change what happened today is to go become a better soccer player."

Connor sniffed the snot running from his nose

"Now, do you want to be a better soccer player?" his father said.

Connor nodded.

"Okay, when we get home we'll work on passing the ball—"

Buzz. Buzz.

The vibration of Connor's cell phone brought Connor back to the present and his prison of a bed. Passing a hand over his cheek, he removed any trace of emotion before lifting the device to his ear.

"Hello?"

"*Oh, Connor?* Praise God!" his mother said on the other end.

"Hi, Mom."

"I'm so sorry, I ran home just—"

"Mom, it's okay. I know you were here the whole time."

"Baby, I was, I really was! I'll be there soon." Her voice sounded laden with panic. "Do you need anything?"

Connor sighed. He wanted a hole. And Death. But he knew his mother needed a mission and to be needed.

"Sure. Why don't you bring me a cheeseburger?"

"I will. Don't move!"

"I don't think that will be a problem." Connor said. "See you when you get here." He hung up his phone.

HIS MOTHER ARRIVED. CONNOR had to watch her cry over him again and again. Shame plagued him as the good woman shed tears on his behalf. She should have time to mourn her husband but instead had to toil for a son who didn't deserve it.

Connor wasn't hungry, but he forced down the food she brought. He thought the woman should have at least one victory. She had spent twelve unflinching hours at his side. Her secret service detail changed. One team's shift ended and another's began.

"Mom, I'll be fine. I'm just going to sleep. Go home for a while and rest—"

"I don't need rest!"

Connor smiled and shook his head. "I'm just going to be here sleeping. Get your rest so you can take care of me."

"I don't need rest to take care of my son!"

"I know you don't, but it would make me feel better. Do it for me?"

She eyed Connor.

"Seriously. Mother. Go home. And do what you need to do. I'll still be here when you get back."

When she tilted her head, Connor knew there might be hope of getting her to leave. "I *promise* you, I'll be fine."

After another few minutes of coaxing, she left and Connor sat in the silence.

Fewer nurses walked the hallways and in the distance, someone cried. The lights of other buildings in his view gradually came on as the hospital fell asleep.

What's wrong with me? I'm so strong, but I can't hold onto anything.

His eyelids were oddly heavy for not having done any activity. Stillness was its own sleeping pill.

A knock on the door roused him. He pulled his eyes open and corrected his slouched posture.

"Come in."

The door opened as a short, soft-statured man stepped into

the room.

"Hello, David," Connor said.

His father's former aide stood at the far side of the room, watching him. He seemed to be waiting. A moment of heavy silence fell before David spoke.

"It's weird to see you this way," David said. "I never thought something like this would happen to you."

"Me, either."

David leaned back against the far wall. "The way the Senator talked about you, spoke of you to other people." He shook his head. "I guess I started to believe you really were invincible."

"It seems I'm letting all sorts of people down," Connor said, appreciating David's bluntness. Too many had tiptoed around him since he arrived at the hospital.

"Yes, you are." David nodded and took small, gradual steps forward. "And you just never could give anything, could you? You were wild and free. And they all loved you for it. Their lives became hell because of you, and all they did was thank you."

"I never asked them to."

"But they did." David moved closer, his face tired. "And they loved you for it."

"I couldn't help that."

"Yes you could. But chose not to." David grabbed the foot-rail of the hospital bed. "Don't you think I'd like to live like that? Don't you think we all would? But maybe being a good man is not forcing those who love you to deal with it."

Connor slowly nodded, once. "Maybe."

David pulled his shoulders back and tucked his hands into his pockets. "I don't know why. But despite my better judgment, I used one last favor and cleaned this up for you. You're not getting your legs back, but there's no criminal charges." David shook his head. "I'd let you rot, but this is what the Senator would have wanted. Maybe he's rubbed off on me more than I thought."

David straightened his head and looked Connor dead in his eye. "But this is it. Do you hear me? We're all out of tricks. There's no cavalry or reset button when you mess up next time. I'm out of favors. This was the very last one. If you mess up again…" David shrugged his shoulders. "No one's coming."

Connor exhaled as he looked at the short, dedicated man. "I got a feeling I won't be up to much trouble anymore."

"Well, if anyone without legs can figure out how to mess up everyone's life, it's you." He took a step away and dropped his head. More silence.

"What will you do next?" Connor said.

"I'll be managing a different congressman's campaign. He's not your father, but hopefully great things can be done." David looked at his watch. "Actually, it's time for my flight." He glanced up. "Good luck, Connor." He walked towards the exit.

"Hey," Connor called.

David stopped, halfway through the door, and took a step back into the room.

Connor stared into his eyes. "He thought of you as a son," Connor lied. "He told me all the time."

The sternness of David's faced softened. He bit his lip and nodded slowly. And as David walked out of the room just a little taller, he glowed like he could walk through brick walls.

Connor watched the empty doorway, feeling a moment of rest. Then, once again alone and very aware of the present, Connor clenched his fist and stared at his legs. He reached for his wallet on the bedside table.

As he leaned back, his fingers cradled the picture of the girl with eyes of blue eternity.

"I hope you never have a chance to cry for me."

CHAPTER 15

Brynn woke up in San Francisco. A salt breeze flew by and kissed her on the cheek. Balcony doors married her room with the outdoors. She turned her head on the overstuffed pillow and rubbed the sleep from her eyes. Sitting up, she reached for the hotel courtesy robe and wrapped the white fluffiness around her shoulders. It embraced her like a hug from a polar bear. She slid from the sheets and stood, her muscles waking.

She crossed the room to the balcony and looked out on the city toward the bay. Dark blue Pacific waters tossed and turned, decorated with ships passing to and fro. Great bridges spilt the ocean from the horizon. From the shore to the cliffs, buildings cloaked the land in such organic fashion, it was as though the hills birthed forth the city. Songs of seagulls complemented sounds of the urban hustle.

Brynn let go of the railing and turned back to her room. At the bedside table she retrieved her phone. Among the messages and emails she missed as she slept was one from Kyle: "Good morning, darling. I hope you slept well. Conference breaks at 12. Interested in lunch?"

"Yes, please," she typed.

Soon after, while she brushed her teeth at the bathroom sink, her phone buzzed.

"12:15, top of Lombard Street. Join me in the cliché!"

Brynn tossed her phone onto the bed and took a shower, rinsing and repeating until steam covered the mirror. After dressing, she descended the stairs to the lobby and offered a smile to the concierge before stepping out into the street. She glanced at her watch: 9:38 A.M.

She purchased her caffeine fix from a barista cart, sipping the beverage as she sauntered the sidewalks.

Suited men chatted on cell phones while racing towards office buildings. At the same time, a much slower lifestyle passed by. Individuals in worn clothes performed or created art on every street corner. Old men carried boxes of goods they hoped to peddle. Some individuals just sat and watched the world. Street musicians tried their hand at exchanging melodies for coins.

Brynn followed a group of artists around a corner and found a street lined with galleries. All appearing equal, she stepped into the nearest one. That gallery led to another, and another. Wall after wall, display after display, she found the traditional mediums, of paint, charcoal, and sculpture. She also discovered experimental works in mud, crayon, and shattered glass.

She stopped before a painting that hung alone. Against the bare white wall, the work seemed a riotous explosion of color. The gallery lights failed against the daylight that came through the window.

Brynn looked the painting over. The entirety of the image was luxurious folds of a stage curtain, as though a play had just ended. Towards the right third of the image, a small boy in a baseball cap and jean jacket held the curtain open, peering through to backstage. The small opening revealed flashes of wonder and mystery from the far side. A young girl in pigtails stood a few steps back, watching the boy look through the gap.

I wonder if he's going to pass through.

Brynn's legs fatigued. She sat on a bench and continued studying the painting. A glance at her watch let her know it was 11:45. The time shook Brynn from her contemplative state and sent her running from the gallery. Brynn looked to the cable car. But not knowing the routes and fearing tardiness, she hailed a cab.

As the driver pulled up to her destination, she handed him the cash he had earned. Kyle sat on the concrete base of a streetlamp. He stood as she approached.

"Hey, how's the conference?" Brynn said as she embraced him.

"Not bad. But if they didn't give us the lunch break, I was ready to cause a scene." He took her hand. "Shall we? I just want to show you off."

"We shall." She followed him down the street.

He held up a flower. "I got this for you, and I didn't pick it from the garden directly behind me."

Brynn looked at the flower in his hand and then to the garden behind him. The flower was an exact match. She laughed as she accepted it. "Of course, you didn't!"

They moved along a sidewalk and found a café that only sold seasonal food. After ordering, Kyle lifted the pitcher of iced tea and poured Brynn a glass. "So what have you done today?"

"I went to a few art galleries. Nosed around."

"Anything cool?"

"Yeah." Brynn smiled. "Some pretty unique stuff."

"That's great. It's good you're getting the chance to check out the neighborhood. And while you've only been here a few days... any thoughts on of San Francisco?" He ran his finger across the hand she rested on the table.

"It's *quite* a city. There's so much to do and explore. But I still feel like the texture of the city is small, like every inch of it is the part 'locals go to.' And the weather here is unreal." She took a sip of her tea.

Kyle gave her an adoring smile. "They should make that the city's motto—"

Out of nowhere, a large shaggy dog shoved its nose against Kyle's thigh. The animal was a mess of curls and fluff. Kyle turned to face the animal and reached out his hand to stroke the beast. It continued its nasal inquisition.

"Why, hello there, fella'." Kyle laughed.

The dog climbed onto Kyle's lap and went after his face with an aggressive tongue.

Kyle chuckled. "You're so shy!"

The owner, a man of average height and curly hair struggled against the leash. "Kirby, heel!"

Next to him, his wife held up her hands, palms forward. "I'm so sorry!"

A child giggled from the stroller she pushed. The owner finally pulled the dog back. "I'm so, so sorry!"

"Forget it. No big deal!" Kyle laughed more. "Honestly, I'm fine." He watched the family as they continued on their afternoon stroll.

"Cute kids." He said as he turned back to Brynn. "Could you see yourself raising a family here?"

"It seems very possible," Brynn said.

"I guess first you'd have to find some guy to marry you." Kyle said, narrowing one eye.

"I guess."

"Somebody who wanted to spend the rest of his life with

you." Kyle smiled.

"That would certainly help," she said.

He emitted so much calmness and confidence. "Because forever is a long time."

"A very long time." She shifted in her seat.

Time slowed down as the moment became lethargic. Her heart raced. Kyle nodded and reached for his chair, scooting back.

Brynn jolted. *He's going to propose!*

But Kyle only reached for his coat hanging on the backrest. "Ready to go?"

Staring blankly for a moment, Brynn then nodded her head. "Of course."

As they meandered along, Kyle was talkative. This pleased Brynn, as she could respond with mutters and nods, instead of trying to focus and summon an actual answer. Her mind was still riding the roller coaster that began at the café.

The next day as her plane lifted away from San Francisco international airport, Brynn gazed out the window. A flight attendant informed the cabin of drink selections and a movie played in the background. The actions and sounds blended into a bland two-dimensional background.

In her head, she felt committed to Kyle. She liked feeling that way. He was a good man. He took care of her, was kind, and made her feel special. The proof was before her in the array of her favorite magazines he had bought for her to take on her flight back to Texas.

Brynn toiled and pondered well into the beverage service, eventually growing tired of her considerations. So she slapped on headphones and partook in the in-flight movie, trying to shake the questions.

The plane's landing gear tugged the runway at Houston Hobby Airport. She walked past the luggage carrouse as her mother pulled up to the curb. Brynn put her bags in the back and climbed into the passenger seat, then gave her mother a quick hug.

"Hi, honey. How was your trip?" her mother said.

"We had fun."

"What'd you think of San Francisco?" Her mother pulled away.

"It's a nice city."

"Nice?" Brynn's mother spent more time looking at Brynn than at the road. "*Nice?* Give me details! What did you do? Where did you go? What did y'all talk about?"

Brynn felt as though she had a never-ending list of topics she'd rather discuss. "Mom, I'm really tired. Can we talk about this some other time?"

Her mother pursed her lips and looked her daughter over, suspicion in her eyes. "Well, all right, but don't think you're getting out of this conversation. I *will* bring it up later."

Brynn grinned and looked through the windshield. "Thanks for picking me up, Mom."

"*Will* be bringing it up later," her mom said.

Once home, they entered through the garage door.

"Is Dad enjoying his conference?"

"Talked to him earlier." Her mom tossed the keys onto the table. "He's with Jim Duggins from his fellowship. They found a cigar club."

"Looks like the boys are out on the town." Brynn said as she dropped her bags and kicked off her shoes. The couch beckoned her. She proceeded to have a date night with an old movie and quart of ice cream.

Later, she opened her eyes and the movie channel was well into infomercials. After climbing the stairs, she fell into her old, familiar bed.

★ ★ ★

FIRST THING THE NEXT morning, a soft knock resonated on her door. Her mother pushed it open and entered the room.

"Hey sweetie, how'd you sleep?"

"Just fine. What's going on?"

"Well, I just got off the phone with Juliet West's assistant, Karen. Do you remember her?" Her mother sat on the foot of the bed.

Brynn knew who the woman was. But she remained confused as to why her mother would ever bring up the West family.

"Yes, I remember her. Is this about whatever accident Connor had?" Brynn tried to sound indifferent and forced a careless yawn.

"No, no. God knows where he is. No, Karen called to ask me a favor. Ever since the Senator died, Juliet has stayed with her brother's family. She apparently hasn't been back to the house. Too painful."

She folded her hands in her lap. "It's understandable. She needs someone to go and gather clothes and stuff, for Juliet. She also wants the family's photo albums. So I'm going to go take care of that and I'll be back this afternoon."

Brynn sat up. "Just give me ten minutes. I can go with you."

"*No.*" Her mother leaned forward quickly, then stopped, and eased back. "No, that's fine."

Brynn rolled her eyes in humor. "Mom, don't worry. Like you said, Mrs. West's son is God knows where. Over it. Nothing is going to happen. It'll be faster if I come along anyways. Then you and I can have lunch at La Luna."

Her mother narrowed her eyes and tilted her head. "Ok. But if you need to leave at any time, just go."

Brynn laughed. "I won't hesitate."

At 10:00 AM, mother and daughter turned down the Wests' street. Brynn blinked twice, unsure if they were on the correct road. The area looked different when not spilling over with cars. Once her mother pulled into the driveway, Brynn got out. Their SUV looked small sitting by itself. As Brynn walked up, she kept her eyes up as she always did, waiting to address secret servicemen. None addressed her. There was no one to protect.

Her mother pulled a key and inserted it into the lock. It clicked open and the door swung wide. The two stepped inside, after which her mother typed the combination into the alarm system.

A chasm sat where once did a home. Without interns, staff, and security, the house had an empty, barren feeling; like the remains of a once legendary castle. Brynn knew it was in her head, but she swore the air smelled stale. The halls waited, silent as a crypt to the world.

This place was so happy once.

"Do you think Mrs. West will sell this house?" Brynn said.

"I'm not sure. I haven't heard anything." Brynn's mother nodded as the walked down the hallway. "How about I get her clothes and you find the photo albums? Karen said they were proably in the library."

"Sounds good," Brynn said.

Brynn's mother walked down the hallway. The door to the

library loomed sturdy and hung adrift. Brynn remembered the night she last saw the senator there, conducting the masses in a coordinated effort for a better tomorrow.

As she put one foot in front of the other and entered the room, her steps creaked. In the empty house, the noise seemed all the louder. Goosebumps peppered her arms. She looked around the floor. Scattered papers lay in wait. She pictured the staff dropping everything the moment they heard something happened to their boss, no doubt racing to his hospital. The light coming through the window was now unbroken by the silhouette of the politician.

Brynn had seen the photograph albums before. She'd seen her own picture in them. She turned to the shelves built into the wall behind the senator's desk. They reached to the ceiling and seemed as steadfast as the foundations of the earth.

Brynn found the albums, ten of them on the middle shelf. She smirked at a mom's tenacity to document every moment of a child's life. As she circled to the other side, Brynn pushed the desk chair out of the way. She pulled the volumes from the shelf. Her foot struck something. Looking down, she found a box full of papers under the senator's desk.

The side of the box read, "stuff that kid is up to."

Brynn sat down and pulled out the box and began searching through its contents. The senator had paid very close attention to his son's life. She found pages and pages of Connor's missions, exhibited by photos, transcripts, memos, and schematics arranged in folders. Discovering sheet after sheet of destruction, a great weight settled on her chest. No wonder Connor had never talked about the things he did. Words couldn't describe them.

Noticing the documents arranged by date, she reached her

hand out, hesitated, then continued. Her fingers danced over pages until she found the date she was looking for. She pulled the file.

"OPERATION DOVE HUNT" Opening the file, she found detailed schematics of the rescue operation that had pulled her out of captivity. An odd swirl of emotions passed through her. She hadn't thought about the horror in so long, and reading the experience two-dimensionally was like reading a history book. It didn't seem real. She didn't feel as though she had starred as the story's leading lady.

Marveling at the abundance of information the SEALs obtained before ever arriving, Brynn passed over the many documented dead insurgents from that night. She flipped another page and looked in what could have been a mirror. Under "HOSTAGE," her picture appeared along with her personal profile. As she read remarkably personal details about her life, she wondered who gathered all that information.

So Senator West did know about what happened.

She didn't find much information on the team who came for her, only their names. Brynn flipped to her favorite part of the story and read the part of the transcript when Connor came out of the dark. *That* moment felt real, the moment when he found her in the night and lifted her from the ground. So long ago… such a different time…

Brynn heard a sound and guessed it was her mother. She replaced the file and returned the box under the desk. She sat still and waited. When her mother didn't reappear, she reached for the box again and withdrew the last file added. She knew what this file meant. It would be her answer for what happened at his end.

She unfolded the papers. The first page was a letter from

a high-ranking government official expressing condolences for the trauma sustained by the senator's son. Next she found a transcript of the mission. She read of Connor and the team members who found their deaths.

With each passing sentence, moisture in her eyes grew, until tears fell. She cried not only for Connor, but also for the families who lost their soldiers. Awe overwhelmed her as she read of heroism that humbled her. Their hearts fought beyond where their bodies could carry them.

And she read the tale of Connor, full of bullets and shedding blood on a lonely mountain. She learned of the betrayal and the vengeance sought.

How did he survive?

Then she turned to the last page. She lost her breath and covered her mouth, fighting to refrain from weeping.

A crystal clear photo depicted some hospital tent emergency room on the other side of the world. Connor lay on a table with his shirt cut open, so much blood spilled that a puddle gathered on the floor. Surgeons poised over him, wielding every conceivable instrument. His body waited limp and lifeless. Tubes and wires passed between him and machines. The respirator over his mouth tried to breathe life into him. His arms hung down, numb. The surgery light overhead bathed him in light and held him, cradling him in space.

Sadness swamped her. She had seen him after this, striding tall and strong.

How could anyone carry on after such things?

Then she bit her lip as she saw what his broken hand clutched as he lay on his deathbed. There, cradled in his fingers and soaked in his blood, was a little wallet picture of her. The one she given him years and years before.

Her breaths trembled and quaked. He had taken her with him to the battlefield.

"Brynn?" Her mother's voice called from down the hallway.

Brynn shoved the file back in the box and used her sleeve as Kleenex. She fought the tears away.

"Brynn, where are—" Her mother stepped into the room and looked at her. She shook her head at her daughter. "This is *exactly* why I didn't want to bring—"

"Relax, Mama, I'm just crying for Mrs. West." Brynn said. "Must be lonely to lose your husband."

Her mother looked at her and lowered her shoulders. "I know. I can't imagine." She peered up at the albums behind Brynn. "Are those the ones?"

"Yes." Brynn stood and lifted the albums from the shelf.

"Good. Let's get out of here," her mother said and led her down the hall, through the door, and away from the house.

The phone in her pocket vibrated. Brynn lifted it out. A message from Kyle read, "Hey, babe. What are you doing in Houston today?"

"Missing you," she texted him back.

CHAPTER 16

"Can you feel *that?*" Lee cradled Connor's right foot with one hand and with the other, poked Connor's big toe with a needle.

"No." Connor leaned against the backrest of the therapy table, arms crossed.

Lee moved the needled to the heel and looked up from the other end of Connor's legs. "How about now?"

"Nothing."

"Okay, let me try something else." Lee stood. "I'll be right back." He walked off towards the offices.

Connor rolled his eyes. He sat in the long room and surveyed the blue floors and gray walls. Stationary bikes, treadmills, weights, rubber bands, and a host of other bizarre-looking contraptions lined up in rows. Fifteen other patients ran through drills with their therapists. Connor had counted them many times. Some lay on mats, stretching. Others went up and down small flights of stairs. Still others sat while therapists applied pressure, wincing when pain became too great.

The general conglomerate of white hair made Connor feel like the drastic junior of the group. An adult contemporary radio station droned in the background.

Connor laughed to himself. One of the drawbacks he hadn't realized about being kicked out of the military was that he lost access to Veterans Administration hospitals. At least there, the facility might seem more like the weight room on base. It might have felt more familiar or comfortable.

But Connor knew he was lying. Regardless of the discharge, even the military would not fit anymore, after all that happened.

"I'm back." Lee approached, wielding some sort of contraption. He plugged it into the wall and held the other end to Connor's foot. "Anything?"

Connor shook his head.

Lee ran it up Connor's shin. "Still nothing?"

"Still nothing." Connor nodded.

"Hmm…" Lee raised an eyebrow.

"Yes?"

Lee sat back in his rolling office chair. "I don't know what to tell you."

"That's okay. It's been seven weeks of this. I think I lost this one." Connor seized the bars on the side of the therapy table and the armrest of his wheelchair. His upper body dragged the rest of him from the table until he fell over into the chair. Reaching down, he took hold of his legs in turn and pulled them into the footrests.

"Same time tomorrow," Lee called after him.

Connor wheeled down the hall and away from the warm atmosphere of the clinic. Beyond the waiting area, he reached the tile floors of the hospital, dodging gurneys as he rolled. He wasn't able to push through the double doors on his own so he waited until an orderly came along. Once through, he stopped in front of the elevator and waited for the steel doors to open.

A young nurse at the nearby nursing station peered over the counter. "Sir?"

Connor turned his head towards her.

"We don't really allow patients to use the elevator by themselves." Her eyebrows pushed together under a wrinkled forehead. She pouted her bottom lip, like she sympathized.

"Oh, honey, don't bother," one of the senior nurses, Miranda, said. "That boy will just do whatever he wants anyways." She shook her head and rolled her eyes before turning away.

With a light ding, the elevator arrived. Connor pushed his way into the steel box, then rode to the ground floor. There, he found a back hall he liked because it was sparsely occupied, and pushed his way through the exit doors to find himself on the bottom floor of the hospital parking garage. All eight stories of it. The glossy concrete smelled of mildew and swamp after the recent rain. The lack of cars led Connor to the assumption that visitors were few in the hospital at this hour.

Connor reached into his pocket and pulled out a pair of fingerless gloves. He touched his wheels, running his fingertips over the steel rims.

He pushed the wheels forward once. Then again, and again. Each time seizing the rims and cranking them while bending at his core and pushing his chest back and forth. He struggled to keep his momentum going so he wouldn't get stuck mid-incline.

He blew through the first climb and tried to wheel quickly across the flat part of level two. His arms felt a little worn after the second incline and the first drop of sweat fell from his forehead. With each passing floor, the muscles of his body burned more and more.

"Don't stop. Don't lose this part of you," he said on the last incline when his muscles argued with him.

The dull sky shone above the top floor. With a final shove, Connor reached the highest point possible in the structure. The wheels slipped from his hands as he coasted to a stop.

He'd performed this routine every day for the past week and it still wasn't the escape he hoped. It only made him tired. Doing it again didn't sound like something he'd like to do. So he descended all eight floors, turned around, and climbed the castle again… three more times.

Before rolling back into the hospital, he stopped to wring the sweat out of his shirt. Then he went inside and took the elevator up to his room.

In his bathroom, he lifted a plastic chair and set it on the tile under the showerhead. Using a yardstick, he tried to shove his socks, shoes, and shorts off. His shoes did not want to cooperate as he maneuvered the yardstick in all directions.

"Come on, damnit." Connor clenched his jaw, all the while the button to summon the nurse hung inches away. After ten minutes, he got them off. He turned the shower handle.

The faucet spat out water. Connor leaned out of his chair into the water stream. He put one hand on the balance bar and another on the plastic chair. Pivoting at his waist, he swung his top half forward and out of the wheelchair. His legs dragged across the floor.

Next, he tried to swing his butt around to the plastic chair. But the chair slid on wet tile before shooting across the shower. Connor's balance failed and he fell. He smacked hard into the shower floor, under pouring water.

"Shit," he whispered as he punched the floor. He felt like a dead fish. He lay in the downpour.

I hate this.

An hour later, he emerged from the bathroom, clean and in a change of clothes. Tired of the wheelchair, he decided to climb into his bed. But looking at its height, staying in his chair seemed so much easier.

These thoughts scared him, causing his face to flush. He never considered the easier path before and didn't know what that meant.

I'm losing myself.

Bedrails in hand, he hoisted himself and utilized every muscle in his upper body to move into position. The landing wasn't graceful. He lay back after lifting his legs onto the mattress.

The warm light of a low sun came through the window and reflected off the floor throughout the room. Gifts people sent, and those some of his military friends had brought, filled the corner table. Connor looked at his watch; his mother would be there in an hour. He clicked the remote and the television came to life. Connor kept it on mute. He flipped channels through meaningless dribble.

"Boy, this sucks."

Connor jerked his head towards the door. "What?"

A tall, wiry man with aged, sunken cheeks stepped from the doorway into the room. His eyes gleamed with a certain healthiness. A little smirk clung to his face as he waved his hand over Connor. "This sucks! Losing your legs."

Connor drew his head back. "Uh, can I help you?"

The man tossed a thin black box towards Connor, which Connor snatched out of the air.

"What's this?"

"Just something I got once," the man nodded to it. "For being foolish."

Connor took his eyes off the intruder and studied the container. He popped open the lid. Black velvet lining intrigued him and a golden shimmer told the story.

The medallion was a star encircled by a woven rim, unapologetically brandishing the likeness of Minerva under the banner "Valor."

Connor read the script at the bottom, "Presented to Lt. William James McIntery."

"Actually now it's *Father* William McIntery," the stranger said. "But you can call me Mickey."

"Medal of Honor." Connor looked at him. "What'd you do?"

"Oh, nothing. Just pushed harder and farther than most would. Saved a few lives. Like you used to."

"Special Forces huh?"

"Yeah. And back then, we didn't rely on all these gadgets like you pussies." Father Mickey grinned.

Connor chose to cut him slack because he was a former soldier, but he didn't enjoy the man's forwardness or forced familiarity. "What do you want, Father Mickey?" Connor kept his face still.

"I want to talk to you about losing your legs. Cause you're not just losing limbs, you're losing a lifestyle."

Connor rolled his eyes and looked away but Father Mickey shuffled sideways to stay in Connor's field of vision, forcing Connor to look at him.

"Lots of us tough guys come back injured, oftentimes worse than we think." Father Mickey pulled back his sleeve and revealed a misshapen forearm. The limb missed a chunk of muscle.

Connor frowned. "It's hard to compare that to no le—"

"Oh, boo-hoo." Father Mickey shook his head. "Connor lost his legs! I got news for you, kid. You ain't the first and you won't be the last. The only question is: are you going to let this ruin the rest of your life? You won't win by wallowing."

He reached into his pocket and produced a card. "Listen. Here's my number. Now I'm not saying today, or tomorrow, or even this week, but get over yourself and give me a call. I want to help you through this."

"I'm out of the military. Aren't you supposed to help soldiers?"

"Brother, you and me both know it's not words on a piece of paper that make you a soldier."

"I can do it on my own," Connor said.

"Maybe. But you don't *have* to. Now, give me that back. I *need* it." Father Mickey reach out and took the Medal of Honor. He paused and looked down at Connor with a whimsical expression. "After all... it's how I pick up chicks." The man turned and disappeared as suddenly as he appeared.

"What just happened?" Connor blew out a long breath and scratched his head. He went back to the television and flipped around for a while.

An hour later a knock came at the door. "Connor, honey?"

"Hi, Mom." He pulled his mouth into a small smile.

"How are you, sweetie?" She walked in and leaned against his bed.

He didn't want to answer that question, so he looked at the man behind her. "Who's this?"

"Hi, Connor. I'm Reagan Marble. I'm your—"

"Dad's estate attorney. I've heard of you." Connor shot his gaze between them. "Why don't you two have a seat?"

The pair scooted two chairs toward him and sat down.

"What do you need, Mr. Marble?"

"Well, as you probably heard, we opened your father's will yesterday." His words slowed and Connor felt the man search his face. "It's understandable you couldn't be there for obvious reasons."

"Obviously." Connor had told his mom his body hurt too much. But in truth, he preferred the seclusion.

"*And that's okay.* Long story short, no surprises, your father left everything to you and your mother." He unfolded a binder and pulled out papers. "All you have to do is sign these and it will all be in your name." He set the documents on Connor's lap.

Connor took the pen and jotted his signature on every line.

"That'll do it." Mr. Marble looked from Connor to his mother. "Now I don't want you to worry. My office will handle everything so that ownership and title of everything passes smoothly."

He turned back to Connor. "Lastly, the only thing Ben did not pass jointly to you both was this." He lifted a small travel suitcase and handed it to Connor. "The contents of this are solely for you."

Connor manipulated the bag in his hands.

Mr. Marble gathered his things. "Thank you. I've intruded long enough." He walked to the door. "Good evening." He disappeared.

Connor and his mother stared at the mysterious bag. Connor took hold of the zipper.

"No, wait." His mother picked up her coat. "I'll give you some privacy. Dad left that to *you*."

"Mom, that's crazy. I don't care if you know what's inside."

"No." She held up her hand. "He left that to you and you alone." She stood back and exhaled. She looked so calm, so peaceful. "I trust him. I always have." She headed out of the room. "I'll see you tomorrow, sweetheart."

Connor never found words as she left. Sitting there alone

with the heirloom addressed solely to him, he tugged at the strap of the heavy bag.

He slid the zipper down the sides and around the corners and slowly peered inside. Notebook upon notebook filled the bag. Some were cheap, spiral bound, and comprised of many colors. Others were leather and stately in fashion. Each one of them had dates on their covers, encompassing years.

"February 18th, 1960-July 7th, 1961." He read on one with spiral binding and a creased cover. It seemed the earliest date he could find.

He opened the first page. "02/18/60" marked the upper right corner. Handcrafted words, some misspelled, draped the page in faded pencil. Connor read.

"Hello, my name is Benjamin West and I am 15 years old. Today in class we learned that many great men in the past kept journals as an exercise in reflection. I too, wish to be a great man. So here it is, day one. The goal is to write in here at least once a week. It'll be a miracle if I keep this up."

Connor felt as though someone tossed a lead blanket over him. He pictured sitting beside his fifteen-year-old father while Ben first laid words on the page.

Befuddled, Connor had never realized his father kept a journal. From the multitude of volumes, it seemed the senator chronicled his entire tale.

Connor continued to the next entry. That entry led to the next and another after that. Page after page described his father's musings on his freshman year of high school as a fifteen-year-old, including a successful run at class president.

"I think becoming class president had a lot to do with interest. That is to say, I have an interest when I speak with people. It's pretty easy for me to be interested in anyone I talk to. People are fascinating. Now, they may be wrong and I disagree with them. Yet, it's still a story. As long as I'm interested, it helps. I remember what they say. I remember who they are. I remember what they want."

Connor read through a summer job and his father's first kiss. He read into his father's sophomore fall before reaching for the next journal. Connor noticed how often his father drifted into wonderings of what life would be like if he didn't have need of a cane.

Three volumes in, and his father was a senior in high school, an incumbent class president, and entrepreneur.

Connor reached for the water on his bedside stand. 3:00 a.m. flashed on the alarm clock. Choosing to ignore it, he read,

"Picking a college is such a big choice. Sure, all these colleges offer the same education, more or less. But who knows how my life will be changed by those I go through four years with. I hope I find those that make me best…"

So Connor continued. Pages later,

"Yale University has issued me a double-wide, handicap dorm with a private bathroom. I *will* turn this into party central…"

A few paragraphs after that,

"First party. Just happy no one died…"

By the time the hospital buzzed again with morning traffic, young Benjamin West was living in a fraternity house with Jase McGee, who would later become his father's best friend for the rest of his life.

Despite his efforts, near the end of his dad's senior year, Connor could stay awake no longer and finally closed his eyes.

He woke that afternoon and prepared himself for therapy, during which the therapist and he practiced going from wheelchair to passenger seat. Already possessing ample upper body strength, Connor handled these exercises with ease.

That night, after a two-hour visit with his mother, Connor resumed his wanderings in his father's life. The next section was dated the day he began law school,

"I don't feel ready for law school, but who ever does?"

The entries of that year were full of the 22-year-old's horror stories, warring with the countless hours the program required.

Notebooks later, a graduated Ben had conquered and finished law school at the top of his class on his way to incredible opportunities.

"Today, I met the girl I'm going to marry. Just like that and out of the blue! No planning, no set up, only an instant. She had me in a smile. Her name is Juliet… haha, I don't even know her last name! I'll play it slow and cool, but it's surreal to already know today and for the rest of your life, you're going to be with someone who completes you. Just being around her will make me better than I've been or ever would be without her. She is my other half, my whole heart. She is home to me."

In pages and pages of lyric, Connor watched his father transform into a poet who filled the rest of that journal. Connor skimmed these parts, not wishing to intrude on a moment between lovers.

The next booklet told of his father's job as a judicial clerk, then constitutional rights lawyer before beginning his political career as a state congressman.

As Connor flipped to another page, he read the entry's date. A signal went off in his mind. He stared at the date.

"The day I was born," Connor said aloud.

The entry read, "Juliet and I had a son today, there are no words sufficient…"

Connor read on, noting how half his father's writings transformed to the subject of Connor.

"Heroes are few, and fear rampant. I want so much more for Connor. I want him to be brave and strong. He has potential to be anything. I don't *just* want him to be protected, I want him to be a threat. Weakness and fear prohibit most from experiencing all they should. I will do my best to make him strong and brave so that he can live more than most dare or dream…"

Book followed book that told of Connor's childhood and rearing years through high school and college. His father documented every chapter in great detail, underlined by a constant theme of gratitude that his son was so able to accomplish things. But around Connor's 16th birthday, the sentences began to hint at a worry that Connor might be too much.

He followed his father's words through his time in the navy.

They were proud but fearful of what seemed to be his son's unchangeable destiny.

"Something drives him, something deeper and scary to most. He is the kind of man who makes history…"

The story continued into his father's viewpoints on Connor's discharge from the Navy.

Connor flipped a page and found one final two-sentence notation, describing a successful meeting with a special interest group. Searching further, Connor sought more. But no words came and he arrived at the back cover. It was dated shortly before his father's death.

Stapled inside the last page was a loose paper, ridden with holes as though attached and detached many times. Connor thought of all the other stapled pages he had seen in the other journals, always at the end. He guessed for years his father meant for this page to be the last thing read. His father must've kept moving it to the next journal as they were completed, always intending this to be the final message.

Connor slowly reached his fingertips towards the page and unfolded it.

"My son."

Connor pulled back, surprised to hear a voice from the grave. And the voice echoed.

My son,

I love you so much. From the first day you opened your eyes until now, I've been out of my mind. It's an odd thing, instantly loving someone you just met. Watching you grow and become more than I could have possibly imagined has been the joy of my life. There were so many things I expected when you were born. I expected to love you, to watch you succeed. But I never expected to look up to you. I thought being a father-son combination would more akin to master-apprentice. I never thought you'd blow me away in such a fashion and leave me speechless.

Some would say I lived my life to the fullest and accomplished such great things. But really, I've always felt secondary. I've let this damn leg hold me back. I've felt as though my soul and heart were meant for one thing and my body couldn't keep up, and so I've lived this life instead.

But in the end I regret nothing. For this life has brought me your mother and it has brought me you.

That said, I wanted more for you. I wanted you to reach the heights I could never attain. And now you've succeeded. Long ago you attained fearlessness. And that has led you to experience life to a higher degree than most could hope or dream.

Selfishly, I've lived through you. And somehow in making you all I missed out on, I have robbed you. I only wanted you to be free of my shortcomings. Yet, in doing so, I fear I have robbed you of the things that make life worth living.

If you're reading this, I'm gone. And I thank God I died first and never had to bury you. But if I am gone, then this last thing I charge you: let it go. Let slip away all the hate and power I've raised you to possess. Breathe instead. Please experience the things that make life worth living. You've fought fiercely, now love fiercely. You've taken life, now give and give generously. You've destroyed, torn down. Now build.

You've tried and triumphed, stared into the abyss and not blinked. You've got nothing left to prove. You're more than anyone I've ever met.

I know the world needs heroes. But you've done your part. You've stepped up for your fair share of years and defended the weak. Now it's someone else's turn. So let it go: all the passion and war I instilled you with.

I'm sorry I was never brave enough to tell you this in life, but we can't all be as brave and invincible as Connor West.

So live, Son. And forgive, Connor, forgive. Starting with yourself. Then forgive me for making you into a machine. And redeem my mistakes, by becoming more human than I could possibly imagine. Be more than you ever thought you could be. That itch has nothing left for you. You've already beaten it.

I love you so much. And by God, take care of your mother. She is the best of me.

Your father,
Ben West

The tears in Connor's eyes blurred his vision as he read and reread his father's letter. He never realized how isolated he was until his father's words highlighted the ways in which he felt alone. Weeping was new to him and yet it gave him hope. Perhaps he could be more than a war machine. Perhaps he could be human.

Then, he wiped away his tears. For despite his newly found revelation, he was still Connor West.

After weighing all matters at hand for hours upon hours, and days upon days, he at last reached for the card on his bedside stand and with delicate moves, dialed the number.

"Father Mickey? Hi, it's Connor West. What are you doing tomorrow?"

Part 3

THOSE DAMN

UNBREAKABLE ONES

CHAPTER 17

The clock blinked 1:45 P.M. Brynn shook her head as she scrambled around her house in search of her keys. A car horn barked outside. The taxi had arrived.

"One minute!" she yelled, aware the cab driver wouldn't hear her. Tossing aside a couch pillow, she caught a glimpse of the small metal keys as they glistened on the cushion. They rattled as she lifted them into her purse.

Rushing to the door, she found today's mail piled under the slot. She scooped the entire lot into her bag. The taxi beckoned her again.

After casting a final look around her house, she opened the front door to pouring sunshine. Brynn took up her suitcase and slung her handbag over her shoulder. The driver stood next to the cab's open trunk. She waived at him and locked the front door.

The driver helped lift her bag into the trunk.

"Austin-Bergstrom Airport, please."

The driver nodded before putting the car in drive and progressing down the road. Open windows let in beautiful Austin air. Brynn withdrew her phone from her pocket and scrolled through recent messages. A message from her mother said, "Fly safe! Enjoy San Francisco!"

Brynn had grown accustomed to her bi-monthly trips to the

West Coast. Kyle was out there now, so she thought she should get out there as often as possible until something happened. She would've guessed she'd have more enthusiasm for the trips but she also realized every moment of her life couldn't be a dazzling romantic rush. Logically, she needed to spend as much time with Kyle as she could. And today, she was excited to see him.

Traffic was light. All Brynn had to do was blink twice and then she arrived at the airport. The driver pulled up to the curb. Brynn climbed out, paid the cabby, and made her way through security.

A little girl in front of Brynn pushed on a bag bigger than she. Navigating the object through the line seemed a more difficult task than the child anticipated. Brynn smiled at the little girl's uncoordinated attempts to reach her goal. The child's parents spent more time chuckling and enjoying the child's adorable struggle rather than helping her.

Eventually, Brynn passed through the scanner and entered the terminal. Gate A-9 lay ahead. People lined the benches while others stood and leaned against columns. It seemed many were headed to the Golden Gate city. Voices droned on the PA system and televisions played CNN. The air smelled of recently mopped floors.

Brynn settled back into a seat, watching massive jets pull up to the jet-ways. A calm passed over her, knowing she wouldn't miss the flight.

Brynn looked over the crowd. She noted a group of high-schoolers in matching tracksuits, a band of Rastafarians, and an old couple that held hands, connected as though conjoined twins, the husband sleeping

Studying her ticket and the clock, Brynn realized she had twenty minutes until boarding. Considering her options, she decided to read her newest book. As she rifled through her purse, she found an envelope in the pile of mail she brought from home. As a trashcan sat near, now was a good time to read through the correspondence.

The first envelope appeared sterile. "You've been approved for a new credit—"

Brynn tossed it. The next item was the alumni magazine from her alma mater. She threw it into the recycle bin, never giving it a look. Then, a small postcard informed her it was time for her dental checkup.

Casting that note aside as well, she read the next envelope. Someone had inscribed the address by hand. Brynn grew curious at the prospect of a personal letter. She opened the letter and unfolded page.

"Connor?"

Speaking his name, thinking of him, seemed to be only daydreams. It felt odd that none of the other passengers reacted at how strange it was for Connor to send a letter.

Didn't they understand?

Shaking off the initial intense pulse of her heart, she endeavored to read the letter as one reads a textbook.

"BRYNN ANNA GRACE."

She heard him say her name.

Brynn Anna Grace,

Words seem cheap, but I hope you are well and happy. And wherever you are, I hope the sun is shining.

I hope you have a reason to smile.

If you've already thrown this letter away, or don't read another word, I won't blame you. In light of what I've done, such action would be merited.

I don't know what I'm trying to accomplish. Many things have changed since last we spoke, things I've never experienced before but I'm learning a lot.

Brynn, I want you to know something. I want you to know that I'm sorry.

She glanced up, searching for a reaction from the strangers sitting next to her. But they weren't part of her situation. Brynn looked back down.

I've owed you an apology for a long time. But until now I have let some deranged mixture of pride and denial hold me back. Maybe even hope. I know now that I've always been destructive, costing more than I'm worth to you and my family.

And you caught the worst of it because I took you for granted. Thinking back on the way we were and the way I am, every single time I called your name, I knew we were doomed. Yet time and time again, I lied to myself that I could have it all and in doing so, lied to you. I consciously condemned you to suffer. And you truly suffered. I should have stayed as far away from you as I could, from day one. From that first second.

So finally, a lifetime in the making: I'm sorry. I'm sorry

for every moment, every selfish action and thought, for every scar on your heart. I'm sorry for all the time I stole from you. I'm sorry for treating you in a way you didn't deserve and for not treating you in the ways you do deserve. I'm sorry for all things you missed because I distracted you. I'm sorry for every tear and pain.

From the very first day we met, you've always been a loyal and kind friend. You championed and fought for me endlessly, no matter how many times I threw mud in your face. I am the man who ruined your world

You're the finest and best person I will ever know. Causing you pain is regret I'll carry with me always.

From here on out, I wish you well and I wish you the best. Please find happiness because no one deserves it more than you. I hope your life unfolds to be more wondrous than you ever imagined.

So go forward and remember to smile, for in your smile exists the power to make a stranger's day. And if years from now I see you in the street, I hope we can greet each other as friends; no hate, no anger, no fight, just memories of good days. Give my best to your family and tell your dear, sweet mother that you and I have put down our gloves and give her all of my love.

For now and for all I time, I am really, truly, sorry.

Stay Sweet, Kid,
Connor

Brynn stared and stared. Her eyes rolled over the last few phrases three times before she backed away from the letter. Her fingers clutched the parchment so tight the page crinkled in her hands. Pulling away from his words arriving back in the terminal was as stark a contrast as jumping through space and time.

Her body ached with exhaustion despite not moving an inch, and panted. She felt as though she'd run a marathon.

Was I waiting for this apology?

She'd been a willing and hopeful participant. Did she feel he owed her this? She knew she was owed this. But did she feel she was owed this? She had yelled at him, fought him, pushed him away, and come back to him. Only to once again fall into him and push him away. He was good at causing her heart to ache. But was she ever really mad at him in all of it?

I was never mad at him.

She was mad at the world, the entire universe, because Connor was the way he was. In the moments she experienced, she was angry things couldn't work out. But she was never mad at him. In the end, she realized she just felt bad for him, for he would never know rest.

But something in the letter sounded different; it sounded like peace. As a deep breath filled her lungs, she felt rested and happy. Was this closure?

"Now boarding Zone 2," the flight attendant said over PA system.

Brynn walked towards the line of passengers and held her ticket out for the gate officer. As she stepped through the door, the smell of airport food court faded, replaced by the odor of old carpet. She dragged her little suitcase down the ramp behind her.

The flight attendant's big smile shined through the plane's open door. Brynn stepped inside, hunching over despite the fact she wasn't tall enough to bump her head. She nodded to the crew and took her aisle seat in the second row. No matter how many times she flew, she always felt first class was a treat.

That letter…

In the window seat next to her a woman slept. Without an obligation to exchange pleasantries with her row partner, Brynn pulled out another magazine if only for the distraction.

But her thoughts ran wild.

Brynn turned pages, unaware of what transpired on the page before her. She'd stare at a picture for minutes, never processing the image it portrayed. Every now and then, she looked up to observe more passengers loading. Then her eyes would fall to the printed text, before looking up again to realize only seconds passed.

Outside her cloud of thoughts, the heavy thud of the airplane door sealed them inside. The sound echoed in an eternal and consequential way.

She kept trying to decipher something from her magazine, but the words spun and jumbled, cast into incoherence. Another hour passed, and days, years even, but only a minute. She looked up.

"What am I doing?" Her words hit her. She glanced to the right and to the left, and said to no one in particular. "I love him. I always have and always will."

I'd rather be miserable with him than happy with someone else.

Then the lightning shot through her.

Suddenly the plane felt very small and suffocating, and it wasn't big enough to contain her heart. These abrupt and sudden thoughts pummeled her. Yet, they reassured her. They had the potential to rescue her from the dull veil she had forced herself to wear. But she needed space to process.

The door was closed but the pilot hadn't started moving. So she grabbed her purse and hurried to the bathroom at the front of the plane. The latch locked and the light flickered on.

"What's happening?" Brynn said to the empty space.

You know what's happening. This is the moment you've been waiting for. This is the moment you're going to rescue you from yourself. You love Connor. You can't spend a lifetime without him.

"But Connor will break my heart over and over again!" Brynn said aloud.

You'd rather feel that heartache than anything else in the world.

Staring at her reflection, she took a deep breath. Life surged within her, all its wonderfulness and all its pain. Standing there in the airplane bathroom, Brynn Greene felt more Brynn Greene than she had in far, far too long. It wouldn't be a happy ending, but it would be an ending that made her happy.

There will be repercussions. Your mother will kill you and you'll break Kyle's heart.

"They'll get over it," she said. And they would.

Right then, all she wanted on earth was to be in Connor's arms again. The grin on her face reflected liberation from the lies she'd spoken into her own ears for the last year.

Suddenly, Brynn jostled sideways, losing her balance. The aircraft had pulled away from the jetway.

"Oh no!" she said. She couldn't go to San Francisco. Connor wasn't in San Francisco. She needed to be where he was.

Brynn considered her predicament. She was in the bathroom of a plane taxiing down the runway, taking her farther away from him. The first step was getting off the plane. But how?

What would Connor do? He was so good at situations like

this, tearing down something carefully constructed. *Yes, what would Connor do?*

"I have to get off this plane!"

Brynn didn't know why, but she dug through her purse. As she shifted through its depths, she found something she'd forgotten, something that didn't make sense to her. Security must've missed it in the airport. Perplexed by its presence, she pulled the little matchbook out and read the cover.

Creek Don't Rise. Her life folded over itself as she remembered back to the tiny café at which she and Connor sat in Montana, and the haphazard way she took the matchbook from the bowl. She ran her thumb over it. She looked in the mirror.

"I don't know," she had once said to him. "I heard you were a wild one."

He had smiled at her. "You should try it sometime…"

She grinned, reassurance and excitement flooding her heart. Brynn looked at the lady in the mirror. "If I'm going…"

She tore a match from the booklet. "Then I'm going, crazy."

With a devilish smirk she borrowed from a boy she once knew, Brynn slid the match across the booklet. The orange cinder emblazoned and engulfed the tiny wand. And never more alive since the day she last held him, Brynn cast the fire into the trash.

Don't think. Just do.

Brynn emerge from the bathroom, calm and collected. She settled into her seat and waited for it all to come crashing down.

Just like Connor showed you.

A breath, a beat, and then…

The still calmness of the plane ripped open as alarms sounded and red lights flashed. The commercial airliner transformed into an Armageddon bunker, just as she intended.

Crewmembers scrambled frantically. Shrieks and murmurs rose from the passengers. All turned their heads to and fro in search of an answer for the madness. Chaos flowed. Passengers shouted each other's names. Mothers grabbed for their kids and husbands grabbed for their wives. Some clutched their bags. Whimpers thundered through the hull.

But there was no time for that.

"Everyone stay calm!" an attendant said. "I'm sure it's just a glitch."

Smoke began to pour from the bathroom.

A trembling young man in front of Brynn stood and grabbed a flight attendant's collar, shaking her. "We're all gonna die!"

"He's right!" Someone else shrieked.

"Yeah!" Brynn called to stir the madness.

"Sir, please stay calm. We are trained to handle this!"

"No! We're all gonna die! We gotta go!" The man shook as he grabbed the handles of the emergency exit. All those around him twisted and cringed, shrieking.

"No, sir! Let me do that!"

"NO TIME! We're going to die!" He yelled and yanked on the red handles, while others jumped to assist him in his struggle with the door. People scrambled over each other.

Brynn couldn't fight her grin. Connor would be so proud.

Explosive as fireworks, the door hissed and opened, spewing the pressurized cabin into the great outdoors. Fresh air charged inward and flooded the cabin.

"We have to get out of here!" Another woman in front trembled like a crazy person. She bent and reached for the lever at the same time as one of the attendants.

The plane spewed a giant inflatable escape slide. Its tremendous folds spilled away. The person next to Brynn was already scrambling over her to escape.

"EVERYONE! Please take off your shoes and move towards the exit!" the flight attendants yelled. Other exits and slides deployed.

So Brynn followed the ebb and flow of people. She looked at the yellow slide, her route, her first step in the pursuit of *him*.

Take me away. She jumped and fell into the air. Her legs swung forward and bathed in the freedom she claimed.

She bounced twice as she collided with the slide, racing down the yellow path. Then her feet met the concrete of the tarmac. She ran towards the terminal, the sun lighting her way.

"This way, ma'am!" An aid worker waved her toward a secure area.

"SORRY!" She yelled and shoved her way past. "I have to go this way!"

There was only one direction for Brynn.

"I'm coming, Connor," she whispered to herself and giggled with excitement. The door surrendered to the wild one as she pushed her way into the terminal.

CHAPTER 18

Their eyes were on him. They lingered on his every word. The attendees sat upright, as though to honor him. Occasional coughs and stray camera flashes broke the amorphous stillness of the crowd, but reverence prevailed. Pulling the words from his memory, Connor spoke into the microphone.

"My father once said, 'Everyone's waiting for a hero. But I won't. Someone has to act. And *I am able.*'" Connor paused and let the wisdom sink in.

Grand pillars held the ceiling over the groomed crowd below. With love he could see in her eyes, his mother watched from her table near the front. She smiled with a head held high and demeanor calm. One of her friends sat behind her and placed a hand on his mother's arm.

Connor raised his head again. "For the longest time, I thought he meant we should become as strong as we might, to be as able as we might, so we can be the hero. I thought he meant we should seek strength."

He shot a look over his shoulder at the giant banner of his father hanging behind him. "But now I don't think so. Now I think he meant being a hero is acting in the small moments, the little opportunities. It's taking time to mend, to fix, to rebuild. It's about acting in your own way to make the world better.

Everyone has something they can do. One need only to find what it is and do it. To never stop searching."

He glanced back at the crowd. "That's my hope for this scholarship program: that those receiving it would learn just that. In some bright tomorrow, I hope they learn how to be heroes, in their own place, at their own time. I can think of no better way to honor my father."

Connor shifted his wheelchair. "And so with this first year, the Benjamin West Scholarship Program is sending twenty children of fallen veterans from inner city Houston to colleges and universities throughout the state. Surely such great things shall come of this. Thank you for giving. And thank you for remembering my father." Connor nodded and rolled back from the microphone.

A first clap led others and soon applause filled the space. The energy seemed infectious as those gathered stood in continued ovation. Before wheeling off the stage, Connor took one last look at the crowd, intent on forming a forever memory. Then after a deep inhale, Connor pulled away from the light.

"All right, thank you, Mr. West," said a woman who took the mic after Connor.

He lost her voice as he passed through the stage exit and down the side hallway before stopping at the door that led back into the room. He waited for conversation to begin again before making his move, not wanting to interrupt any of the speakers.

Guests rose from their seats and began to move about, mingling and chatting. Connor wheeled through the door and toward the gathering.

"Connor, thank you so much for speaking today," said Henley Rae, the chair of the scholarship's board, as she took Connor's hand.

"Don't thank me," Connor said. "You and your people have done all the hard work. Thank you." Connor smiled as best he could and continued towards his mother's table.

"Moving words." Someone else patted him on the back.

The controlled ruckus of dishes, silverware, and moving chairs mixed with the buzz of laughter and conversation. He neared his destination.

"Not bad for a gym rat." Father Mickey smiled over a glass of wine. The priest looked as joyful as ever.

"These words is confusing me." Connor flexed his bicep.

Father Mickey laughed. "Yeah, yeah. I'd still never vote for you."

Connor wheeled farther until he found his mother. She sat encircled by attendees. They watched her every word. Between her answers, she looked out the corner of her eye and over the shoulders of her interviewers at Connor. She nodded and gave the most subtle of smiles.

Connor stayed and spoke with any and everyone who wanted to engage him. It was the best way for him to help.

"You look a lot like him, you know," a voice said during a lull.

Connor turned towards the voice.

"Hello, Senator Ford." Connor nodded. "How's Tennessee?"

"Business as usual." The aged man pulled up a chair and sat down. "I was sorry to hear about your accident."

"Well, when you act foolishly, these things happen."

"Still can't be easy."

"I've made my peace with it. I deserve this and I can still do what I need to do."

"That's a good attitude because it seems there is still a lot for you to do." He took a sip of his drink. "I miss him… your father." The senator pulled off his glasses and rubbed his eyes. "We always sat by each other so we could rip on the more asinine bills. There's this little dive by the Capitol, a place called Roman's. We ate lunch there every Thursday."

He looked up. "Maybe if you're ever in Washington, I'll take you there."

"Deal." Connor stuck out his hand.

Senator Ford shook it before standing. "I appreciated what you said. About what it means to be a hero. One time I was with your father as we spent weeks trying to pass a law. We failed. Late that night we split a bottle of bourbon in my office. I told him I was really upset. I told him I wanted to leave a legacy. You see, we get so little done in D.C., I wanted one good thing for people to remember me by. And I'll never forget what he said. He said, 'It ain't about being remembered because most everyone forgets you. Only a few people remember you. So life must be about the moments with those few."

"That sounds like him," Connor said.

"Indeed. And then your father hopped a redeye back to Texas so he could make it to *that one's* garden party." He nodded towards Connor's mom.

"Yeah. That's him." Connor swallowed.

"Well. Take care of yourself, kid." Senator Ford nodded and walked away.

Connor sat and pondered the senator's words, as one-by-one, the crowd filtered out. Soon after, he said goodbye to Father Mickey and his mother.

Connor waited until the final guest disappeared. He hated when people tried to help him, so he hoped to navigate the building without seeing anyone. The grand ballroom grew cavernous.

He entered an elevator and pressed the lowest button on the panel. The doors opened with a ring. Marble floors passed underneath. Once clear, he tapped the handicap button and the entrance to the parking garage swung open.

The door to his van opened. A wheelchair lift unfolded and lowered to the ground. Connor pushed onto it. The lift raised him and the chair so he could enter the van. Inside, Connor shuffled into the driver seat. He turned the key and the vehicle came to life. He pressed the steering wheel accelerator with his thumb. The van pulled forward.

The sun and blue sky shone overhead. Connor enjoyed the mild temperature. With no commitments the rest of his day, Connor drove past his old high school and alongside the park where he used to play. That seemed lifetimes ago. Streets paved with memories rolled out before him until he rounded the corner towards home.

Then the world didn't make sense.

She stood there his in driveway, simple and lovely.

He fought his heart, convinced it lied to him. But between blinks and disbelief, she remained, watching him.

She waited, her posture slight yet steady, small yet giant. She was a focal point, in control of the background.

"Brynn…" he whispered.

He stopped the van on the far side of the street and stared at her over his arm propped on the steering wheel and through the open window. He feared that any movement might make her disappear. "What are you doing here?"

He wondered what to do. Perhaps she was there to give him the berating he deserved or perhaps this was a moment in which they could forge some sort of civility—

My legs.

Though he no longer shied from others seeing him, somehow Brynn was different. Connor didn't want her to see him this way. He felt as though she and he were already discussing things through the looks they exchanged, so he swallowed and nodded to her. Then Connor turned and lifted himself from the front seat into his wheelchair.

As he sat in the dark back of his van, he was well aware this was his last opportunity to stay hidden from her. Or this was his last chance to experience her. And if this were his last chance, the last time for them to breathe the same air, he would hold nothing from her in hopes that she might find peace. After all, this was the way a girl like Brynn deserved to be treated. This might be his one moment in time to get it right, his only chance.

He inhaled and pressed the button. The automatic door slid away, light pouring through open seams. The lift extended forward. The mechanism worked. It took ages.

He rolled his chair forward out of the van and paused on the grate. Raised on this pedestal, he felt to be declaring "this is me" to the world.

Their eyes locked every moment as he pushed himself across the street and up the circular drive, a million miles in every inch. She seemed a vision so far, yet stood before him.

He stopped before her. Try as he might, he could not read her.

"Hello, Brynn." He relaxed in his chair and gazed up at her. "It's nice to see you." His words came with an odd pace.

"Connor." She looked at him, biting her lower lip and holding the outside of her arm. "I didn't realize how serious your accident was."

"Well, you know, I was acting stupid. I got what I deserved."

"It happens."

He cracked a smile. "For certain. How are you—"

"Shut up, Connor. I need to say something." Her hand dropped to her hip.

Connor closed his mouth and sat at rigid attention. Her words might hurt, but it would be good for her to let them out. And he would survive. So he waited.

"I just... I..." She drew in a deep breath and squared her shoulders. "What you do to me is inexcusable, you know? And it hurts Connor, it hurts every time."

"I know—"

"I'm not finished." Brynn shifted her stance. "I will never have back the time I've spent waiting on you or hurting over you..." Something twitched on her face. "You're no good for me, Connor, and never will be."

What was that? Between her words? A grin?

Silence grew and mounted. But then Brynn's shoulders broke and slumped. She looked down and shook her head.

She laughed. "But I guess I am just an idiot, Connor. Because for some reason, you always wreck me and break me, and yet, I miss the misery. No matter how far I run, you're beside me and in me. And I know, Connor, I'll spend more time hurting than being happy. I know I'll cry. You'll break my heart over and over."

She opened her eyes and raised her head. "But that's the life I want."

Connor's eternities split. He lost control of hope as in a dared belief, he smiled. Surely this could not be happening. His hands shook and his stomach twisted. A small and subtle laugh escaped from him. *Is she saying what I think she's saying?*

It must have been infectious because Brynn smiled as well

and laughed it away. "Shut-up," she said playfully. "I'd rather be miserable with you than happy anywhere else. I guess maybe I'll drown or I'll learn how to swim."

Connor waited, paused on a razor's edge. The anticipation consumed him. He only gazed at her.

"Well, say something!" She tossed her hands up. "Don't you get it? I'm here. You get to be self-centered and reckless and still have me. Because I love you, Connor West. I love you!"

Weight fell from him. "You're too good for me."

"I know." She smiled.

With those words, Connor refused to contain himself. He'd lost enough to know what it meant to have something. This was Brynn. This was *Brynn*, damn it! And he would never screw it up again.

She paused, starring at him, eyebrows level.

Heartbeat. Heartbeat. Heartbeat.

"Oh, Brynn…" He let everything flow into his grin, drunk on the ecstasy of the moment. "Your mom is just going to hate me." He smirked.

"Stop!" She giggled. The richness of completion poured over them like sunlight. "Now what did you do to yourself!" She slugged him on the shoulder, looking at his wheelchair.

"Oh you know, *motorcycles*." He smiled and shrugged.

She chortled and rolled her eyes. "Meathead."

Life surged in his veins. He remembered how it felt long ago. Not when he could walk, but how it felt the day he met her. The first time he really lived.

"Marry me, Brynn."

Her smiling face broke to bewilderment. "What?"

"Marry me. Now, today, and for the rest of your life." He took her hand. "We'll go to the courthouse. After that, I'll give you any kind of ceremony you want. Take all the time you need to plan it. We can celebrate with everyone. But let's go, right now. Because you are the best of me and I am the rest of you."

Her crystal eyes glossed over with moisture and emotion. She nodded slowly, biting a quivering lip.

Connor couldn't walk, but his soul could fly at the speed of light. In disbelief of reality, he pulled her into his lap. He could smell her, feel her, touch her.

Brynn glowed in the still air as he cradled her delicate chin in his hand.

"Hey," he said.

"Hey," she said.

Then he kissed her in a mess of smiles, feeling her breath.

"Come on," Brynn said. "Let's get out of here."

Connor spun his chair and wheeled them down the driveway.

CHAPTER 19

Pristine folds of ivory fell away from her waist, cascading away like a crystal waterfall. These waters were unapologetic in their majesty.

Brynn's eyes followed the fabric that flowed recklessly up to their source, where the dress narrowed and cradled her waist, never to let her go. She looked further at the A-line as the faille fabric clutched her torso, before holding fast at her bust and allowing her shoulders and arms to shine.

The hair stylist promised that once he was through, Brynn would never want to cover her hair with a veil. And now, looking at the elaborate braids woven into the white rose over her ear, Brynn was happy she had trusted him.

"You must be the most beautiful bride there's ever been," her mother said from a chair in the corner.

Though she'd never say it aloud, Brynn felt tempted to believe her mother.

Bridesmaids' voices hummed in the background. The smell of hairspray and perfumes hung pungent in the air while a subtle heat came from the vanity lights.

"You're just so stunning it could..." her mother whimpered.

Descending the step from a full-length mirror in the wooden frame, Brynn reached for the box of tissue and offered it to her mother. "Don't cry, mom."

Brynn's mother took the tissue and dabbed her eyes. "Pay no attention to me, I'm just being dumb." She cleared her throat, her face growing stern. "It's not too late, you know. You can still walk out of this."

Brynn laughed, "Yes it is." She held her hand up and brandished her wedding band. "Remember, we're already married."

"I'm pretty sure courthouse weddings don't count," her mother sniffed.

Brynn smiled. "I'm pretty sure they do."

"Says who?"

"Oh, you know, the state of Texas, the country, pretty much everyone." Brynn shrugged. "And besides, I love him."

Her mother sighed and rolled her eyes. "I know you do."

A knock came from the door. Bridesmaids, bride, and mother-of-the-bride all turned and looked.

The wedding coordinator stepped inside. "We're ready to begin."

A warmth of excitement welled deep within Brynn's stomach and rose. She looked back at her mom.

"Well, they can't start without you." Her mother stood and rolled her shoulders back. "Let's get this show on the road."

Brynn wrapped her arms around her mother. "I love you, Mom."

"Okay, okay. You're going to get my mascara all over your dress." She stepped back and looked her daughter over once more. "Here we go." Her mother turned and passed through the door.

The maid-of-honor lifted the ivory train and carried it as Brynn followed the group outside. In the empty foyer, the wedding party stood in line. Their posture froze rigid as they prepared for their journey down the isle.

Her mother's parents, Brynn's only living grandparents, stood at the front of the line. Behind them waited her mother and Mrs. West.

Mrs. West, in her eternal grace, looked back at Brynn and gave a radiant smile. A calm smile. A strong smile, and nodded.

Brynn waited, making sure to remain invisible through the soon to open doors.

Soft steps approached. Brynn turned to see her father and his restful presence.

His eyes smiled. "You're supposed to be my little girl. You're supposed to be in pigtails and on your way to preschool. You're supposed to be begging me for another piggyback ride. What happened?" He took her hands. "Now you're all grown up and my favorite daughter is getting married."

"Dad," Brynn tilted her head. "I'm your *only* daughter."

He raised his eyebrows regally. "Doesn't make it any less true." He swallowed hard as a wave of seriousness passed over his face. "Now listen to me."

Brynn waited, as the music inside the church whispered through the doors. "Yes, dad?"

"Brynn, I want you to know how proud of you I am." He blinked as moisture accented the rich color in his eyes. "We're standing here and you're about to walk down there and marry that boy, who I don't completely understand and probably never will. He's done things and behaved in ways—" his voiced choked. "Well, the world washed its hands of him long ago."

He took a deep breath. "But the point is, Brynn, you never truly gave up hope, even when you pretended to. From the first day you saw him and through every good and bad day that followed."

Brynn didn't fight her tears.

"You wouldn't listen. And it wasn't pride or stubbornness. It was hope. Hope guides you, Brynn." He hugged her. "Keep on never giving up, for all of us. I can only imagine what a world we could live in if there were more people like you, hoping for the rest of us."

Brynn wiped her tears. "Dad..."

He cleared his throat. "Enough of that. There's a young man waiting for you at the other end of this." He shifted toward the doorway to the sanctuary and offered his arm.

Brynn nodded and took it. Then she turned and faced the large, redwood doors. They stood sturdy and held back the forever that waited on the other side. Next thing she knew, the wedding planner and her assistant seized the handles.

Then a moment. A pause. A breath before the leap.

With a nod, the doors were pulled open as two worlds meshed. Brynn's dreams and reality became one.

Connor had promised her she could have the exact wedding she wanted. And she did. Not a detail lacked. Through the doors, she fell into the fairytale.

The guests stood in their pews within the stone church. Friends, family, acquaintances, new and old, poised respectfully for the bride. Under their eyes, locked on her, smiles waited.

Great, open windows bid the autumn air to come inside. Colors of the fall balanced against the rock, and the scent of spent leaves spun every which way. A low sun came from the west.

The pianist and his stringed quartet thundered Pachabel's "Canon in D," breathing new life into the anthem as the notes weaved to and fro.

At the end of a long and sacred walk over red carpet, Father

Mickey stood up at the altar, smiling and cradling his Holy book. Four soldiers, present and past, formed a line to the right. And four of Brynn's favorite women waited to the left.

And there, sitting in his wheelchair at the bottom of the altar steps, waited the legend, the story, the controversy: Connor West. *Her* Connor West. Posture straight and shoulders facing her, he sat taller than most men stood. Calmly, he smiled at her. His lips parted and gave way to his quarterback grin.

The length of the church couldn't hold her back. She took every one of those steps at her father's side, counting down until she could be next to him. And as she strode, she knew she had made this walk in her heart years ago. But no one would believe a child could understand what love and forever meant.

Her heart rejoiced as she reached Connor.

After his opening greeting to the congregation, Father Mickey said from the altar, "Who gives this woman to be married?"

"Her mother and I." Brynn's father said. He turned to her one last time and gently laid a kiss upon her cheek. Then he nodded to Connor and joined Brynn's mother in the front row.

Taking Connor's strong hand, Brynn turned and settled into a rose-covered wicker throne, a piece of art made just for this occasion. She and Connor held hands and sat across the aisle from each other, waiting on Father Mickey.

She loved staring into his eyes. She had noticed their change. For they had the same strength, the same energy, the same passion and unconquerable fire. The irises still burned green. But now there was no wall. He wasn't holding anything back from her. She could look into them and read the depths of his soul. The mystery departed and there was nothing left for her to wonder. Nothing left to make her anxious.

He was all those feet away yet his gaze embraced her. Connecting with him, she felt so worshiped, so loved, and so celebrated.

"Friends, family, guests," Father Mickey began. "I know Connor and Brynn want to thank you for joining them today. This is a special day and they're so excited you're here to officially enjoy their marriage with them. Brynn will tell you without hesitation that she's loved Connor from the day she met him. That, since eight years old, she knew this day would come." Father Mickey gestured towards her. "And Connor will tell you that talking about feelings is for women and artists."

The crowd laughed.

"They say some survive life while others live it. They say that to really know what love is, what good is, what hope is, one needs to encountering hate, evil, and hopelessness. Connor and Brynn have done this and more, experiencing moments that have led them to this day. I wager few can appreciate the beauty in this day as can Connor and Brynn."

He looked down at Connor. "You know, Connor, there are two names that God shares with men. That of 'father' and that of 'husband.' The mention of 'husband' comes when He compares Himself to a groom anxiously awaiting his bride: the church. I hope you realize how important is the job you undertake."

The priest turned to Brynn and smiled. "Brynn, the Bible compares a good woman to precious stones, something to be sought and searched for. I hope you realize what a prize you are."

To both of them, he said, "Love is such a cool thing. It makes you crazy, to behave counter-intuitive and act against your own survival. It makes no sense and all the sense in the world. It gives strength and weakens. It heals and hurts. It's a mystery and yet perfectly clear. It terrifyingly crippling and fantastically empowering."

The priest continued quoting verses and stories as he made marriage sound so beautiful and promising. Brynn heard some of it, but mostly she and Connor conveyed without a word "I love you" over and over.

"Today, Connor and Brynn have elected to recite their own vows."

At the mention of vows, Brynn readied to pour out her heart. But Connor shifted in his seat when he was supposed to begin. Instead of speaking for all the crowd to hear, he leaned in to her and whispered, "Come on, Brynn Greene. They deserve to see how beautiful you are." He smirked.

Wondering at his cryptic words, Brynn watched Connor take a deep breath and grab the arms of his chair. Never losing sight of her, he pushed downward and grinded his teeth behind his smile, squinting slightly as he fought gravity. Then slowly, steadily, he rose. His knees trembled. But inch by inch, his legs straightened.

Amid her gasps and gasps from those in attendance, Connor West stood before her.

Brynn grabbed her chest while her tears flowed in jubilee. A standing Connor took her hands and drew her up to him until she stood before her groom.

"Connor," Brynn stammered. "How... when—"

"Shh... we ain't there yet." Connor turned, arm-in-arm with her, swallowed hard, and took the first step up to the altar.

Between her crying, joy, concern, and bewilderment, she could feel his body straining. She watched his face as he focused intently on each step, one-by-one, and rising. Brynn helped him on his left. Lt. Ryan helped him on his right.

And despite her disbelief, and before she dared accept this was not a dream, she and her groom stood at the altar, in front of all. The building erupted in applause as Brynn wept and laughed.

"I can't believe it!" She smiled at him over the cheers.

Connor smirked from the corner of his mouth and winked at her. Clutching her hands as though for dear life, and softly as though mid-stride while dancing to a tried and true song, he gazed into her eyes.

"My dear, sweet, Brynn," Connor began as the crowd settled to silence. "I'm so excited to be at this altar with you." He drew her hands into his chest. "On the precipice of our lives together, I can hardly stand still. From the day we met until now, you're the best person I've ever known."

His words came slow, graveled, and intentional. "The way your eyes shine starlight and the way your heart breaks over the suffering of strangers. Your laughter and your thoughtfulness. Your spark. I don't deserve to speak your name, much less spend every waking morning with you. Countless times I've shoved you away. And despite me, you've chased me down. You've stood strong in whatever has come your way. You're so brave, Brynn. So brave… baby, you're my hero."

He lifted her hands to kiss the back of them. "And now I'm here and give my word to love you in the way you deserve. I will have eyes for no one other than you. I swear to pursue you every day and make you the queen of my life. I'll die for you, kill for you, and live for you. I promise to hold you through rain and laugh with you in sunshine. I promise to make you feel my love, whatever comes. I promise to listen and not just hear the things you say. I promise to make memories, overcome struggles, and survive losses. And in the still moments, when it is only you and

I… I promise to understand I am the luckiest man in the galaxy, for I get to pass my days with you."

Connor reached up and wiped a tear from Brynn's cheek with a tender thumb. "I love you, Brynn, to the end of time. And beyond."

As he slid a new wedding band over her finger, her whole being quaked. She felt complete. She read the Latin engraved in gold. It meant, "The invincibility of two hearts combined."

As the swoons of the audience passed, Brynn tried to begin. But her words failed, lost to quivers of emotion.

"That's all right," Connor whispered for only her to hear. "I'd stand here with you forever."

She spent a few seconds gathering herself before clearing her throat. "Connor. Some say you're a wild one and I wouldn't have it any other way. Because I know you love me. It's written on every breath I take. You give me courage and push me in ways and towards adventures I never would have believed. And in the end, I'm a better person for it. Every day with you is the best day of my life. And the only life I want is one alongside you."

She squeezed his hand. "Connor, I promise to never look to any other than you. I promise to be a good companion and to trust you, and to trust in you. I promise to care for you and let you care for me. I promise to follow you wherever you will go, and to celebrate your wild heart."

Brynn watched him through the moisture filling her eyes, as she bit her trembling lip. "I'll never leave and always stay. You have my heart, now and forevermore. My love for you is unbreakable."

She held his gnarled and worn hand, sliding a titanium ring over his third finger. The symbol of promise rested next to his missing little finger, a remnant of a ferocious history.

Once again, Connor dabbed tears from her cheek.

"And with that," Father Mickey spoke loud and clear. "By the power vested in me by God and the holy church, I now *gladly* pronounce you still: husband and wife. Connor, kiss your bride!"

To a chorus of celebration, Connor gently cradled her neck in his hands and pulled her in. She tasted his lips.

"Woo-hoo!" The room shook in cheers.

"Ladies and gentlemen!" Father Mickey beamed. "Mr. and Mrs. Connor West!"

In the midst of applause, husband and wife turned to the crowd. Connor hoisted her hand triumphantly into the air.

All continued clapping as Lt. Ryan helped Connor down the steps and into his wheelchair. He pushed while Brynn held Connor's hand, walking down the aisle and through the doors: in victory.

CHAPTER 20

A dust-laced wind blew across the land and up the front steps. Sun-infused clouds billowed above the tree line and provided a backdrop to the ancient barn. Then, all was quiet.

Connor swayed back and forth effortlessly on the bench swing, breathing in a scent of dry foliage. This was his favorite time of day. He soaked in the stillness. The quiet was louder than thunder. He and the land were companions.

The screen door screeched. He turned his head.

Brynn followed her pregnant belly out onto the porch. She pressed her hand against her lower back as she took small steps towards him, smiling. The old home creaked beneath her.

"Hey there, bright eyes." Connor said. "How's the little guy doing today?"

"He's kicking like he wants out."

Connor helped her to sit.

"It's like he can't wait to face the world." She eased back and looked at him.

Connor touched her stomach. "Well, if he's anything like you, the world will be lucky to have him." He brushed dark locks behind her ear.

She rested her hand on his leg. "Did you hear from your mom?"

"Yeah. They've still got her busy fundraising. She's worried they want her to run for office. She can't make it this weekend, but she'll be here next Thursday."

"Perfect! Just in time to meet her grandson."

"Yep. Just in time." Connor stroked the back of her neck.

"I can't wait to show her this." Brynn presented an old photograph from a stack of materials she carried. "I found it in the study in the bottom of the corner desk." She held it up for Connor. "Isn't this your mom and her parents?"

Connor studied the black and white image of a young family. A man, Connor's age, grinned with wise eyes towards the camera. Even in the grainy resolution, one could see the energy that burned in them. The man's arm hung around a beautiful woman. Dark, untamed hair wrapped over her shoulders.

"Oh, yeah." Connor nodded. "That's Grandpa Jake and Grandma Ellie." Grandma Ellie cradled a big-eyed, blond toddler. "And there's Mom."

Connor pointed. A boy with a clever little expression stood in front of his parents. "And there's Uncle Charlie. You know, they say grandma named him Charlemagne, but everyone else just called him Charlie."

"How sweet." Brynn touched the frame.

"I'm not certain on the details, but I'm pretty sure Grandma lived in San Francisco before Grandpa brought her here to Crane, in good ol' west Texas."

"Was he a cowboy, too?"

"Worked this ranch every day of his life. Took it further than anyone else ever has. But since he and Grandma passed, things sort of closed up around here." Connor looked across the pasture at his family's land. "But we'll get there. We'll get it back."

He took a deep breath. "Speaking of, I've got to meet the boys and check the bottomlands before dark." He let out a sharp whistle and waited.

The patter of hooves approached from the side of the house as a charcoal stallion came into view. It stopped a few feet beyond the porch railing and shook its mane.

Brynn erupted in laughter. "How long did it take to teach him that?"

Connor chuckled. "This is actually the first time it's ever worked."

Brynn laughed again.

"Well, baby." Connor kissed her cheek. "See you at sundown." He stood and stepped onto the railing, before hopping onto the back of the horse and into the saddle. His boots met stirrups.

"You know, you kind of look like you know what you're doing." Brynn's lips curled over her white teeth. "Not bad for a kid from Houston."

"I've been around." Connor winked at her.

"Just come home safe."

Connor grabbed a handful of reins and looked at his cherished wife, his whole world, sitting there on the old west Texas porch.

"Brynn West, there ain't no flood, fire of hell, or force on this earth that could keep me from coming home to a girl like you." And he meant it.

Brynn bit her lip, holding back a huge smile. She lifted her little, sweet hand and blew him a silent kiss.

He touched his fingers to his lips and returned the same. Then Connor turned his horse, sunk his heels, and raced the wind.

ABOUT THE AUTHOR

After Alex Reed graduated from Baylor with a degree in Political Science and Communication, he moved to Austin, Texas, drawn to the city for its music and cultural scenes. As he always enjoyed creative writing, he began with short stories and published his first novel, *Burning Son*, in 2013. He likes to focus on heavy character development and finding heroism in unlikely places.

www.ingramcontent.com/pod-product-compliance
Lightning Source LLC
Chambersburg PA
CBHW071234260626
47161CB00003BA/854